MW01087305

WHERE THERE ARE TWO OR MORE

The following stories have been previously published:
"September Dance," *The MacGuffin*, Summer 2014
"Heron in the Garden," *Red Earth Review*, Summer 2014
"Us vs. They," *Pembroke Magazine*, Spring 2014
"Tea and Oranges," *Driftwood Press*, Winter 2014
"Three to the Vine" (formerly "The North Comes for Dinner"), *The Lablettex*, Spring 2013

ISBN-13: 978-1-942515-00-5
Library of Congress Control Number: 2015933090

Fomite
58 Peru Street
Burlington, VT 05401
www.fomitepress.com

Cover art - *Skeleton Series Two*, Lynnda Tenpenny (www.ltenart.com)

WHERE THERE ARE TWO OR MORE

ELIZABETH GENOVISE

Fomite

Burlington, VT

For Chris

CONTENTS

The First Fog

It is September, and it is the first brush Kirsten, Conrad, and Josiah have had with death. They are twelve years old—Kirsten and Conrad Lawson are twins, and Josiah Clayton has been their friend since the second grade. They live in the small mountain town of Canton, Tennessee, and when the car wreck happens out on Norris Lake, it is the talk of the town for weeks.

It was a spectacular wreck, involving four teenagers, all of whom lived within a block or two of Kirsten and Conrad. The reports said nobody had been drinking, but that the driver lost control of the car in a heavy fog, and the sedan went careening into the lake. The teenagers had planned to camp there that night. As the story went, the car plummeted into the water, and Owen Christianson, in the backseat, unbuckled himself, used their camping ax to shatter his window open, and somehow got his friend Lena out of the car with him. She'd been knocked out, but he swam with her to the surface and got her safely to the shore, leaving her only when he was certain she was breathing. Back under the water, he was too late to save the other two. They said the driver, Elisabeth (who once babysat for Kirsten and Conrad) had died on impact, and her boyfriend, Lane, had drowned before Owen could get to him.

The story was fascinating enough as it was, but there was more. The gossips said Owen's head wasn't right after the accident because he insisted in the hospital and later on television that when he surfaced from his last attempt to save them, he saw them walking across the lake, holding hands. He said they looked like mist but he knew it was them. His mother, on live television, asked him to stop saying what he was saying. He wouldn't. He said that the car had fallen into the part of the lake known as the Loyston Sea, where the old town of Loyston was buried underwater when the government first created the lake. He said it was no coincidence: his friends were still in the world, just not the one we are familiar with. They were only living in another town.

Now, Kirsten, Conrad, and Josiah are discussing it all in the backseat of Josiah's parents' car. Or really, the twins are; Josiah is watching the back of his parents' heads. Ehron and Rachel Clayton have been taking the three of them out more and more, and only last night, eavesdropping, did Josiah understand why.

"Charles Lawson is good for exactly nothing," Rachel was saying to his father when Josiah got halfway down the stairs. "This is bullshit, all this talk about him coming with us tomorrow. How many times have we heard this one? You know what Marta told me? Last week, he was gone four days. Four days! It's only a matter of time before he just disappears entirely."

"Give the man a chance, Rachel," Ehron murmured in his low, easy tones. "They're his kids, not ours."

"Bet you a fried chicken he goes on a bender tomorrow. I want chicken at our campsite—no more of those cheap hot dogs. They could be full of possum meat for all we know."

Ehron was laughing, but Josiah just sat there on the stairs, thinking about his friends.

Now Kirsten is saying with her characteristic ferocity, "I believe Owen. I know he's right. I knew it the minute he started talking."

"Me too." Conrad's urgency mirrors hers; he is leaning forward. "I wish I'd been there. God, I wish it had been me."

"That's a strange thing to say, Conrad," Rachel interjects from up front. "You wish you'd been in that horrible accident? You wish you'd seen your friends die?"

He looks at her with open disdain. "I wish I'd been Owen. Because of what he had the chance to do. And he wasn't lying when he said he saw them on the water."

"I know he wasn't," Kirsten says, nodding emphatically.

Josiah, next to her, shifts a little to look in her eyes, which are cat-green in the September sun. "That's crazy, K. How can you say you *know*? They even said his head was screwed up after the accident."

"I just do." She is fingering the pendant of a necklace, holding it as though afraid it will be taken from her. Josiah has never seen her wear jewelry, and it looks odd over her boyish clothes. It's also an opportunity to change the subject, so he asks her about it.

Conrad speaks up: "Oh, it's something she stole from Mom. She was going through Mom's old boxes again last night. She's obsessed with that thing."

"I didn't steal it. She said it was fine." Kirsten holds the pendant up to the light, and Josiah sees that it is actually a bubble of clear glass, containing the fine, amber-colored grains of something familiar.

"They're dandelion seeds," Kirsten explains. "The pieces, you know? When you pick them up when they're all skeleton-like and blow on them? Some woman caught them and put them in glass. It's like they're still moving in the wind." Her fists closes around it and she sits back.

Conrad leans forward, his dark hair falling into his eyes. "I think she's right. Not the dandelions, Owen's story. Don't you remember that Cherokee story about the banquet under the river? That story I told you guys the last time we camped?"

"Not really," Josiah mumbles, but he does, and the story terrified him so much that be begged out of fishing trips with his father for weeks afterward.

"The people underneath would call up and try to get them to come down and join them," Kirsten supplies eagerly.

"And they had a choice, but if they leaned over far enough, they would fall in and the people at the banquet would take them," Conrad finishes.

The twins have a matching fire in these moments, and Josiah is instantly excluded. He doesn't understand their passion for stories like this. Irritated, he tries to divert the conversation again: "Dad, what are we grilling at the campsite?"

"Not grilling tonight," Ehron says, looking at him in the rearview mirror. "Picking up fried chicken. Your mom's got a hankering."

Josiah sits back, ashamed. He looks worriedly at the twins but they are talking heatedly about Owen Christianson again. Conrad is saying, "I trust him because the guy's a hero. He could've died going back under like that. How do we know what we would have done?"

"You would have done it," Kirsten promises. "Me, too."

"I hope so."

THEY CAMP AT INDIAN BOUNDARY, a stunning sapphire lake concealed deep in the mountains near Tellico. Now, the lake is bluer than ever, fringed with blushing woods. This forest and the lake's clean waters are familiar to the children, as the site of countless cookouts, swimming trips, fishing excursions, and campouts since their early childhood. The place is a wilderness, utterly isolated, but the children have no sense of this. They see only the familiar fishing docks and the gently-sloping beach cut out of the woods, and smell much-loved barbecue and woodsmoke. They choose a site right on the lakefront, just a short walk from one of the docks, and pitch their tents around the fire ring. Josiah struggles with his tent as the twins blithely pitch theirs a few feet away. He watches their movements out of the corner of his eye, always impressed by this, their almost silken solidarity, the way they make the tent rise like it is a living, winged thing.

When the tents are up, the Claytons set out the chicken they've picked up on the way, and everyone sits down at the picnic table, Josiah noting his mother shaking her head as she sets out the food. He wants to ask, *Is Charles Lawson on a bender*, and, *is he going to abandon Kirsten and Conrad and their mother* but instead he asks for gravy for his mashed potatoes and then passes it to Conrad. Conrad heaps the gravy over his mountain of potato and says, "Look, it's Canton Mountain. Did you know, my dad thinks they might try to mine it one day? He says they might cut it open and rip the coal out." He stabs his plastic fork into the potato mountain and it bleeds gravy.

"That will never happen," Kirsten says sharply. "They'll never do that. Not to our mountain."

"You got that right. I'll kill anyone who tries," Conrad says grimly. He pats the mountain back into place with his bare hands.

"That's enough," Rachel says. "Let's try not to talk about things dying for awhile, okay? Let's pray."

Josiah puts his fork down and lowers his head. His eyes cut left toward the twins who are both rigid, staring at the table, eyes forward. Rachel thanks God for the meal and for their togetherness and then they start into the food.

Ehron waits a beat before saying, "You kids could pray with us, you know."

"My dad does that when he's drunk," Conrad says unexpectedly, looking Ehron right in the eye. "It doesn't mean anything. Just like church."

Ehron swallows and everyone freezes.

"It doesn't mean the same thing for everyone," Rachel starts, but Kirsten cuts her off: "At church they told us only Christ can save you. I believe in Him but not in *that*. *That*'s a crock of shit."

"Kirsten," Ehron says, but Kirsten talks over him: "Because only you can save yourself."

"No," Conrad corrects her, "only another person can save a person. That's what Christ meant when he said, 'where there are two or more.'" He looks hard at Ehron. "Did you know Owen Christianson? My dad said he took drugs and he got busted stealing like ten times. But he saved that girl, he turned into somebody else when the car hit the water. If you tell me he's not saved then I don't know what God is thinking."

"I would never tell you that boy was not saved," Ehron says gently.

"Anyone can do it," Conrad presses on. His dark eyes are gleaming; his hand grips the table's edge. "Anyone. My dad helped somebody out of a burning building once when he was like twenty. He told us that. He could do it again." The he stops, looking down into his lap.

"Like hell he would," Kirsten mutters and her face is also down, almost level with her plate. Her fist is tight around her necklace again.

"Two things I'd like to clear up right now," Rachel says with bare-ly-restrained calm. "One: no swearing. Put an end to it. Two: faith in God is enough, do you understand? There is no list of things you have to accomplish to be saved. If you believe, you will be saved. That's all there is to it."

Josiah watches his father—this, too, he has heard them argue about at night—and Ehron is quiet until his eyes lift to meet Josiah's. "And you—what do you think, son?"

The twins' brazenness is contagious. "I think it's a crock, too," Josiah says softly.

He feels the twins turn to stare at him, and his neck flushes. His mother's mouth is agape, but he continues: "I mean all that stuff about heaven and the afterlife. Spirits and angels, I don't believe it. This is what's real," and he lifts up his chicken leg and tries to grin. His grin falls; he means it. He has to believe it. The chicken leg, he can handle; the thought of an afterlife makes him sick with fear.

The twins exchange disappointed glances, and Josiah is confused.

"You're just scared," Conrad mutters, reading Josiah's mind as he often does.

"Enough," Rachel snaps.

Kirsten's hand finds Josiah's under the table. "I know why you think that," she says. "I really do, but I this is not the only real thing. That couple who died? Doesn't it make you feel better to know they're walking on water, or walking around on those streets under the water? Instead of being dust where they could never be together again?" Her eyes are suddenly wet, and Josiah squeezes her hand back, feeling something inside him flutter.

"I think this whole group needs Sunday school," Ehron says. Rachel glances at him, irritated, but he is smiling faintly: "I think we're all a little crooked in our theology if you want the truth. I'm just glad you kids are giving it some thought." He meets Josiah's eyes again. "No son of mine, in particular, is going to go through this world without thinking. Even if he thinks this world is all there is."

"We are going to have a serious discussion when we get home," Rachel says firmly to her son. "Keep that in mind while your father is being so cavalier."

"Good word," Kirsten comments, and they finish the meal without saying much else.

As THOUGH THE CONVERSATION HAS EXHAUSTED THEM, they spend the rest of the afternoon in near-silence. The Claytons relax on the beach, sipping Cokes, while Conrad and Josiah splash in the water, enjoying the last chance they have to swim before it becomes too cold. Kirsten, who fears water, walks along the beach, bending over to examine tiny stones and hoarding many of them in her pockets. These are their usual habits: Conrad swims out the furthest, always exploring; Kirsten collects, and walks about with her pockets bulging; and Josiah wavers between the two of them, wanting to be with them both but unable to fully enter the world of either.

When night falls, there is a deep chill to it, and the five of them sit around the campfire in their parkas. Ehron toasts marshmallows on sticks and, as usual, burns most of them. The children are wan from exercise and they lie on their backs, talking quietly. The smoke blots out most of the stars, but every so often a determined one pierces the smoke with its blue light, and Kirsten will point to it.

They all go to bed. Josiah listens as the twins settle themselves into

their sleeping bags and he watches the faint, bobbing glow of their flashlights as he arranges himself in his own bag. When they go quiet, he
drifts off, thinking for some reason of the dandelion seeds trapped in
Kirsten's pendant.

He wakes awhile later to the twins' low, hushed voices. He can feel
that it is the deep center of the night; the campground is hushed, the
stars almost audible in that way they are audible only in the mountains.
There is no light coming from the twins' tent, but Josiah can hear them
moving, and he unzips his door. A watery fog has fallen over their campsite and he can just barely make out their silhouettes as they emerge
from their tent. They move stealthily, no longer speaking, and they both
jump when Josiah climbs out to meet them. He blinks through the mist.
"What are you guys doing?"

"Look at this," Kirsten says softly, waving at the fog. "We want to
explore."

"Coming?" Conrad asks, starting toward the woods. Josiah follows,
just behind Kirsten, and they enter the woods. Josiah suppresses a shiver.
It is the first fog he has even seen like this, and he has no idea where they
are going.

THE FOG CHANGES AS THEY MOVE CLOSER to the water's edge. It thickens
and whitens, becoming a shroud, something Josiah feels the overwhelming urge to push away with his hands. The twins are barely visible in
front of him, and neither has brought a flashlight. Only in rare patches
is the fog thinner, wispier, and this makes it eerier to Josiah, because he
can't make sense of it.

"This is different," Conrad murmurs somewhere ahead of him.

"What is," Josiah hisses.

"This fog. It's not normal."

"It's just fog," Josiah gets out, but already, his throat is tightening
with fear. He reaches for Kirsten's hand, and she squeezes but then lets
go, walking ahead.

"Where are we going?" Josiah asks.

"To the lake. I think," Kirsten says. "I can't really see it anymore, though."

"I couldn't really see it to begin with," Conrad admits.

They walk on, stumbling over roots. Every so often, the twins will stop and listen for the lake, and they can just barely hear the water lapping the shore. The darkness is almost complete, but silvery in the fog, and as they walk on, Josiah realizes he can no longer see his own hands. He feels that he is breathing in water.

"I think we should go back," he says.

"Hang on," Conrad responds. "I'm going to walk toward the water and we can just follow that back. You wait here."

Josiah listens to his friend's footsteps and reaches for Kirsten. "I think we're lost," he tells her.

"I know. I wasn't going to say it to Conrad."

He can't see her, so he reaches for her again, and she surprises him by pulling him up tight against her. "Josiah," she murmurs into the gray mist, "did you mean what you said before, that you don't believe in any of it?"

"I think so." His hand finds her hair; he lets it linger there.

"So if I died, or Conrad, that would be it. We'd just be gone to you."

He thinks he hears her voice break but doesn't quite believe it. To the best of his knowledge, Kirsten has never cried in her life. "Don't say it like that," is all he can get out.

But she has pulled away from him, and he hears her footsteps, twigs cracking. "Hey," he says, starting after her, moving blindly. "Where are you going? He said to wait for him. Kirsten!"

It shocks him how abruptly she seems to vanish. The fog has thickened again, and Josiah crouches down to look at this own shoes, reassuring himself that all this is real. Then he rises and starts left, in Conrad's direction, thinking that if he can find the lake, he can make it back to the campsite. He tries not to think too hard about the fact that the lake is surrounded by endless woods, that a person could wander for miles, for days, out here and never reach a road or house. Indian Boundary is suddenly a stranger to him—a place without boundaries at all—and something in Josiah chokes up.

He holds both hands out in front of him as he walks, calling out the twins' names every so often, but uncomfortable with the sound of his own voice in this wilderness. He hears the scramblings and scratchings of small animals, and he thinks of bears. An owl calls, the cry piercing the sky above him. Twice, something swoops by him, dark and velvety in the night, and he knows these are bats and that bats are harmless, but he ducks both times and shudders.

He keeps stopping to listen for the water but he can't hear it. He moves faster, still with his arms out, but it is cold, and finally he walks with his arms wrapped around himself. He crashes into an enormous tree and the blow stuns him. For a long moment he stands still, letting the shock of it reverberate through him, and then he reaches out to touch the tree. The rough stubble of bark soothes him; he looks up, straight up along the tree's trunk, and for just a moment, the fog opens and reveals to him the tree's spiraling limbs, curving up and away toward the stars, and the starlight illuminates the limbs in silvery blue and makes them dance. In this image Josiah sees other, familiar images: a map of rivers crisscrossing, a photograph of human veins in his science textbook, a bouquet of wild cauliflower in his mother's hand, waiting to be washed. What he sees above him is savagely beautiful, but at the same time comforting in its familiarity, and he stays where he is until the fog returns and he is blind again.

"Kirsten," he calls out. "Conrad."

No answer.

He walks on, thinking he can now hear the lake. He has already forgotten the beauty of the tree, and is trembling again with fear.

Stop it. You are not going to die out here. But he can't stop the thought that he could die, and that if he did die, he might not deserve a second chance in a second life, if such a thing even existed. His worry is that he is spoiled, that life is too easy, that there is something deeply amiss in the way he lives. He is twelve years old, and he believes himself to harbor an unshakeable habit of choosing the easy way out of everything. He fears that he is only Josiah, and that he has never saved a thing.

KIRSTEN HAS HEARD JOSIAH'S VOICE but instead of going toward it she continues on in her original direction. His voice assures her that Josiah is fine; it is her brother she is worried about. She has wild and terrible visions of him falling into the lake, breathing in the blue water, lying there cold and drowned in the morning. Conrad has disappeared before— once, after their parents fought through the night, he ran away and was missing for two days, and another time, he wandered off during a hike and didn't come back for hours—and each time, something clenches up in Kirsten and she believes this time he will not come back.

"He is half of you," her mother once told her. "That's what happens when you're born together. If one of you goes away, the other one isn't the same."

It is a familiar feeling. Something shifts in Kirsten when she is without her brother. When he did a summer camp for baseball last year, she spent the summer drifting around, lost on trails in the Canton woods she used to know down to the last tree. She couldn't remember the names of birds. It worried her, as though what her mother had said were literally true: if something ever happened to Conrad, he would be forever in a place she couldn't follow, and she would never know where she was anymore.

I can do without my father, she promises herself, as she often does. *I can take care of myself and Mom too when he's gone. Nobody needs to take care of me. But not Conrad, I can't do without Conrad.*

She calls his name and there is only a rustle of wind in response. She clutches at her necklace, wishing she had light to look into it. Her pants feel heavy—they are still laden with the stones and tiny shells she salvaged from the lakebed earlier—and she moves slowly. For the third time since she separated from Josiah, she sees a tiny flicker of light, and stops still.

"What are you?" she murmurs, stepping toward it. The light is misted, domed with the fog, and minute as her fingernail. It blinks, vanishes, and returns. Kirsten follows it until she sees a second and third glimmer of light and realizes they are fireflies. Something brushes up against her body, and she jumps. She is walking through reeds now, which means she is closer to the water. She stops moving and watches the fireflies. One of them lands on the tip of what looks like a cattail just beside her and its tiny blue-green glow illuminates the cattail and creates a tiny tree out of it. Kirsten, mesmerized, bends slowly to take this in, and on impulse, gently pulls the reed up from the ground. Amazingly, the firefly stays put, and Kirsten, her eyes wide with wonder, begins to walk again with this tiny torch held before her.

"Conrad," she calls out again. "Conrad."

CONRAD IS KNEELING IN THE SAND, frozen in place, his eyes on the water. The fog over the lake's surface is as thick as it was in the woods but it is lit from above with uninhibited stars, the massive sheet of them that has always covered this place but only tonight seems foreign and miraculous to Conrad. The fog is lit enough, thinned enough over this water, for its movements and patterns to be visible. On first reaching this spot, Conrad thought he was dreaming; he stepped onto the sand, crouched down to touch its reassuring softness, and then looked up and gasped. He made himself look down and up again. They were still there. People, walking across the water. Couples hand-in-hand, children darting amongst themselves, old men bent over at the waist, groups huddled together as though in conversation. The couples interested him most: they held onto each other as they walked, the mist of their hands braided together subtly but undeniably. They moved like couples across a dance floor: with purpose, but with grace.

"Kirsten," Conrad says hoarsely. "You have to see this."

His first instinct is to swim out to them. He has the idea—it grips him, vise-like—that if he can get hold of them, he can swim them back to shore, and they can live again, here where no one will doubt them. He imagines they can be returned. He imagines that if he does this, he will be someone else afterwards: someone not like his father. Someone who reaches out instead of vanishing, someone who chooses the other person first, always.

He feels, in the deepest core of himself, that he is already running out of time. He has told no one, not even Kirsten, about the strange things that have been happening to him over this past year: moments in which his body falls, out of his control, his mind knots up, his limbs become separate from him, he loses time. The moments happen without warning and he cannot find the pattern. He has done his research in secret, at the old library in the next town over, asking his mother to drop him off there on Saturday mornings so he can work on homework in peace and quiet. The books tell him he must be having seizures. He doesn't know where they will lead but already, at twelve years old, he feels that his hourglass has turned.

Conrad takes off his shirt and lets it drop into the gray mist at his feet. The water is terrifying with its midnight depths, and the figures are moving faster now, their faces almost visible to him. He is shaking, but he heels off his shoes. *I can do this. This could be my only chance. And if I'm afraid and I do it anyway, that only makes it mean more.*

There is a rustling behind him, and he spins around to see two dark shapes moving toward him. His heart hammers but he stands his ground. When the figures reach him, emerging from two directions, he sees that it is his sister and Josiah.

"We were lost," Josiah pants. "We got separated."

"It's the beach," Kirsten says, kneeling as Conrad had, and touching the sand. "You found it. We couldn't—" Her voice breaks off; she is staring at the water. Josiah, too, is silent, his eyes huge.

Conrad is facing them and is afraid to turn around, afraid that what he saw is not as it was before. But he has to turn, and when he does, the three of them are seeing the same thing: the couples moving together, the children running, the old men walking, the groups huddling. Conrad feels a surge of vindication, a wave of something like hope.

"It's real," he sighs, as his sister whispers, "They *do* get to come back. He was right." Her relief is audible, immense. This is everything she has ever hoped to see: proof that there is always a counterpart to loss, a mirror image for every tragedy—the possibility of a returning.

Josiah is silent, trying to control his breathing, his fists tight at his sides.

"I wanted to save them," Conrad confesses, so softly they almost cannot hear him.

"They already are," Kirsten responds.

"Did they save themselves, or did somebody come for them?" He is not taunting his sister; his hushed voice is in earnest, desperate to know.

Kirsten does not answer. Instead she kneels again and Josiah can just make out what she is doing: scooping the sand and stones into her pants pocket, salvaging something from this night. He knows her: her terror right now is not of these ghosts, but that they will forget what they saw, killing these souls all over again. In a flash of insight, he understands that even though he doesn't know why she thinks this way, he loves her for it. And he wants to release her from all this fear, and Conrad too.

Josiah opens his mouth to say, *They aren't real. It's only fog. It's only our imaginations. And none of us are going to die, and we are never going to forget each other, and there is nothing to worry about.* But he can see limbs and faces and there is no way he can utter these words aloud without losing both of his friends. A tremor moves through his back. He closes his eyes against the vision. *It is not real.*

IN THE MORNING, the lake is bright and clear; the deep blues and greens of the trees are mirrored perfectly in the waters, a butterfly effect. The three of them stand on the fishing dock for a long time, gazing at the lake, but no one speaks of the night before. They are silent as they pack up their tents and help Josiah's parents clean up the campsite. They say nothing in the car driving home. Kirsten and Conrad's eyes are on the windows, and they are as far away as birds, unblinking. Kirsten has one hand around her brother's and the other around her necklace. Josiah tries to think of nothing, tries to blot out the vision of those ghosts on the lake even as the twins burrow deeper into their memories. But he will have to think of them again, many years from now, when he and Conrad camp alone in the mountains and when, in the morning, Josiah wakes up and Conrad does not. There will be only silence, no trace of a soul sprung from its casing; just Conrad lying there in his sleeping bag, never to climb out of it again. It is Josiah who will come back to this place, hoping for fog, hoping to remember, hoping that Conrad is not truly gone, and wanting with all his heart to tell Kirsten, the woman he loves, that he has seen her brother again.

Noon in Three Cities

Nashville

TRAVELERS STAYING AT THIS HOTEL might walk by Raven, who is sitting in the lobby with Wheelock's Latin spread open on her lap, and easily draw their conclusions. She is perhaps a college student returning to school a little late in life. She is a woman of compact, contained strength; she is small, with powerful legs, and the flat chest and sleek arms of a swimmer or dancer. A rope of dark hair interwoven with auburn and new silver is slung over one shoulder, and the rubber band she's twisted it with can't hold the mass of it. Her shoulders are hunched over intently rather than in shyness, and when hotel employees pass her, they can't help but wonder who she is, where she's from.

Where she's from. Raven's eyes move over the now-foreign words and conjugations in her old Latin textbook, trying to determine just this. The last time this book was open on her lap, she was twenty, far away at a tiny Midwestern college, a place her father, a firefighter, worked like mad to put her through. He didn't want her at the University of Tennessee, where he said it was "all football hype and no true soul" and where he worried she would turn into one of those girls who decided to settle for an M.R.S. degree, and just become some athlete's wife. At the little Midwestern school, she lived in the leaves. Deepest scarlet, burnt orange, glimmering gold--autumn like nothing she'd known before. She studied late into the night, took long walks in the downtown, made friends with young men who could recite poetry over carry-out pizza. These were, she now knows, some of her happiest years.

This is the Microtel Inn of Nashville and she has been here before. Though the hotel is a chain--not the kind of thing she would normally be drawn to--this particular hotel, and the chain itself, is special. Since her late teens, anytime Raven traveled alone, she stayed at one of these hotels. It was the smallness of the rooms--the suggestion of potential, the sense of each room being a jumping point--and the window seats she came for. She loved the window seats. If she had a dollar for every poem she had written while curled up on one, her gaze often shifting to the window to watch a moonrise or some little drama in the parking lot below, she would be a wealthy woman now, and her daughter Ellie could be at home with her all week, instead of at daycare while Raven teaches literature and the oboe.

The owner of this hotel is special as well. In the lobby where Raven now sits, there are dozens of his framed photographs on the widest wall, all of them capturing the smiles of guests from past years. Guests at the breakfast tables, at the check-in counter, here in this lobby, lounging in chairs. Guests happy to be caught so candidly, in the midst of their travels. Raven's photograph, taken nearly ten years ago, is on this wall. She is considerably darker, her hair even longer, her eyes brighter. In this photograph, she is still single, though she has met Trace, the man she has only this past month divorced. Raven loves the fact that Trace is not in this snapshot, not physically and not in her eyes either. Raven is just Raven in this picture. Motivated and glowing with possibility, happy to be here alone, exploring this gorgeous city. The city of music.

She squints hard at her book, trying to see only the words: *laudo, laudas, laudat,* from the verb *laudare,* to praise. She tries to imagine herself back in the classroom, afternoon light streaming in from the windows facing the campus lawn, the sun warm on the side of her face as she takes notes in the margins. Instead she sees the woman her husband chose to sleep with behind her back, the woman who helped to break her small family into two jagged pieces: Raven and Ellie making one, Trace, the other. The still-fresh bitterness rises up like bile. This woman of all people. She has a face, Raven thinks, like an egg with the features drawn on with weak pencil. She is as transparent and ductile as Jell-O. No. She won't think like this. What's the point?

Her friends have told her: move forward. Move on. Raven thinks this is faulty. She wants to go back, not into her early memories of her romance with Trace, but before that. Yesterday after work, after she'd picked up Ellie from daycare, Raven went deep into the cardboard boxes in her closet and dug out the ringing reminders of those past years: photographs from solo travels. A tiny ceramic lighthouse. A bar of milky soap, smelling strongly of herbs whose names she no longer knows, bought from a roadside peddler. Sheet music she used in college. A citrus perfume an old roommate had given her. The smells alone made her swoon with want. Then Ellie was calling for her, wanting a snack.

I have a daughter, she told herself fiercely. *I can't afford to do this.* But she was afraid. She knew she had to do something. So she took a sick day from work and got right back on the highway after dropping off Ellie this morning. She shot straight down I-40 West from Knoxville to Nashville, one of the many cities she once visited alone. She checked into a room and didn't tell the receptionist that she planned on leaving before nightfall.

Things she is fairly certain her husband never knew: she loves the smell of diesel, the purr of engines on planes, and the feel of mulch in her hands. Extremes please her—mountains or the ocean, powerful storms or dead-still days, wild thorny roses and koi moving in tranquil figure eights in a pond. When on her own, she preferred ten-mile backcountry hikes to nature walks, and spent more time writing poems in oaky-smelling lofts in city libraries than browsing in bookstores. Everything was a mission; nothing was offhand.

Now, she wonders whether things would have gone differently, had she told Trace more about herself as she was before they came together.

He knows so little of her past. She has come to understand why she kept these secrets from him: these passions and journeys of hers represented her best. She guarded it, too frightened to grant him access. She did it so that an event like this--his leaving, his betrayal--could only hurt so much. After all, he hadn't had her best; and so he could not have rejected her best. She can safely say now that her strategy did not work. She should have been herself, no matter how sharp the angles might have seemed to Trace, who always seemed to love life so rounded, so cavalier.

The life of extremes and of deep commitments was what her father passed down to her. He died putting out a Knoxville factory fire eleven years ago, the last man willing to fight a blaze that had driven out all the rest of his crew. Snippets of Latin are coming back to Raven now as she remembers her father; she runs her fingers over her lips, leans over the book. Her father would not allow her to live a lukewarm life, and though she had sometimes resented his pushing and pulling, it was because of him that she had struck out so boldly on her own. He was not threatened by her boldness, nor by her findings out in that world; he let her be who she was. *Donum est magnum,* she remembers. The gift is great. It may be all she has left.

She leans in close to her book again, her hair falling over the pages, and finds the verb *ire*, to go. Her lips move over its complicated conjugations even as she watches new guests come through the glass doors, awkward with duffels and backpacks. Everyone laden with baggage, everyone on a trip that is only that: a trip. A short, vivid season in an otherwise uniform life. This couple, now passing by her, in their sixties at least: an escape from the duties of children and grandchildren, a renaissance in their marriage, a nostalgic visit to the city where they fell in love. This family of five: on vacation, where the father can think about something other than what he makes, where the mother can take a break from the endless cleaning and the rides to lessons and games, where the youngest girl, so timid-looking in glasses and braids, can get a few days away from the anxiety of school. When there is a home to return to, a husband or wife, any journey you make boomerangs you back. You aren't really free; you are in orbit, circling always what you left. Dizziness rushes over Raven. She doesn't want the kind of freedom she has now. She wants her family. Gravity.

She turns a page, and an old index card of hers falls out. The phrases there, in her deeply slanted writing, pierce her:

Poterant non superare (they were not able to overcome)
Potest non remanere (he was not able to remain)
Videre non poteramus (we were not able to see).

She shoves the card back where it was and starts turning the pages, faster. The Wheelock is well-worn. She used to know her way around it the way she knows Nashville's streets and the way she still knows this hotel. It feels as good in her hands as a gas pump does, or a hotel key, or a pen—symbols of her old life. But she can't find the infinitive *to love*, is shocked that she can't remember it, and the glossary in the back was the victim of a long-ago coffee spill, so that the words look blurred and ancient beneath the tawny stain. It hurts to look at them. She flips through the first chapter again, thinking this is where it would have to be—such a simple verb, such a staple verb—but her eyes are blurring, and she can't find it. A clerk, passing by with an air of crucial business, hesitates and then backs up.

"Do you have everything you need, Miss?" he asks, bending toward her.

"A postcard," she hears herself say. "Do you sell them?"

"Sure we do. There's a rack up at the front desk."

"Thank you."

She sets her book down and crosses the lobby. From the many glossy cards on the wire rack, she chooses two: one of downtown Nashville at night, the other of sprawling Percy Warner Park. She asks the clerk for a pen and hovers at the desk for a long time, trying to ignore the other woman's frank curiosity. Her problem is that she knows neither where to address them, nor what to write on them. She is at a loss for words. Words could not keep her father alive ("Don't go to the firehouse today," she would tell him as a teenager; "Stay home"), words could not keep Trace with her ("Don't throw away this marriage—we've hardly begun, and joy is a thing you have to work at"), words could not lift her own blinders ("Dear Journal: Trace has been so distant lately, but it must be that he's working too hard").

Finally, her pen moves. The first card, she addresses to her husband's new apartment. The second, to the house she grew up in with her father, though she has no idea who lives there now. On both, she writes, "Wish You Were Here." She signs neither.

"Will you add these to your outgoing mail?" she asks the front desk clerk.

The woman holds out her hand. "Of course we will." Then, smiling slightly, "Just out of curiosity, is that your picture on the wall? I see them every day, you know, and it gets to where you recognize a face. That picture, right there. The dark-haired girl. Is she you?"

"No," Raven says, with feeling. "She's not."

Asheville

TUCKED CASUALLY INTO A DIM CORNER of the Sidestep Café in mountain-fringed Asheville, Trace almost looks like he belongs. An overly-complicated iced drink, something shot through with "green caffeine," herbs, and pomegranate, sweats on the tiny table he leans against. He's haloed by a massive abstract painting done in red, brown, and yellow acrylics, and on the wall to his right is another bright maelstrom on canvas, this one faintly like a jungle landscape but on second glance not like anything at all. His clothes are right: hemp shirt, cargo pants, low boots. His salt-and-pepper hair is rakish. Most notably, he carries a green leather journal, which lies open and blank on the table, dangerously close to the widening pool of condensation from his drink.

Trace forces himself to take a long sip from his tea and then pushes it away. He swallows the gulp—it's too cold, too sharp—and tries to breathe in and breathe out, slowly, tightening his right hand into a fist and then releasing, an old trick he uses to stop a panic attack. He was in a panic this morning when he woke up in his new apartment just a few miles from here. It wasn't the first time he'd woken up there, and the place was filled with the furniture he and his lover had chosen together, but this morning, he was alarmed. The feeling was so strong that he thought of the time when he gave himself alcohol poisoning in college, drinking too much whiskey at a party, and ended up waking in a hospital bed, his stomach twisting in agony after having been pumped the night before.

He sits back and tries to look at ease. He watches the other patrons, a mix of young and old, but all with the same look and manner. They are carefree in a way that Trace has only recently begun to question. He wonders when they work, if they work. He is curious as to what their plans are, or if they all believe that they will stay here forever, wearing their organic clothes, shopping for local art, and strumming guitars on the streets. Each time Trace has caught himself thinking this way since he moved here, he has stopped himself: *You're being paranoid. You're overthinking it all. Just enjoy it. This is exactly where you belong.*

Still, his hand shakes a little when he reaches again for his drink. Two young women sit down at a table near him and they are so laden down with silver jewelry, they sound like ice cubes rattling in a glass. Both wear brightly-painted necklaces and hemp skirts, their hair highlighted, their tops tight and revealing. The jewelry irritates Trace, but he decides that his irritation is only the voice of his ex-wife, not his true feeling about the look. Raven never wore costume jewelry, or anything that didn't have some kind of meaning for her. A necklace was a part of her; a ring, a tiny world of memories contained on her finger. These women look a great deal like Trace's lover, Serena, and he reminds himself of how attractive he really finds them.

But again, the anxiety: he is tense at the prospect of coming home to Serena tonight. She will want to know how his job search went today, though she won't really care if he found something or not, and she will want to have sex. He is on edge just thinking about this last, fearing another moment like last night's: the horrible white blankness he'd peered into in the moment after he finished. He didn't know what he was seeing but he knows he doesn't want to see it again.

One of the café's perky waiters stops by his table. "Need anything else?" he asks brightly. "Want a shot of sugar in that?"

"Do I look like I need it?" Trace asks, trying to smile, and the waiter gamely responds, "Oh, I just thought I'd ask. I love sugar in anything. You just let me know."

He hurries off, and Trace looks down into his drink.

For the second time this week, he finds himself wondering what his father would have to say about a place like this. Like his wife, Trace was raised by a single father—a good man, a hardworking man—and it was a thing he and Raven had bonded over, a thing that set them apart from the other people they knew. Trace's father had been a window-washer. He was a man of few words, usually too tired to talk at the end of the day when Trace got home from school. But he was steadfast in everything, even food. Trace's best memories of his father involve the two of them eating together. Chinese buffets were the old man's favorite, but the two of them had a shared love for a simple Arby's sandwich, and sitting at this table now, Trace can taste it. Thin slices of savory roast beef thickly layered inside a soft sesame seed bun. The heat of the foil wrappers, the little cushion of red sauce his father would pinch open and spread in a perfect circle on the underside of the bun. He can see his father across from him in the booth, a little hunched over in his plaid or checked shirt, but happy: "They're always so darn good," he'd say, or maybe, "Gets me every time."

He wouldn't understand this place. He wouldn't understand what Trace is doing here. How he could be here.

The panic is rising in Trace. He fumbles for the pen in his shirt pocket and leans over his leather journal, flipping it to yet another blank page.

He came here to write or sketch, the way everyone else seems to in this town—to express himself. But when he presses the pen down, nothing comes.

His wife could do this. Every damn morning at sunup: there she was, typing away, or hunched over a notebook. "You have to commit," she had explained to him once. "It's like painting or acting or anything else. You have to commit."

That lighthouse-like persistence was what drove him mad. It was sexy at the beginning and then he couldn't take it. The weight of everything in her world, the way nothing was easy. Serena was nothing like that. The way she was late to work every day, the fact that she'd gotten an arts degree but hadn't touched her pottery wheel since, the thrown-together last-minuteness of her was what he loved. The girl had a memory-foam soul, immersed fully in the now but reshaping herself immediately after the pressure of a moment had gone. Sex too was simple, requiring no taxing journeys into a shared past, into other moments—and it required no real promises, either. Sex was an island. Everything they had was. And an island, Trace knows, is the easiest place for a man to live.

The truth was that he had been in love with ease since his teenage years. He refused to be ashamed of this. His series of addictions—he counts them now, the way some men might count the women they have slept with—were not signs of some flaw in him, but rather a manifestation of a wilder man, a man who liked to leap headlong at passing fancies, enjoy the moment, live for the hour. He tells himself that he still is that man and that is why he belongs here. This is a city of people who live for the hour. They are like space travelers, floating, rootless. Trace writes, *It's beautiful,* and stares at the words in dismay: his penmanship looks like a ten-year-old's.

He presses on, though, writing, *Trust me, Dad, I made the right choice. You would want me to be happy. Raven will be fine and Ellie is with her. I swear when Ellie is older and can understand, I will take her out to Arby's and tell her what happened and why I had to leave.*

The blank pages in this book sent excited chills down his spine the day he bought it, in an artsy little bookstore a few blocks from here. Now, the expanse of ivory in front of him seems endless. A tundra. His hand is shaking again.

"It's the caffeine," he murmurs, and one of the girls at the table near his glances his way.

He flips to a new page and creates a heading: *Things I Want.* Then he starts his list:

To design homes like I always wanted to.

To find a job that taps into my passions.

To never sit down in a cubicle in my life.

~~*To see the world.*~~ *To see the world with Serena.*

~~To experience~~

~~To learn to speak French~~

To learn to speak

HE STOPS. His phone is vibrating in his pocket. For a second he thinks it might be Raven calling before he remembers what's happened, and then Serena's name is blinking there. He shoves the phone back into his pocket and looks resolutely at his list. Why learn another language, he wonders? Where did that come from? He's never had an interest in this, except for when he was a child, and dreamed about having a secret language with his friends, something only they could share. The closest he ever came to that was the language he and his father developed for church: during prayer, Trace's father would hold his hand, and he would squeeze in elaborate patterns—codes that Trace would have to send back with his own squeezes. He loved it. He was probably eight years old, maybe younger, but he has never forgotten it.

He writes, *Pursue a spiritual life.* Then he laughs out loud at this, his short bark drawing more looks his way. The cliché of it sickens him. He glances up and around, taking in all the abstract art, and suddenly, that's what this whole place looks like to him: a cliché. A cliché, and nobody here knows it. They all believe so fervently in their own originality. But Trace's father, if he were here, would squint at these ridiculous paintings and say, "What are they supposed to *be?*" Because it didn't matter to Trace's father what a thing looked like. It only mattered what it *was.*

The old man died of a heart attack on the living room couch one night when Trace was eighteen. Trace was just outside on the porch, smoking a cigarette. For years, he wondered what would've happened had he skipped the cigarette and stayed indoors. He might have called 911 just in time, or heard his father's request for an aspirin (a request Trace only imagined, but still sometimes hears in his sleep). Suddenly, the need to hear his father's voice is urgent. Trace takes out his phone and closes the message announcing Serena's missed call. Of course, he cannot call his father, and it's just as well: what would he say? How would he justify the fact that he's left his own wife and child?

There is Raven. He could call her. He could tell her everything, the whole horrifying truth that has been slowly dawning on him: He doesn't want the newfangled drinks, the herbal iced teas. His relationship with his lover is like the art in this place—paint flung on a wall, a child's fingerpaint mess. Being with Serena is like relaxing by the pool after a long day of work. But he is empty without the work, the farming and the logging and the reaping that is love. He needs a mirror to reflect back to him the best parts of himself—the parts that are like his father, strong and true—and Raven was that mirror. The mirror is gone and instead there is trompe l'oeil, a phony landscape leading nowhere. But he can't call her, can't write her, can't get out a single word. What's done is done.

He gestures at the waiter, who hurries to his side. He says, "Can I just get a plain coffee? Just a plain coffee with cream and sugar."

"Of course."

Coffee with cream and sugar. Road trips with Raven. Winter nights, curled up with her by a window. A sweet treat after a long walk. He can't wait another minute for it. He is standing, moving toward the waiter, taking the cup from him. He tastes it and it isn't sweet enough.

"Could I put in more sugar?" he asks stupidly, seeing the rack of packets near the counter even as he asks.

"Of course."

And he does. He rips open packet after packet, spilling the crystals into his cup, tasting his drink after each one. But it is never sweet enough. He cannot find the taste he's looking for.

Knoxville

AT THE BRIGHT STARS DAYCARE in west Knoxville, Ellie is one of the last children anyone would notice upon first walking in. It is not a fancy, corporate daycare, but a small-scale place, a throwback, with an office by the door, a playground outside, and two large rooms equipped with plastic toys and play stations and coloring tables. Two women run each room, and in Ellie's room, it is Glinda and Bee. Bee, younger and sweet-natured, tends to do all the talking to the parents, and she is the one to prepare activities for the children and hand out the snacks. Glinda, gray-haired and silent, spends hours behind the desk at the room's entryway, either disinfecting crates full of toys with a bottle of Lysol, or organizing the walk-in closet that is her personal domain. Glinda is in charge of which toys go out and which ones stay in the closet, so that the selection of items available to the children depends largely on her mood. When patient, she lets them have the crayon sets, the washable paints, the puzzles. When irritable, they only get the larger, blockier toys, like the pretend stove with its clunky plastic pots.

The reason that Ellie is hardly noticeable is that she rarely speaks. Glinda calls her spacey; Bee suspects there is something more there and tends to fend for Ellie when she can, though she doesn't understand Ellie's silence any more than Glinda does. She can't know that the reason Ellie speaks so little is that this last year of her life, watching her parents' love for each other dissolve but not understanding why or how, has left her in a state of constant listening, as though for clues.

It will be years before someone identifies it, but Ellie has synesthesia—overlapping of the senses, a brain map bright with crossovers. Color has smell, smells have color. Music creates both colors and distinct shapes in her mind; at five years old, she is already understanding what it is that makes certain kinds of music triangular and other kinds circular. She knows that the circle-music makes her calm and that the triangle music is upsetting but also beautiful, sharp and thrilling in its sadness. The first time she told someone that the wind tasted gray-blue, she was laughed at. In this room, telling Bee that she wished they'd turn the music off because it was so yellow and white that it hurt her head, she sent the woman into a panic. Her mother was called, but no one could explain just what they thought was wrong with her.

Left to her own devices except for the rare hour when there is an organized activity, Ellie has wandered this room a thousand times and memorized every object in it. The play stations are like tiny worlds: the dress-up spot, the pretend kitchen, the puzzle and game shelf, the giant carpet with the train-track design on it and the cars to go with it. Ellie knows that there is a chewed-on plastic slice of bread hidden in the fake oven and a tiny toy soldier jammed into the trunk of a model car. She knows that the puzzle showing the fairy castle is missing seven pieces and she knows that there is a translucent stone from the fish tank in the office wedged into a thick storybook nobody reads. This last thing, she knows because she did it herself. She was struck by the beauty of those stones and waited her chance for weeks to steal one. She didn't need to own it, but she did need to see it and hold it, and bring it to the light.

Noon is her favorite time of day, first because of lunch. She hates the soggy cookies Bee hands out for snack, and so she holds out for lunch each day. Her box is a delight—fire-engine red, her mother's choice— and inside are treasures. Fruit snacks that also let the light through, like gems. The Teddy Graham crackers whose marbled surfaces fascinate her. The sandwich, its white bread moonlike when she looks at it closely enough to see the craters.

But the best part of noon is that this is when Glinda switches out the toys and sends out new ones. It is Ellie's ritual to ask for the plastic dollhouse and the Muppets at this time of day. There are five Muppets, a family of little rubber figurines that nobody else ever asks for or notices, and they are exactly the right size to live in this house. Once she has what she wants, Ellie will search through the big Tupperware bin that holds all the smallest toys, and find the furniture. There isn't much, but she takes enormous satisfaction in hunting down the pink plastic beds, the blue dresser, the TV, the sofa, the dining room table. When the house is furnished and Ellie is alone with it, she peoples it with the Muppets.

Today, she finishes her lunch and waits her turn to talk to Glinda. Glinda is angry, as she often is. She is telling one of the boys to stop badgering her, they are never going to have squirt guns in this room. A girl asks for the Play-Doh and gets a similar response.

"Oh, Glinda," Bee is saying from the lunch table, which she is cleaning. "Let her have it. It's not that messy, really."

"You aren't the one who cleans it up."

Bee shrugs.

Ellie stands on tiptoe to look at Glinda, who is bent over one of the shelves in the walk-in closet, rummaging through a bin. "Miss Glinda?"

"In a minute."

Ellie looks at the placard above the closet, which reads, *TOYS AND SUPPLIES*. She notes that the letter 'A' is red, just as it was yesterday, and that the 'D' is blue, but knows better than to ask about the colors. She already understands that nobody else sees this. But it makes sense to her. The letter 'A' *feels* red, always has.

"What do you want?" Glinda finally asks.

"The same," Ellie says, struggling to hold her ground. "The plastic house. And the Muppets?"

"Every day of the week," Glinda mutters and turns her back on Ellie, rummaging again. She comes back with the house, but that's all, and Ellie hesitates.

"I don't know where the Muppet figures are," Glinda says roughly. "I don't know if we have them. I don't feel like looking through ten bins for them today."

Stunned, Ellie just stands there.

From behind her, Bee says softly, "Jesus, Glinda, give the kid a break. Her parents—"

"I know all about it. Life's not perfect, better they figure it out sooner than later."

As the two women enter into a low but impassioned argument, Ellie backs up, retreating to her usual corner, where she sets up the house and then digs deep into the Tupperware bin. She finds the pieces of furniture one at a time. As she arranges them in the house, she thinks about what Bee said. Her parents. But there is only one parent. She is down by one. And with her father gone, the air in the house tastes different. The music her mother plays makes so many triangles, it hurts. It is a different world. Already, at five years old, Ellie is wondering if it is possible to resurrect forgotten colors, to recreate a taste.

The house is ready but there is no one to live in it. Ellie's hands flail a little inside the small rooms, as though moving the ghosts of the figurines from place to place, but it doesn't satisfy. She glances back at Glinda, who is sitting at the desk. Suddenly she is determined to get those Muppets, no matter what. If she could just have them in these rooms, for an hour or so…

She sits quietly, and anyone watching her would think she was staring blankly into space. But she is thinking furiously. She is rehearsing what she will say, composing her speech with care, weighing the options. When she rises, she moves with new confidence toward the desk. She is young, and she believes she can have her family back in this plastic house if only she says the right thing. She walks bravely forward, because she still believes in the power of words.

Heron in the Garden

Each Saturday that Heron comes home from Whitsun College to visit with his parents, he can't help but note the painful contrast between his mother's garden and the gardens at his school, which is a sprawling campus set in the foothills of the Smoky Mountains. He can remember being six or seven and finding this garden beautiful, fascinating even, with its mixed flowers and translucent stones and little gnomes peering out from behind shrubs. Today, as he pulls into the driveway in the car he spent the last three years working to buy, his mother stands up from a patch of weeds and waves.

"Your father's cigarette smoke is what kills 'em," she says as Heron comes up the walk. "My flowers. I swear, weeds grow just because they're dirty-natured like smoke and they love it."

"Aw Mom, come on." Heron rubs her shoulder and grins. "You know that's not even possible."

"Bet you ten dollars it is. How was your week?"

"I'm starting to like my composition professor," he tells her. "The one I wasn't too sure about? He's turning out to be pretty amazing. He read one of my essays out loud to the class on Thursday."

"You're kidding me. Which one was that?"

"The one I wrote about Dad and me. 'How to Survive in the Wild with Grace.'"

"That's incredible, honey. You have to tell your father. And how's your roommate? Benjy?"

"Ben, Mom. He only goes by Ben."

"Oh, right. He still okay to room with?"

"He's fine."

His mother points at the porch steps. "You set down. I'm gonna grab you some limeade. Your father's out getting the car looked at again. Somethin's wrong with the muffler. It sounds like a train coming down the line."

Heron sits on the concrete steps and his mother lets the screen door slap behind her as she goes into the house. He is trying not to cringe at the way she speaks, which for the first time in his life has begun to trouble him. Whenever he comes home, he can't help but imagine his friends at Whitsun—a private liberal arts school he never could have afforded without a scholarship—reacting to the words, "You set down." He wonders what they would think about this front yard. The back-yard is a whole other story: along the treeline are ancient models of backcountry shelters his father taught him to make when he was a boy, along with a sharpening block and a proudly-displayed board of ropes and cords Heron made out of tree fibers, also under his father's instruc-tion. Back when the old man was younger and didn't smoke so much, he made it his personal mission to pass on to Heron everything he knew about the mountains, including how to live in them. Heron's childhood and early teens years were spent pitching tents, hiking the national park trails, fishing in trout streams, and hunting.

He laughs quietly to himself now, remembering the mixed expres-sions on his classmates' faces as Dr. Weston read his essay: they were piqued, but confused. What he'd shared with them was a part of his life he knew he had nothing to feel shame for. But this house...he shakes his head, imagining what his roommate might say about the yard. Not that he has thoughts of bringing anybody here, to the old duplex in Townsend's backwoods, where the people who share a wall with his par-ents sell drugs out their back door.

He glances over at the neighbors' matching porch, and as if on cue, the door opens. The drug dealer's girlfriend dumps her baby daughter on the concrete landing and then goes back inside, slamming the door. Heron waits a few beats before climbing down his own porch. He doesn't know exactly how old the baby is—she might be a year old now—but she is young enough that she can't hold her head up very well. Heron has never heard her cry, and suspects it is because she already understands it to be pointless. The drug dealer and the girlfriend do this all the time—sit her on the porch and then leave her there—and the first time he saw this, Heron could only stand there and stare in disbelief. What hurt most was that she just stayed where she was, head down, the posture of her unformed body the very picture of defeat. Heron has seen the drug dealer grab her up roughly by one arm; he's seen the man practically throw her into her car seat the rare times they went anywhere with her. But even this was not as horrible as seeing her just sit there, a little hopeless lump on the concrete, and so he'd gotten into the habit of going over there and picking her up, and taking her around his mother's garden.

At the beginning, he was terrified that the drug dealer would come out and shoot him, worried that he might say something to *make* the drug dealer shoot him. The third time he picked up the baby, the mother opened the front door and rasped at him that he'd better not be taking her anywhere. Heron said simply, "I'm not, just here in the yard." He spoke the words without rancor—the baby's head against his shoulder softened him—and she watched him awhile before closing the door again. She must have decided he meant it, or found the free babysitting convenient, because she never opened the door on him again. Heron learned to relax a little, and speak to the baby in low tones as he showed her things. Now, he crosses the short distance between the porches and lifts the child off the concrete, feeling her hands grabbing up fistfuls of his shirt as he adjusts her in his arms.

He carries her into his parents' garden and makes for the scraggly crabapple tree where his mother's chimes hang. Murmuring, he tinkles the chimes for her, and is satisfied to see her reaching out for them, her blue eyes brightening. She makes some burbling noises and he wonders when she will start using words.

"The poor thing," his mother says from behind him. She sets his glass of limeade down on the tiny rock bench beside the crabapple tree and reaches up to rub the baby's head. "Why do people like that have children, I wonder."

"You know why," Heron says bitterly. "For the checks."

His mother shakes her head. "It'll be fall soon. It'll be too cold for them to leave her out there like that."

"I saw him wrench her arm once, you know that? He's disgusting."

"I know."

Heron bounces the baby gently as she continues to explore the chimes. He has thought many times about calling DCS and filing a report on his neighbors, but is terrified for himself. Surely they would know who made the call.

"I hate it when it gets cold," his mother goes on. "My garden looks terrible then."

Heron laughs, and she looks at him in confusion.

"Sorry," he says. "It's just—well, it's not exactly an English garden even in summer, right?"

His mother hesitates, then smiles faintly. "Not exactly."

"I'm just teasing," Heron says quickly. But his mother's attention is on the baby, and he has the same sensation he has nearly every weekend he visits now: that he can't seem to stop himself from saying cruel things, or at least thinking them, and he isn't even sure why.

"How are things with that girl?" his mother asks. She opens her arms for the baby and Heron hands her gently over.

"Alyssa. We're going to the homecoming dance together," he says, and he can feel the back of his neck reddening. This has been on his mind all week: the fact that Alyssa Harding, a sophomore that he'd been eyeing since the first day of the semester, chose him for the homecoming dance. His roommate has referred to the situation as a cosmic miracle.

"You really like this one, don't you?"

"She tested out of everything and started as a sophomore. Did I tell you that? She's doing a business major and a music minor. She's from the coast."

"Hm. What does she play?"

"Her minor's in Voice. Her mom was a singer," Heron tells her, thinking of the day he first saw Alyssa: through the thick glass window of a practice room. She had her head tilted back and he could just hear the pulse of her voice through the wall. When she noticed him, she kept on singing.

"Oh. Does she know much about the mountains?"

"Hardly anyone does at Whitsun," Heron says with a laugh. "But I'm going to show her some things."

"You should." His mother hands the baby back, and Heron hefts her partly over her shoulder, feeling the little head come to rest near his neck. "She's an angel," he says quietly.

"Alyssa?"

"This one," Heron says, patting the baby. "I wish we knew her name."

"Good luck askin' them. I wouldn't dare."

Heron's father's ancient pickup coughs its way up the driveway and comes to an abrupt halt.

"Carson, it still sounds like shit," Heron's mother calls out.

"Oh, don't I know it." Heron's father moves heavily out of the truck and embraces both Heron and the baby. "Good to see you, son. Good to see you with her, too. The little thing misses you when you aren't here."

"Go on, set her back over there, hon," his mother says. "Let's go inside a minute and have a snack or something. Carson, did you know his professor read his essay out loud to his class? The one about all the things you taught him."

His father, red-eyed from last night's shift at the Mayfield factory, grins at him. "Hell, son. I hope you didn't use my name. Go on, put that baby down. She'll be here when you come back out."

Reluctantly, Heron brings the baby back to his neighbors' porch, and as an afterthought grabs his sweatshirt out of his car and arranges it underneath her. He touches her smooth cheek and she gives him what he hopes is a tiny smile. When he turns around, his parents are waiting for him, and he follows them inside.

The kitchen is a mess. Molding garlic on a string over the sink, piles of dishes, brimming ashtrays everywhere, stacks of Tom Clancy novels forming small cities on what was once the breakfast table. His father sits down in his rocking chair beside the kitchen counter and his mother goes into the refrigerator and starts rummaging around for snacks.

"So the professor read your essay," Heron's father says, folding his hands in his lap. "That is something. What did everyone think?"

"I don't think they'd heard much like it til then," Heron tells him, grinning.

"Good. Maybe you can teach them something."

"You'd be the one teaching them, Dad. It's all stuff you told me. I even used your line: *Learning how to survive to save only yourself is never enough. If all you do is rescue yourself, you aren't saved at all.*"

His father swats at the air, as if at a fly. "Come on. You better not tell 'em you're gettin' ideas from an ignorant old man. I didn't even get through high school math, you know that?"

Heron says, "They don't need to know that. You still know things nobody else does."

His father harrumphs and then looks at his mother. "Do we have any coffee for him? He's probably drinking coffee now."

"I'm fine," Heron says. "Actually, I need to go grab some more clothes out of my room before I forget."

"It's your room, son," his father laughs. "It's not like you need permission."

In his old room, Heron turns in a circle. The threadbare rug, the old posters on the wall from teenage obsessions of his, the sagging bookshelf that reveals the whole of his literary journey, from CS Lewis' Narnia to Steinbeck's California—a journey taken more out of desperation than out of a real love for the literature. These books were his only way out of this place when he was younger, other than those trips to the rivers and into the backcountry with his father. He reminds himself that this duplex, this neighborhood, is not going to be his life anymore. Now that he is on the track he's on, there will be no factory jobs like his father's, no babies being left on porches next door.

Quickly, he rifles through his bureau drawers and finds the sweaters he knows he is going to need soon at Whitsun. Secretly, he is hoping to end this routine of coming home every single Saturday, and he doesn't want to need anything from here.

He kneels there holding one of his old sweatshirts and breathes in the mixed scent of cigarette smoke and cheap detergent. It is a smell that he loves but cannot admit to loving, and as he holds the shirt to his face, he is overcome with the same panicked confusion that has been taking him in strange moments out of the blue since he started at Whitsun. Then he recovers himself, and returns to the kitchen, where he coaches himself not to say anything about his father's coughing, or the sound of a shotgun going off in a distant neighbor's yard. He blinks back the sudden wetness in his eyes when his father asks, in deeply respectful tones, what he is learning at Whitsun, and what the instructors are like there, and what it looks like on campus with the leaves starting to turn—as though it is Heaven itself Heron has been disappearing to all this time.

When he finally does leave, the baby is gone from the neighbors' front porch, and so is his Whitsun sweatshirt.

THE FOLLOWING SATURDAY is the homecoming dance, and Heron tells his parents he has too much to do and can't come home for his usual visit. His mother tells him, "I was hoping you'd help me in the garden, but I want you to have a good time. Show that pretty girl somethin' she ain't seen before, like you told me."

"I will," he promises, and he means it. He is going to take Alyssa to the most beautiful place he knows, a secret place he has visited alone many times since his early teens, when his father showed it to him. The place is called Look Rock—a white lookout tower perched high above the western Smoky Mountains, at the top of the winding Foothills Parkway road above Townsend. He has already explained to Alyssa that after the dance, they will go back to their dorms and get some sleep, and then he will pick her back up before dawn so they can make the drive to the secret place. But she knows nothing more than this, and the mystery of it all is lending an air of both romance and authority to Heron, which he would enjoy immensely if his roommate weren't so bitter about the whole situation.

Adjusting his suit in front of the floor-length mirror in their dorm room, Heron sneaks glances at his roommate, who is hunkered over in the bucket chair next to his bed, wearing the woolly pullover he always lounges in. Ben is making his way through the assigned reading for their Political Economy class, a highlighter in hand, but hasn't turned a page in twenty minutes. He does not have a date for the homecoming dance—a fact they have both managed not to address over the course of the past week.

"Alyssa Harding," Ben says at last, snapping the textbook shut. "You know, I've been trying to figure it out, how you of all people pulled it off. A sophomore. And I think I know."

"What do you mean?" Heron meets his roommate's eyes in the mirror and their gaze holds.

"It's all that mountain-boy crap. The way you dress—those shirts? Where are you getting them from? And your accent, and all this talk about the country, and camping by the river, and Hemingway-type shit that girls go crazy for. That business in your essay in Weston's class. That's why they're all into you. That's why you've got Alyssa hooked on you and you've barely seen her outside of class. I mean, where does she get a chance to know you? When you're stalking her in the music building?"

It is the most Ben has said to him in one sitting since their first night in this room. For moment, Heron just studies him in the mirror.

Ben says, "I hit the jackpot, huh?"

"No," Heron says. He takes his suitcoat off, feeling suddenly overheated. "It's not true. I talk to Alyssa all the time."

Ben laughs. "Notice how you make no move to contradict anything else I said."

"I meant, none of what you said is true. I'm not putting on an act."

Still laughing, Ben tilts his head back and looks at the ceiling. "Oh, right. Heron, if you really were some country boy, you wouldn't have gotten into this place to begin with. And look, what's with the name, anyway? Is that another thing you just put on? Nobody names their kid after a bird."

Heron sits down slowly at his desk. "It was my mother's idea. She loves to garden. She told me that her perfect garden would always have a heron in it, so she gave me the name."

"Wait, you're serious?"

"Serious as a heart attack," Heron says, then bites his lip—it is one of his father's clichés, and it embarrasses him every time it slips out.

"Okay, okay, let's say that's really your name. But how long can you keep the rest of it up? This country-boy adventurer crap."

Heron reaches for his suitcoat. "I have to go. I have to go pick her up."

"Whatever you say. Go easy on her."

"Right."

In the car, Heron reviews the conversation word for word. The idea that after all of his hard work to fit in here, the others might think the truest parts of himself were actually the projected ones—he can't wrap his mind around it. He wonders if Alyssa thinks the same way Ben does, and believes that all of his stories, his efforts to bring what he knows into their world, are merely calculated attempts to win others' attention.

He refuses to believe this. Since arriving here, he has felt certain that he could pick and choose which parts of himself to keep and which to discard. He could leave behind the embarrassing facts of his upbringing, but hold onto the things he loved, like the knowledge his father passed on to him, and the awareness of the land's beauty. This last, he knows, is what really matters: his sense of having an inside understanding of the mountains. Any time in his life that he has felt insecure, the intimacy he has with that beauty has been a rudder to bear him through the moment and back to himself. The scissoring of trout in amber water, the way yellow leaves make figure eights as they fall from poplars, the pungent sleep of a bear in its boulder den—these things make him feel pure and infallible.

As he pulls up in front of Alyssa's dorm, he feels sure of himself once more. He is positive that Alyssa is interested in who he really is. She knows that he is different from the others at Whitsun, and her interest in him is proof that Ben is wrong.

ALYSSA KEEPS CLOSE TO HERON at the homecoming dance, although there are plenty of others to talk to, and more than once she's asked to karaoke up on stage. She wears a pale pink dress that flutters at the shoulders and falls gracefully along her hips. Her heavy blonde hair is partly taken up in a silvery band of some kind, and every time they dance, the light trembles there. Heron can't help but bask in all the attention, though he knows it is only by proximity that he has earned it. The two of them speak little; each time Heron tries to talk, Alyssa leans in close and shushes him, telling him to just move with her. He can hardly say no, and they sway through one song after another as other couples move around them.

Only when they take a break for drinks does Alyssa initiate conversation: "So when the dance is over, we split? And what time do you pick me up again?"

"Five AM," he tells her, grinning around his water glass.

"Oh my *God,*" she moans. "Why does it have to be before dawn?"

"You'll see."

"Do I stay in my dress? Or are you expecting pajamas?"

"Do whatever you want."

"I'll stay in my dress. Might as well get some use out of it. I'll never wear it again."

"Good. I'll stay in my suit. Just try to get some sleep before I come get you."

"I'll do my best." She takes his elbow and nudges him back toward the dance floor. "Ready?"

The song is a slow one, and Heron tries to create a little gap between them as they move so that he can talk to her. "Alyssa," he says quietly, "tell me something."

"Sure, Heron."

"Do you think my name is made-up?"

She laughs, her head rocking back a little. "I always wondered."

"Well, it isn't."

"Okay."

"I'm from Townsend, right by the national park. That's where we're going. Have you been out there?"

Her brow furrows. "I don't think so."

Heron opens his mouth to tell her more about where they are headed, but she cuts him off: "You know, I bet I know where you grew up. One of those big chateau-looking houses that are way up on the mountainsides by the national park? I can remember them. It was like somebody started off building a log cabin and then decided to make a castle instead."

Heron knows which houses she is talking about—they are actually on the eastern side of the park, far away from Townsend—but he has seen them, too, and as a child often imagined what it would be like to live in such a place.

"Will you show me?" Alyssa persists, her face turned up to his. Her skin is flushed in the warm light of the dance floor, and flawless as wax fruit.

"Maybe a different night," he tells her. "We have something else to see first."

They dance, and Heron tries to focus only on the smell of her hair and the feel of her body against his.

AT FIVE O'CLOCK IN THE MORNING, Heron returns to Alyssa's dorm, and she is there, sitting on the curb in her pink dress.

"This is crazy," she says excitedly as she climbs into the car.

"I know. Did your dorm monitor see you?"

"No way. I'm way too slick for her."

Heron laughs. "Of course you are. You cold?"

"I'm okay. How long of a drive is this?"

"About a half hour. Not too bad."

"All right."

They are quiet as Heron navigates first the highway and then the smaller, winding roads leading into Townsend. When they start the sharp ascent up Foothills Parkway's hairpin turns, Alyssa sits up straight and tries to peer into the darkness outside her window. "This road is scary," she murmurs.

"It's okay. I've driven it a lot."

"Can your engine handle this?"

It embarrasses Heron that his engine is in fact audibly struggling, but he smiles. "It'll be fine."

The climb is long and Heron takes the curves slowly and with his brights on, watching constantly for deer. He tells Alyssa a story about hitting a deer once in his father's pickup truck, and then bringing the deer home with them afterwards, and then stops when he realizes how quiet she is.

"You brought it home? To do what?" she asks at last.

"Well, to eat it. It's the law in Tennessee that if it's a fresh kill, I mean on the road, you can take it home with you."

"You just hauled roadkill back with you and what, skinned it right there on the porch?" Alyssa is laughing, her head thrown back. "Oh my God. You are so full of shit, Heron. I love it."

"I'm not making this up," he insists, but she squirms over to his side and hooks her arm into his.

"I love your stories," she says reassuringly.

Heron is quiet. They are nearly to the top, and his determination to prove Ben and his own nagging suspicions wrong is overwhelming. He sits up high in his seat, squinting at the road, looking for the spot. When he senses it ahead of them, he slows the car dramatically.

"Are we there?"

Heron brings the car to a careful stop in the grass on the side of the road. "We're here."

Alyssa points at the woods—black, opaque—and says, "You're kidding, right? There could be bears. Or all kinds of scumbags doing God knows what in there."

Heron laughs. "There won't be. Just come on." He coaxes her out of the car, and the moonlight washes over the pale pink of her dress as she lets him take her hand. He helps her up the narrow trail that moves gently uphill through the woods, and he tries not to notice when she curses under her breath—something about her shoes. She seems nervous. But to Heron, the woods are welcoming, embracing them; the silence of their walk is a kind of meditation or prayer, readying them both for what is to come.

Finally, he can see the lookout tower ahead of them—an unlikely thing, a shocking thing if you weren't looking for it, especially in the moonlit dark, with its spirals pearly white. It is like a great conch shell deposited atop the mountains by some colossal wave. He feels rather than hears Alyssa's gasp.

"It's a lookout tower," he explains softly. "Anyone can come up here, but hardly anyone does. I think people just don't know it's here."

Alyssa holds tightly to him as they begin the ascent to the lookout. Heron knows just how high up they are, but decides not to tell her, wanting her to see for herself when the first light comes.

They stand together with their elbows propped on the ledge, peering out into almost complete darkness; there are just a few scattered lights from Maryville and other towns in the distance. It is much colder here than it was in Townsend, and Heron takes off his suitcoat and drapes it over Alyssa's shoulders. She adjusts it and he thinks he sees her smile.

Then she says, "So what are we doing up here again?"

Her voice is surprisingly loud, and a little shrill, a thing Heron has never noticed before. But he rubs her shoulder and says reassuringly, "It's going to be worth it—you'll see. Just wait a little while."

Alyssa makes an impatient movement under his shoulder. "I wish you'd just tell me."

"I can't. That would ruin it."

"You sound so excited."

Something in her tone troubles him, as though she is implying that his excitement is somehow infantile. The same anxiety he felt with Ben in his dorm room rises up in him and he has to fight to swallow it back down.

"I *am* excited," he says with an effort.

Alyssa says nothing. Heron is relieved. Their voices up here sound too loud to him. Intrusive. Like the world of night that orbits this tower has its own demands, and might depart from them with all its beauty if they break its unspoken laws.

"Wait a minute," Alyssa says. He feels her hand move against his back, then up under his shirt; the coolness of her skin sends a tremor through him. "You don't have devilish plans for us, do you? So soon?"

Confused, Heron opens his mouth to respond, then stops as her hand comes around in front and dips just below the waistband of his dress pants.

It is a thing he has fantasized about more than once. But instead of arousal, he feels a kind of panic—like they are about to miss out on something terribly important.

"Hang on," he says, tugging on her hand. "Just hang on. Just wait. Watch the mountains."

In the darkness, Alyssa's silence is unreadable. Heron tries not to think about this as he scans the horizon. And then, there it is: the first rose-gold spark, like a tiny flame burning in a single tree on a distant mountain. His hand tightens around Alyssa's. The spark takes. The trees around it seem to blaze softly, and as it always does, this first sighting shakes him deeply. It is as human and hopeful as a campfire in the wild, as rich in faith as a man of some ancient time praying to a sun god. Then the flood begins: rose around the rims of the sky, rose brushing the tree tops, rose falling into the ravines and calling up the mist. Swaths of precipitation disguised as low clouds flirting with the earth fill the coves and valleys. Every few minutes, another version of the world is revealed, which is the way Heron imagines creation to have looked to God in those first few hours. Violet and amber and blue pour down the mountainsides like the sky's overburden and pool in the rivers. And when the sun ascends the staircase of Mt. LeConte and pauses on the landing, it erupts into a six-pointed star whose brightness knocks both Heron and Alyssa back a step. The light is so utterly clean, so perfect, it sears Heron's heart.

He has to tear his eyes away from it all to look at Alyssa.

What he sees on her face staggers him. It is the same polite but frozen expression he has seen on people's faces when talking to salesmen over the phone, or trapped in some taxing conversation with a complaining relative. She is struggling to look interested and impressed, and of course, all that really shows is impatience and confusion.

"You do this a lot?" she asks finally, offering him a small grin.

"Sometimes." He tries to grin back. It feels so false, it seems like it has to be ugly, but Alyssa's smile widens.

"So *now* are you going to tell me why we're up here?" She pulls him toward her, hands on his waist. In the new light, her makeup is dry and caking around her eyes, and he can see that the color of her skin is not really hers, but a shade of cream or powder she has applied and must apply every day.

"We should get going," he says. "Your roommate's going to be worrying about you."

"Are you serious?" She shakes her head. "You really are something, you know that? You're a nut." She says this playfully and reaches up to tousle his hair, but he can tell that she is as irritated as he is. Their walk downhill through the trees is rushed, nothing at all like the climb up which now seems to have happened years ago.

They drive back to the college in yet another near-silence. When he pulls up in front of Alyssa's dormitory, she hesitates before getting out of the car. "That was fun," she says at last.

"Yeah."

HE KNOWS SOMETHING is terribly wrong as soon as he turns onto his parents' street. An ambulance, red lights flaring, is parked between their house and the neighbors', and there are a lot of people standing around in their driveways, looking on. For a moment he thinks it is his father: *he's had a heart attack. Please God, no.* But then he sees both of his parents, also standing outside in the garden, in their bathrobes. He swings the car against an open stretch of parkway and leaps out.

"What happened?" he demands of his mother, who stands within the circle of his father's arm.

"Oh, honey." Her eyes are red; she is actually wringing her hands, a thing he has never seen her do. "I wish you hadn't come."

"What is it? What—" And then he looks at the neighbors' house, and he knows. The paramedics are closing up the ambulance, and two police cars are making their way up the street. The ambulance goes abruptly silent, and then pulls out into the road, leaving the scene.

"They found her dead in her crib," his mother explains, her voice breaking on "crib." "At least that's what they told 911. They just got up this morning and she wasn't breathing."

Heron watches as four police officers move past the crowd and into the duplex. They seem collectively disgusted, as though they have seen all of this before.

"They killed her," Heron says through gritted teeth. "My God, they fucking killed her. They starved her or suffocated her or hit her with something. I know it. I know they did."

"Calm down, Heron," his father hisses. "The cops are here, all right? They're here. They're gonna ask them all about it."

"It's not enough," Heron cries. "They killed her, Jesus Christ! You know they did."

As if hearing him, one of the officers reappears, and moves directly toward them. "You live here?" he asks, gesturing at their house.

"Yes," Heron's father says.

"You ever see anything that looked like abuse going on over there? Did you ever see either one of them rough-housing that little girl or hurting her in any way?"

"I can't say I did," Heron's father responds, "but my wife and I seen them leave her on the front porch a lot of times. Just settin' there by herself."

Heron's fists are clenching and unclenching. The officer looks at him. "And you?"

"He's always known somethin' wasn't right there," his mother interrupts. "He used to carry that baby around so somebody would hold her. He kept an eye on her back when he was here."

"And you don't live here anymore?" the officer asks, pulling out a notepad.

"No," Heron says with difficulty. "I'm at college."

"Whitsun College," his father adds.

"You knew they were hurting her? And you never called child services?" the officer demands, leaning closer.

Heron has no idea what this could mean for him, if he were to admit that yes, this is exactly what he knew, and exactly what he failed to do. In a rush, he imagines the worst: his scholarship gone, his schooling over. A return to this place, maybe for years. His old room with its cheap posters and nubby carpet.

"I don't know about them hurting her," he says at last. "They would just leave her on the porch, like my dad says."

He can feel his mother's eyes on him but he stares straight ahead, at the officer, who meets his gaze for a moment and then writes something on his pad.

"We might come back with follow-up questions," is all he says before turning around and going back into the house.

Heron watches him go, if only so that he can avoid looking anywhere else. But eventually, he has to face his parents, and to his surprise, they are also gone, moving back into their house. He stands there in the garden and looks down the street and sees the rest of his neighbors, still hovering in their driveways, silent. He looks toward the highway, in the direction of his college, and sees only the flat, dulled light of sun filtered through heavy clouds he hadn't even seen coming.

JONAH

WHEN I TRY TO EXPLAIN TO PEOPLE where I'm working now, their expressions always slide from confusion to incredulity and then right into something annoyingly like pity—that look that says, "You must be punishing yourself for something." I always hurry to fill in the concerned silence that I know is coming, and I tell them, "It's just a placeholder til I can get a job teaching art history," or, "It was all I could find after graduation; you know how bad the economy is." Then I change the subject and hope they've got the sense to let it alone. Usually, they do, except for one time at Wal-Mart when a lady reached into her purse and handed me a pamphlet for battered women (at the time, I had a black eye from when one of our ninth graders punched me with a football).

If you want to understand what my job is like, imagine a New Age school from someplace like Oregon hybridized with a fundamentalist Christian academy. My boss, Melinda, does everything in the name of God, but her pedagogies promote so much independence and self-expression in our students that most of them spend very little time at their desks, and even less time actually learning anything. "Let them do what they feel they need to do," Melinda loves to say. "Let them be themselves, just as God made them!"

"Being themselves" translates into scenes that most educators would find unbelievable. Sometimes I imagine this tiny school as a reality TV show that the whole nation is watching. Honestly, it really is that entertaining, when you can step back from it and pretend it's not your actual life.

Our cast of characters is impressive, with our kids ranging from age nine to eighteen. With four of us teaching here, and the kids divided up into rotating groups of two, three, or four, we each have a set we tend to spend more time with. My set consists primarily of Morgan and Mindy, who are nine and still learning to do math using plastic blocks. Both have a smattering of learning disorders. Then there is L.J., who is eleven. His parents are absurdly wealthy, his father a doctor and his mother a vain neurotic. His ADHD and anger management problems mean that we are constantly talking him down. My older group consists of Kelley, Ralston, Rita, and Tanner. Kelley is sweet but clingy and three grade years behind; Ralston is delicate and sensitive, always desperate for affection, but his self-hatred make him rough to work with; his rich parents barely know his name and have a nanny who picks him up most days. I once heard his mother say to Melinda about me, "I don't care what degree she has, that girl looks like she's been trash, you know? Where did you find her anyway?" Rita fancies herself Gothic, and paints her face white every day, her eyes two black holes in the caulk. She's a classy girl; she's carved the words "fuck" and "cunt" into every desk in the school. She's been expelled from two other schools, once for splashing turpentine into a teacher's eyes. Then there is Tanner.

Tanner is everyone's nightmare—he is eighteen, the child of parents who gave him a Mustang for his sixteenth birthday even though he already had a criminal record. He is violent, and dumb as bricks. He is our chair-thrower, our window-breaker, our food-poisoner (I found glue in my sandwich once), and our hitter. Everyone's worn a mark of his at one point or another. The black eye he gave me in September is healed, but he shoved my head into our flagpole one morning in November, then turned and did the same to L.J. L.J. at least had the right to scream obscenities at Tanner, but not me: when these things happen, Melinda croons, "We have to forgive. Forgive and just love them."

There are no detentions here, no failing grades, no tests. Their parents pay for the report cards that will one day say to some east Tennessee college, "my child went to a private academy, and he got A's." And they pay through the nose. I make about eight hundred dollars a month here, but the parents pay private academy rates, and Melinda collects quite a bounty. I came into this job thinking I'd be helping kids who were underprivileged and desperate—foster home kids, mentally challenged kids forgotten in the crowds, abused kids. It's more like overindulged kids whose disorders are really code words for "spoiled rotten."

It's the second week of January, and over the Christmas break, I told myself I could come back for another semester and not lose my mind in this backwater mountain town in the middle of nowhere, in this yellow house that's been converted into an academy for Knoxville's rejects. Alone in my apartment, with snow grazing the windows, I worked on lesson plans (I do these in secret; Melinda doesn't like the limitations structure places on children) and talked to myself. I took long walks and stopped to pet my neighbors' mangy dogs and cats whose names I've gleaned over time: U.T., Sweet Baby Ray, Forrest, and Jefferson. I convinced myself that I was doing good work at the academy. I promised myself I would not scream or cry or swear at anyone like I had been on the verge of doing for months, no matter what they did to me. I said to myself, "You are there for Jonah, if for no one else."

I live for Jonah. He is the reason I have not torn off my stupid nametag and gone storming out of this place. Now, as I hang up my coat in my tiny classroom (once somebody's bedroom), I hear his heavy footsteps in the hallway, and I catch myself smiling. I am his primary teacher; no one spends the amount of time with him that I do.

"Miss Amelia," his voice booms. He really projects, and my name resonates off the walls. I turn as he enters the room, and when I see him, I have to check my natural reaction to reach out for him. Jonah isn't like the other kids—his problems go way beyond concentration issues or a bad temper—and I know he has a condition, but he's never been diagnosed. Maybe his father would rather not know, and hold onto the hope that this could all change at any time. Jonah gets frustrated easily, and he's not the type to let you hug him, ever. "Not even if he loves you," Melinda once chirped at me. "But he doesn't like anyone here, trust me. Nobody wants to work with Jonah. Maybe you can do something with him?"

Jonah is twelve, big for his age with coarse blond hair and intelligent green eyes. He is the only child here whose family is well-meaning, not to mention poor: his father, a widower, placed him here as a last resort, unable to find a school that would work with him, and the man works like a dog at the paper mill to pay for it. The only way to get Jonah through the day to is to stick to the routines he has come to know and trust. If anything is out of whack, Jonah is the first to panic and get desperate, which is of course the worst way to be at a place like this. I mean, Melinda tells L.J. to walk in circles around the classrooms when he feels antsy, so half the time when I'm teaching Jonah and L.J. together, L.J. is in orbit, weaving around poor Jonah who cannot focus with L.J.'s head roving in and out of view.

Generally speaking, Melinda is right: Jonah does not like anyone. He tells it like it is, and has managed to alienate every student and teacher. He's told Mindy, "Don't come near me, I don't like girls"; to L.J., "Your brain is the size of a seed"; and to Tanner, "I'd rather talk to a pumpkin" (I barely hid my laugh at that one. A gourd? He was spot on). The other teachers, Arya, Jennifer, and Frances, can't stand him. That's how I ended up with what Melinda calls Jonah Recess Duty: during lunch and recess each day, I sit with Jonah in this room, because he refuses to eat with the other students or go outdoors to play games.

Now, Jonah sits back in his seat with his vocabulary workbook in front of him and he eyes me. He is rocking a little, just perceptibly swaying back and forth.

"Well," he says, which is how he starts most sentences. "We're back."

"We're back," I say. "How was your Christmas?"

"Oh, well, we didn't do anything. No money. And my cat got hit by a car."

I stop. "Queenie? Is she okay?"

"She died."

I sit down across from him; he reaches into his jeans pocket and pulls out a beat-up photograph and hands it to me. It's a younger Jonah, holding a fat white cat in his arms, dingy furniture and his father fuzzy in the background. Written on the back in a woman's faded handwriting is *Jonah with Queenie, July 4.*

"This is her?" I ask. "I'm so sorry, Jonah."

"Well, it's okay. My dad said she was pretty old. You can keep that," he adds as I try to hand the photo back. "You keep it."

My eyes are already stinging and it's only 8AM. I tuck the photo in my pants pocket and fight the urge to rub Jonah's shoulder. "I'm really sorry, Jonah. I know it's hard to lose a pet."

"Well, it happens. Where's L.J.? Maybe he's at some other school."

I laugh. "I don't think so."

On cue, L.J. comes shuffling in, dragging his Spiderman backpack across the floor.

"What's in there?" I demand.

"My Christmas gifts," L.J. says smugly. "I brought them to show."

"Wonderful. Let's wait til recess, okay?"

"I knew you'd say that." With a gusty sigh, L.J. dumps the bag against the wall and plops down into his seat.

"It's time to start," Jonah says nervously, pointing at his watch. "Page fifty-seven is where we were before the break. Page fifty-seven."

"Page fifty-seven," I agree, to cut him off. Jonah has a habit of repeating other people's phrases over and over again, particularly when he's anxious. I can hear in a neighboring room Jennifer already begging Rita to please leave Ralston alone, and I stifle the panic that has been rising in my throat since my alarm went off this morning.

AFTER VOCABULARY WITH JONAH AND L.J., I spend forty-five minutes with
Mindy and Morgan, working in a different room. Mindy is quiet, uncer-
tain of herself after the long break, but Morgan can't stay in his chair,
and I spend most of the time coaxing him back to his seat. He jumps up
to look out the window, to change pencils, to examine a stain on the floor,
you name it. By the time we're ready to shift rooms, I've had it with him.

I have to pee and the prospect still fills me with dread. Our bathrooms
don't lock; they are unisex bathrooms, one on each floor of the house,
and Melinda thinks that locks on the doors will alienate the children
from each other. When I go (which is only when I'm desperate), I shove
the big white supply shelf in front of the door so that no one can come
flying in. But today, the shelf is gone, and I stare at the blank space of
wall like I've entered a time warp.

"Fran," I call out as I see her passing by, "where is the supply shelf?"

"You mean the door blocker?" she asks wryly, not stopping. She has L.J.
in tow; he's smacking her leg with a binder. "I have no idea."

"Great." I close the bathroom door and wait. Sure enough, Tanner
bursts in, but instead of yelling "I SAW YOU" like he normally would,
he slams the door behind him and grabs both my arms before I can react.

"You have to kiss me before I graduate," he announces without pre-
lude, as is his way.

"Tanner, let go of me." He's tall, and I hate having to look up at an
eighteen-year-old punk.

"No, I mean it. One kiss. We can do it now, or later."

"I vote neither. Let go."

"If you don't," he says calmly, "I'll put a golf ball through your apartment window. I almost did it before. I was outside your house with a golf
club and a sack of balls." For a moment, his seriousness dissolves as he
enjoys a requisite giggle over "sack of balls." Then he recovers himself:
"I'll put one though your window one night and it'll probably hit you in
the face."

Tanner used to terrify me, but I've built up an immunity. However, the part about knowing where I live makes my hair stand up on end. "How do you know where my apartment is?"

"It's right down the street from my house. On Winston Road."

"How did you—"

"Kiss me now or I'll do it."

"That's the way to get a woman, Tanner. Really hot," I tell him. "Did you notice how hitting me in the face with a football didn't exactly make me fall in love? This isn't, either." I know what works, and sure enough, Tanner lets go. I say, "I'd like to pee now."

Tanner laughs and says, "You looked good even with a black eye." Then he walks out. I watch him walk to his class down the hall—math with Jennifer. He looks like a criminal even from behind, and I know he'll do it, put golf balls or baseballs through my windows one of these nights. I could talk to Melinda, but she'd only lecture me about giving the students every chance to improve themselves, rather than judging them.

My next class is Bible Study, which consists of me reading Bible stories to Jonah, L.J., and two others, Keith and Lila, while they pitch fits and sporadically leave the room. They don't hear a word I read, except for Jonah, who always whips out his Post-It note pad while I'm reading and will create tiny illustrations to accompany the stories. I have several of them: Jonah inside the whale (my Jonah drew this guy reading a book in there; he told me it was a book mapping the anatomy of a whale, which might help him find his way out); Adam and Eve with the apple (Eve has a dialogue bubble saying, "Don't you want to know the truth?" and Adam saying, "I'm scared"); Daniel in the lion's den (he is holding forth from behind a lectern, and his bubble reads, "If anyone can get us out of here, it's me").

Today, we're reading Cain and Abel. If you don't know the story, the short version is this: Cain and Abel, two brothers, make sacrifices to God. God likes Abel's sacrifice but doesn't care for Cain's. Cain ends up knifing Abel in the fields. When I pull out the Bible, Jonah is in his corner, away from the others, with his notepad ready. L.J. has an action figure in his lap and Keith keeps trying to grab it. Lila, whose attention is always a million miles away, keeps shooting looks at the lights above us like they're speaking to her. I read the story, tuning out L.J. and Keith's hisses, and when I finish, I ask the question Melinda requires me to ask: "What is God's message in this story?" I have a big jar of Tootsie Rolls, ready to be distributed to anyone who will answer.

"Don't kill," Keith says immediately, holding out his palm for a candy. I give it to him.

"Don't kill *family*," L.J. adds, impressed with himself. I toss him a Tootsie Roll and he puts it in his mouth without unwrapping it. I know the wrapper will emerge eventually and land somewhere on my person.

Lila stares fixedly into the candy bucket as though there is a holy vision swirling there.

I say, "Jonah, any thoughts? Could I see your picture?"

He gets up and hands me his Post-It note, then returns to his desk. "Well, there was a reason, you know."

I look at the picture: it's just two stick figures, one dressed like a shepherd, the other, a farmer. Abel inspects the sky and Cain seems to be cursing at the ground. I say, "A reason?"

"For why he killed Abel."

"What was that reason?"

Jonah opens his mouth to answer, and there is a cheery knock at our door, which I know to be Melinda's. She pops her head in and gives me a big smile. "Amelia, would you mind stepping out into the hallway for a moment? I can sit with your students. Morgan's made a little mess and I'd like you to get it cleaned up."

I feel my spine straightening and I almost say, "Actually, you can go to hell, you miserable twit," but I get up and go, stuffing Jonah's picture into my pocket with the photo of Queenie. Morgan takes the occasional crap in the middle of the hallway, and Melinda always calls on me to handle it, maybe because I'm the newest addition here and she thinks my hourglass holds more sand. I close the classroom door behind me and spot the little heap of turds on the hallway floor—just a couple feet from the bathroom door—and sigh.

I gather up the turds with some paper towels, deposit them in the bathroom trash can, and spray the scene with Lysol. As I'm finishing up, Kelley wanders up to me, her long dark hair in her face, her poorly-fitting clothes seeming to fight her every move. She is fifteen years old and a complete mess, and though she crowds my space, I can't help but love her.

She squats down beside me and asks, "What happened?"

"Morgan shit on the floor again."

Swearing is the one thing nobody here is allowed to do, and Kelley's eyes light up with laughter; she covers her mouth. "Oh," she finally gets out. "Oh, man. Sorry you had to clean it up."

"Yeah. What an existence, you know?"

"What an existence," she agrees.

We get up and I see her eyeing my hair, my sweater. Kelley thinks I'm beautiful. I don't know what planet she's living on—I've got hair like Anne of Green Gables, an outsized head and a body just as oddly proportioned as Kelley's. But she thinks I've got it all together. She copies everything I do, even steals my phrases, and I want to tell her that I'm nothing special.

"I love that bracelet," she tells me, touching the copper band that has crept out from my sweater sleeve. "Most of the time, I can't see it. But you wear it every day, don't you? Where'd you get it from?"

I push my sleeve back down over it. "It was a present."

"From who?"

I say, "Shouldn't you be in class?"

"Science," Kelley says, making a face. "Miss Frances."

"Well, go on in there. The poop show's over."

She grins and hurries to her classroom at the other end of the hall. I turn back to mine just as Melinda is stepping out of the door. Once that door opens, the wilderness comes spilling out: Jonah and L.J., both screaming, their arms wrapped around each other. They fall into the hallway in a tangled mess and I can see scratch marks and already-forming bruises on their arms. L.J. shouts, "Get off me you fatass, don't you ever touch me," and Jonah lets out a grunt of some kind and bashes L.J. in the head.

"Boys, boys," Melinda cries out, standing there with both hands at her mouth, ineffectual as always. I dart in, making a quick decision to go for L.J. first. He's smaller than Jonah and won't kill me on reflex for touching him. Somehow I get him out of the pretzel of their kicking limbs and start hauling him down the hallway. Jonah, red-faced and shaking, stands up and shouts back, "Don't you ever touch me, don't you ever touch me, don't you ever touch me!"

"Boys," Melinda says. "Apologize to each other now. Forgive each other. Or nobody gets recess."

They ignore her. L.J. shakes me off and I let him go. He storms into the bathroom and slams the door so he can take an angry pee. Jonah shoots Melinda a disgusted look and goes back into our classroom. I say nothing to her as I follow him. Keith and Lila are huddled in one corner, Lila's eyes wet and owl-like.

I open the candy jar. "It's okay, guys. Everything's under control."

But we get nothing done before lunch, and when my little class disperses, I am alone in the room with Jonah, who is visibly relieved.

"What happened, anyway?" I ask him.

"Well, I looked in his backpack, at his Christmas presents," Jonah explains. His gaze wanders longingly to the corner where the backpack still sits. "He said they weren't for me."

"That sounds like something he would say. Look, I'll go get your lunch," I tell him. He nods, rocking a little, and then gets up and goes to the little TV and DVD player we have in one corner. Jonah moves from one obsession to the next, usually spending a few weeks on each one, and his latest obsession is Pearl Harbor. We watch chunks of the movie every day at lunchtime, and he points out all the historical inaccuracies. Jonah hates Ben Affleck and we bond over this, among other things.

The kitchen is a madhouse with everyone seated around the huge lunch table, paper bags and wrappers everywhere, Jennifer on her hands and knees cleaning up a juice spill and Kelley and Ralston fighting passionately over a bag of SunChips. L.J. sulks at one end of the table. Tanner is kneading his ham sandwich into a giant ball, mashing neon-bright Gushers into it so the whole thing looks like a shoddy strobe light, and I wonder where that sucker's going to land when it's all said and done. Poor Arya is struggling to eat her yogurt amidst some pretty stomach-turning comments from the kids about what yogurt looks like. She is too lovely to work at a place like this; she is statuesque, regal, in her beauty. Even as I'm thinking it, Rita says nastily, "She *has* to eat yogurt. Look how fat she is," and I want to slap that Gothic makeup right off her face.

I tell myself to breathe slowly. I am claustrophobic by nature and working here has tested that from the first day. Lunchtime is hard. I go to the microwave with Jonah's mac and cheese and move through the exact process he showed me my first week here. Noodles first, water in next, just slightly above the recommended line; then heat it up, add the cheese, and stir one full minute. The other teachers tease me for doing it his way but this is the only way he will eat. Last semester, I discovered that if he saw one of us making the macaroni with any variations to the process, he would not touch it, and go hungry the rest of the day. I promised him I would do it right and he watched me for weeks before he learned to trust me; now I can make it without him standing here monitoring. I feel pretty good about this. Earning Jonah's trust in any sense takes a lot of labor.

As I watch the microwave's yellow light, I think of our best moment yet, mine and Jonah's: it was one of the few days he'd been willing to go out for recess, and he and I jumped around together on the big trampoline out back. His laugh, big and full-throated, seemed to fill the whole yard as his weight sent me careening into the air and back down. Nobody else was willing to jump with him. Jonah's clumsiness tends to unnerve the other teachers; they can sense disaster coming whenever he does try some physical feat. I hadn't learned this yet. Eventually, Melinda called me back to the house to clean up some mess, and a few minutes later, I heard a cry from Jennifer: Jonah, jumping alone, had somehow fallen through the poles on one end of the trampoline. He was struggling there like an animal in a cage, his leg stuck, and he screamed at Jennifer when she reached for him. I pushed her aside and Jonah let me help him out. He was shaking; I think the shock of it was what had gotten him, not the pain. On the grass, he just sat there with both hands around his leg, trying to get his breath back. I sat beside him, not touching him, and I said, "All okay now?"

He said, "Well, just stay here another minute." I was stunned and I stayed where I was until he said, "Okay, all good now. Well, that hurt. That trampoline is a hazard. That's why I don't go outside." Later, when his father picked him up, he said to me in the coatroom, "You must be something special, Miss Amelia. Because Jonah never once told me about his day until you started working here."

The microwave beeps and I pull out the macaroni and stir in the cheese, watching the clock until the full minute is up. As I pass out of the kitchen, Tanner leans back in his chair and says, "Remember what I said." I roll my eyes and keep going. I notice L.J.'s Tootsie Roll wrapper on my thigh, pasted there with spit.

PEARL HARBOR IS PLAYING when I reenter my little classroom, and Jonah does not look up when I place his macaroni on the desk in front of him. I go into the supply closet and retrieve my lunch from where I typically hide it, behind a barrel of markers and crayons, and sit beside him.

"Well, same lunch as always," Jonah comments as I pull out a peanut butter sandwich and check it for any surprises from Tanner.

"Look who's talking," I point out, and he nods. He picks up the remote and fast-forwards through a mushy scene between Ben Affleck and Kate Beckinsale. He has a deck of cards in front of him—this was a new obsession right before Christmas—but he won't touch it until he's had his fill of the movie. Jonah never invests in two things at once.

We eat, and Jonah is unusually quiet. I say, "Did you do any new investigations over the break, Jonah?"

"The megalodon," he responds and takes a bite of his macaroni.

"Still on that, huh? You just about drove me crazy with that in December," I remind him, smiling. And he really did—he talked about that behemoth fish through every lesson I tried to teach, to the point where I very nearly shouted at him to stop. But I have never shouted at Jonah, and I intend to keep it that way.

"Well, there was no creature like it," Jonah begins, and he reaches for the remote and *Pearl Harbor* is gone, the screen blue. He shoves his cards aside. He launches into a description of what his latest research has uncovered about the monstrous animal, and I listen, amazed as always at the way his brain works. He rattles off facts that graduate students would take weeks to memorize, as casually as though it is just weather talk. He has no idea what his talents are. He just falls in love with ideas, one at a time, and dives in. He lets them take him. It's beautiful. That is the way I used to paint, when I first admitted to myself that I was serious about it and wanted to make a life out of it. In school, I would lose whole days sometimes to the colors, and emerge out of that vibrant coma shocked at what I had made. When Jonah asks, "Well, do you want to see pictures?", I have to say yes.

He asks me to get his picture binder out of the closet, where he too hides things that are important to him, since the other kids have a habit of sabotaging his little treasures whenever they can. I find the green binder and flip through the mad and fanciful pictures he has cut from magazines and printouts until I find the megalodon shark. As I smooth back the page, something catches on my wrist and it hurts.

"Ow," I mutter, and pull back my sleeve.

"What's the matter?" Jonah demands. "Is it bleeding?"

I look; my bracelet has cracked, probably during that wild scuffle with

L.J., and the broken edges are scraping against my skin, creating tiny red lines.

"No, it's not bleeding," I tell him. "Damn L.J. I think he did this."

I look up just in time to catch one of my favorite grins of Jonah's. It's a small one that he reserves for moments like these when we're partners in crime; in this case, my bad language has set it off.

"Damn L.J.," Jonah agrees. "Well, I told you he's an idiot. I told you eight hundred times."

"You did."

Jonah returns to his macaroni. He'll give it a minute or so and then come back to the megalodon. I start to nudge the bracelet off my wrist but stop—it's been there so long that my arm feels too exposed without it. I go back into the closet, find the little First Aid kit that Melinda keeps there, and pull out a couple of Band-Aids. I bandage up my bracelet so it doesn't hurt anymore. Then I look up and around. Suddenly, this room feels smaller than ever, its yellow walls suffocating, and I stand up and go to the single window. I draw back the curtain. It's only a view of the street, but beyond, above the houses, is a glimpse of the frosted Cumberland Mountains. Against the soundtrack of Jonah's quiet chewing and the distant din of the lunch table, I imagine hiking through those woods, not alone, breathing in pine and that strange scent that is only on summits, that unmistakable aroma of trees that love themselves and trust in the worth of their own ageless stories.

I'm almost there, my hand tight in another's, when Jonah says loudly, "Well, why aren't you married?"

I spin around. "What?"

"Well, I don't care. My dad asked me."

"Your dad?"

Jonah jabs his plastic fork into the bright orange noodles. "My dad asked, why isn't Amelia married. Why is she at this school and why isn't she married."

"I'm not that old," I say, trying to laugh. "Who says I need to be married?"

Jonah gives me an unreadable look.

"You can tell him that I just don't—that I haven't—you tell him I'm just not."

"Well, that's not a good answer," Jonah says calmly. He pitches the empty container into the trash can and reaches for his binder.

"Well what exactly is a good answer?" I demand. "What does he want to hear, Jonah? What does he care anyway?" I can feel my face flushing.

When Jonah senses anger, he does one of two things: he takes it up, giving it momentum of his own, or he retreats into dramatic silence, refusing to engage. With me, it's always the latter, which Arya claims is what makes me special around here. But it doesn't make me special. It just makes me feel like shit. I watch him bury himself in his binder and I look back out the window.

"I'm sorry, Jonah," I say to the glass.

There is a pause. I turn.

He is looking at me, those green eyes of his both disapproving and accepting, a look that no child his age should possess. "Well, it's okay."

I have an inspiration. "Jonah, would you like to learn to paint? I mean, paint really well, paint anything you like. I can teach you. I have all the supplies. I know how, I mean, that's what I went to school for, mostly. Did you know that? Your dad wouldn't have to buy anything, I can bring it all in. Watercolor, oil, whatever you want. Would you want to try?"

"No thanks," he says simply. "I hate art class. With Miss Jennifer. I hate when she makes me draw."

I know he does. I know my idea is stupid. I say, "Okay. That's okay."

I'M SUPPOSED TO TEACH HISTORY at two o'clock, and this is the one class where Jonah has to mix with the older group. It's always an ugly scene, since there is bad blood between Tanner and Jonah, between Rita and Ralston, between Ralston and Kelley, and perhaps most of all between Rita and myself. Tanner scares me, but Rita's spitefulness can poison a room. I am no saint -- I have no patience for her scenes. Today, I'm hoping that after a two week break, things will be different, and I start by assigning them new seats. Jonah is next to Kelley, who has a calming effect on him, and Rita is as far away from Ralston as I can get her. Tanner is just to my left, dangerously close to me but a long way from Jonah, who has often gotten the brunt of his fist (or chair) during a temper tantrum.

We're talking about Mesopotamia and I don't blame them for not caring. But as soon as the first balled-up sheet of paper hits my back, I feel heat rising in my neck. By two o'clock, I'm nearly spent. I hate this tiny room—we're underground, with no windows, and the air is stale.

"Can we try to focus? I know it's the first day back, but we need to get through some of this," I say.

"Sure, Miss Amelia," Rita says, drawing out the "e" in my name. Then, "I really like those pants. They look *great* on you. They're just like my grandma's."

I continue writing on the board and something wet lands on my arm. I peel it off and keep writing but my hand is shaking. I hear Tanner mutter, "I dare you to."

I turn around just in time to see Rita mouthing something at Ralston across the room.

"What was that, Rita?" I ask. "I didn't catch that."

"Nothing," she says sweetly, her raccoon eyes finding mine.

I look over at Ralston, who sits with his arms folded over his big stomach. His delicate fingers are laced as though in prayer. Rita has always been his tormentor, calling him "homo" and worse, and suddenly I want to champion him at any cost. "What did she call you now, Ralston?" I ask. "What was today's really mature remark? I'm sure it was deeply intelligent, just really unique."

Ralston says stoutly, "I don't know. I don't care."

I look at Kelley. "What did she say?"

Kelley shrugs, eyes on the floor.

I say, "You know what, Rita? I think we've all had enough. It might be time to grow up."

But Rita only dissolves into giggles, smearing her makeup as she covers her mouth.

Tanner raises his hand; he is smiling slyly. "She said, 'old maid,'" he tells me.

Confused, I look at Rita. "Excuse me?"

But it's Ralston who answers: "She was calling you an old maid." His face is very red, and I realize the mistake I've made—I've embarrassed him by trying to come to his aid, verifying for everyone that he is in fact the "pussy" Rita claims him to be.

Then I really hear his words, and I turn on Rita. "You're boring us all," I say calmly. "Please leave. Go sit in the hallway until you can handle a class."

"I don't think so," she responds, stretching out her legs in their skin-tight black pants. "I'm pretty comfortable right here."

Kelley's cheeks are pink and she is staring into her lap. Ralston won't look at me. Tanner is loving all of this, his whole body tensed for a fight. I glance at Jonah. He is grinning at me, and at first, I think he's on my side.

Then he says, "Old maid." Just like that.

I've dropped my dry erase marker and I bend down to get it. In that moment, Tanner shoots out of his chair quick as a fox and shoves me in the hip. I go down hard on the tile floor. Pain spears through my right knee and I close my throat against vomit. It feels like the kneecap's shattered and for a moment I just close my eyes against the pain. I can hear Tanner and Rita laughing hysterically, and Jonah repeating over and over, "Old maid, old maid, old maid…" I stand up and try not to favor the right leg. I say, "I'm twenty-six," but nobody hears me; they are smart enough to understand how much Jonah's betrayal hurts, and they're reveling in his toneless mantra.

What I want to do is grab Rita by her sleazy black shirt and throw her out the door. Or call the police on Tanner, tell them about his threats, and get him put on probation. Instead I stride up to Jonah and scream into his face, "Jonah *shut the fuck up! Shut up!*"

I've probably said it five or six times before I realize his face has gone flat, and that my voice rather than his has filled up the room. Everyone is silent behind me. Jonah and I just look at each other. I know I've just shattered four months' worth of work with him but I'm too shaken to take that in. I watch as he gets up, overturning his chair as he goes; he trips a little, and the others laugh at him. He goes clamoring up the linoleum stairs and I know he's going to spend the rest of the period in the kitchen, alone at the lunch table. It's where Melinda tells him to go sit when things get to be too much for him.

I start to follow him, but feel Kelley behind me on the stairs. She is hanging on to my sweater.

"What," I say, whipping the word out at her.

She flinches but holds on. "I don't think you're an old maid. Even if your man left you."

"He didn't leave me," I say, shaking her off. "Where did you get that from? What man are you talking about?"

"Miss Melinda told us the day you were sick," she says, her big doe eyes on mine. She's innocent; her lip is trembling. "She said you had a sad love story. She said you'd tell us one day if you wanted to."

"Miss Melinda doesn't know anything about it," I say acidly. I feel sick. I feel like something is filling me up from the inside and threatening to detonate. "I don't know where she got that from."

"So there isn't a love story?" She is disappointed. Her eyes are still huge and locked on mine. I feel myself softening and I reach out to touch her hair.

I could sit down on these stairs with her and tell her everything, cry on her shoulder like I'm the child and she the woman. I want to. I know she would listen.

"No," I tell her. "Nothing worth telling about anyway. Go on back in there, I'll be back in a minute. I have to try to talk to Jonah. I have to apologize. Go on."

She lets go of my shirt. I trudge up the stairs, my knee aching.

JONAH'S ALONE AT THE FAR END of the big lunch table, toying with his deck of cards. He's closed the half-door to the kitchen and I hover against it, propping my chin on my hands. I study him. He ignores me. I wonder if he would forgive me, would come back to me, if I explained everything in terms he could understand.

How do you tell a love story without sounding ridiculous? How do you pluck out the details that matter, that tell the truth? What would I say about Kiernan, if I were willing to try? He was thin and barely taller than I was. He was dark Irish, with pale skin but walnut-black eyes. I still find Irish men beautiful, and my breath catches when I see the familiar down of dark hair against a man's pale arm. Clap a watch on that white wrist and I'm gone. He said "I love you" a lot, in unlikely places like a crowded coffee shop or at the Laundromat downtown where we'd sit together for hours talking against the hum of the dryers. He was a painter like me, and we found each other a few months out of graduate school, both of us wondering how on earth to translate our passions into a living, into independence. He walked into a gallery in Knoxville and came to my side in front of a watercolor as though we'd planned all along to meet in front of that very frame.

When he painted something and let me see it, it was like peering into a mirror. We painted letters to each other instead of writing them. He saw me naked when he saw my paintings; he knew me, as I knew him. He accepted what he saw. We were so much the same—bounced around from foster home to foster home all our lives, holding tight to our brushes like they were our real addresses. I still don't know if I loved him as much as he loved me, but what I did feel sure of was that love of his, the pulse of it emanating from some unseen but promising source, like quartz in a watch. He told me he would give up anything for a house by a mountain lake with me, and a child or two, "even if we couldn't afford a washing machine." He asked me to move in with him and proposed with a tiny blue diamond. He said our children would never know loneliness. I told him I couldn't. I gave all sorts of reasons but I didn't give him the real one: I was certain that this thing we had was a fiction, because people like me didn't get to have a life like this.

I still think that Kiernan must have been something I just dreamed up. That brand of happiness is to me like an unidentified element, a baffling swatch of life that plunges past the radars and that everyone knows has to have come from some rogue planet. I think of him telling me he loved me in the middle of a coffee shop, and I wonder if he actually spoke those words or if I invented them.

And yet I know perfectly well it was all real, because as I stand here, shuddering against this kitchen door, all I can think about is how I would feel if Kiernan had witnessed this day out of my life. I can still hear myself screaming into Jonah's slackened face, and I swallow hard as if to bring the words back down.

I look at Jonah, sitting placidly at the end of the table, cutting his deck of cards.

"Jonah," I say, and he looks right at me.

"The Cain and Abel story? You remember, we were talking about it earlier today? Before everything went to hell?"

He pauses and I can see the beginning of a grin: that conspirator's grin, the one I love so much. "Yeah. I remember, yeah, before it all went to hell."

I hold on tight to the door. "I never got to hear your answer. Why did he do it? Cain, I mean. Why do people do terrible things like that?"

Calmly, Jonah cuts the deck once more. His hands are steady now and his face is no longer contorted as it was a few minutes ago. "Well, he did it," he says, "because he didn't think he was worth anything better."

"You mean, to God?"

"To anyone."

I fish in my pants pocket for his Post-It note picture and study it again: Abel's face raised expectantly to the sky, his shepherd's hook held firmly in one stick hand. Cain, stooped low beneath his straw hat, his mouth a quivering line. I look back at Jonah, who has set down his cards. I know he won't ever let me hold him, and certainly he will never come to me. So I accept his gaze, and try to make it fill the spaces—that look of his that is punishing and yet full of unbearable mercy.

MITHLAND

THE HOUSE IS FULL THIS MORNING, with Livia home on her college's fall break, and Hendley back from boarding school for the weekend as usual. When Mollie props herself up on one elbow to listen for her parents' voices, though, there is only silence. She has been doing this experiment every morning for so long now that the movement sends a familiar pain shooting up one side of her back. She listens harder. It is the thick of autumn in the Cumberland Mountains, and she can at least hear that— autumn's sounds. Hard leaves grazing the sides of the house. Two owls calling to each other—always a sad conversation. There is a row of miniature pumpkins on Mollie's windowsill, gifts from her father, that bump against each other when a rough wind rattles the house. Mollie fears the day when they will begin to rot, and with these morning listening sessions comes a quick overview of her pumpkins' condition. When she is satisfied that her pumpkins are still thriving, she gets dressed.

Giving up on hearing sounds of any kind of improvement, Mollie stumbles around her room hunting for clothes and tries to choose something appropriate. It is Saturday, and her brother and sister are taking her to see the old family land—a place called Mithland, high up in the mountains a little ways west of here. Livia and Hendley have been up there dozens of times, but Mollie has never seen it, since their parents abandoned their care of the place years ago. The first she heard of it was two nights ago over a nearly silent pizza dinner: Livia startled everyone by asking suddenly, "What are you going to do with the old land? Are you selling it?"

"You should probably go see it one more time," their mother told her by way of answer, and Livia actually went pale. It was the first sign of emotion Mollie had detected in her sister in weeks, and she sat up, waiting for more.

When no one else spoke, Mollie felt her self-control going, and demanded loudly, "What land are we talking about?" She hoped to shock everyone with her loud voice, but no one really responded. Finally Hendley explained to her that it was land they had owned for four generations, but her parents had been the ones to name it. Then he set another slice of pizza on their mother's plate, saying quietly to her, "Keep eating, Ma. You look skinny to me," and the conversation was over.

"Mithland," her mother told Mollie later that night as she balanced her checkbook, "is a mythical place out of Tolkien. Lord of the Rings. We were crazy then, your father and me. Crazy in love. We didn't even spell it right—that should have been a sign." She laughed shortly, looked back down at her ledger. "Mithland. We thought we'd *live* there."

Her father, smoking a cigarette on the back porch, told her essentially the same thing. Then after a pause he said, "Have you—do you know what you're going to do? I mean—have you talked to your brother and sister?" He asked the question formally, his tone steady, but the hand that held the cigarette was trembling. Mollie just shook her head numbly, and her father closed his eyes.

"They're good kids," he said at last, and Mollie could see that he was a little drunk. "They wouldn't want to influence you."

Clothes pile up on the bed and the floor as Mollie moves angrily through shirts and pants. She is twelve and nothing fits her right anymore. Her hands work furiously at buttons and zippers, and all the while, she is talking to herself.

"I'll ask them today. I'll make them tell me. I don't care if I cry. I don't care."

Finally she settles for a pair of grey hiking pants and a dark blue long-sleeve shirt. She tugs at her hair in front of her mirror and gives up on that, too, yanking it into a rough ponytail. She looks critically at her face. A putty face, she decides. Beady eyes, pale mouth. Certainly not a face anyone would be tempted to stick around for.

In her best tough voice, practicing, she says to the mirror, "If all they want to talk about is that damned Mithland, I'll kill them."

There is a knock at her door, and it's Hendley, her brother, holding a little maple branch with the leaves still dangling off it. "Good morning, Little Miss," he says to her. "You look ready for the mountain."

Mollie takes the branch, its scarlet leaves like ripe cherries waiting to fall. "Thanks. I guess I am. When are we leaving?"

"Soon as we finish breakfast. Come on, I made eggs. Livia went to gas up the car."

She speaks carefully: "Are Mom and Dad here still?"

His tone mirrors hers: "No, Dad went to work and Mom had shopping. The house is ours."

There is a pause, and in that moment, Mollie looks searchingly at her brother, scanning the old loved features: the wide and expressive mouth, the blue eyes that match their mother's. He is a reader, a very still person, and at his school he wears tweed and old blazers he finds at the Salvation Army. He has a way of speaking to her, a way of moving around the house even, that makes the boys in her class seem like bumbling apes. If there is anyone she should be able to talk to, it is Hendley, even though he is five years older. She is burning with her question, almost sick with it. She opens her mouth. But she sees his face close, and he says, "Well, come on then. It's getting cold."

She puts the leaf bouquet in a plastic cup, fills the cup with water, and sets it on the windowsill before following her brother into the kitchen.

THEY RIDE IN THE ANCIENT SEDAN Livia drives at college, and Mollie sits in the back, feeling the same way she always does with her two siblings:

excluded, mystified, clumsy. Livia drives. Her sister in particular, though she is home less often now, always makes Mollie feel stupid to herself.

From her seat behind Hendley, Mollie studies Livia as she drives, making mental notes as though there is hope that she too might look like this one day. Livia is small like Mollie but carries herself like a young queen. Her long wild hair is in some kind of complicated half-plait and she wears a dark blue hiking dress over heather-grey tights and flat calf-high walking boots. Her glasses change shades with the light and right now they are violet-grey in the autumn sun; behind them, Livia's thick-lashed eyes are two foreign worlds to Mollie, eyes as sensitive as Hendley's mouth but never really revealing of anything. Mollie's gaze fastens on her sister's leather and sterling watch, a thing Livia made by hand, and she feels hopeless.

The two of them, Livia and Hendley, are talking without talking, caught in the private rhythm Mollie has resented all through her child-hood. They are like binary moons, following in each other's orbits every-where, talking passionately into the night about the same ideas, the same places. Hendley's school is just a few miles from Livia's college, and he plans to join her there in a year. To Mollie, they seem so fully formed that she finds them frightening, the way people are frightened of geniuses. She is certain they have it all figured out: what they are going to do next, how they'll navigate the next few years before they are old enough to have their own homes. She wants to beg them to take her with them so that she doesn't end up completely forgotten. But what use could they have for her?

Livia has taken them down a tiny country highway, and with Hendley murmuring reminders, she hunts down a tiny grassy lot in a gap where the mountains rise up in reds and yellows around them.

"This is the trailhead," she announces, meeting Mollie's eyes in the rearview mirror. "It's just a few miles to the cove where the old place is. But it's going to be pretty uphill."

Mollie nods and follows her brother and sister out of the car. Hendley has to move some fallen branches at the start of the trail, and the path is visible but overgrown and thick with dead leaves. Mollie hikes behind Livia and Hendley, trying to watch their feet while also taking in the thick forest around them. The hike is difficult and she tries not to pant audibly, but can't help it. Livia moves like a wood nymph and Hendley too is almost soundless as he climbs. The birches scattered among dark oak, walnut, and cherry look like slender ghosts lost in a crowd of the still-living. Mollie is troubled by them and tries to keep her eyes on her siblings.

When Mollie judges it has been long enough, she takes a big gulp of air to fuel her question: "So what are you guys going to do?"

The question hangs like mist in the forest air but Livia and Hendley continue up the trail. She sees them exchange glances. Hendley says lightly, "We're going to show you the whole place. The house is boarded up, but there is a second trail near the one that leads to the property, and it goes through the woods. There's a hidden waterfall, and a bunker. Family secrets."

Mollie's quick rage at his effort to distract her flutters away at this last remark. "What secrets? What do you mean, a bunker?"

"It was a Civil War bunker. They used it to hide soldiers who wanted out of the war. Soldiers from both sides," Livia explains, turning to face Mollie at last. "That was our family. They fed any soldiers who found the trail to the property and let them wait out the war if they wanted to. They wanted to help them get home."

"Where is it?"

"Hidden. You can't see it from the old house. You have to take a separate trail to a place where the stream forks. We'll show you." Livia's wide eyes behind her glasses are flashing; she is alive with some intensity Mollie can't fathom. "It's beautiful. Not the bunker, I mean, the forests there. The way the trail is carved out. It really is something out of Tolkien. I've looked into the history. Can't figure out if it just happened that way, or if the first settlers planted those groves deliberately. In some places, it just doesn't make sense. It's like art. It couldn't have been an accident." Out of breath, Livia nods as if to close the conversation, and turns back to the trail. Hendley follows suit and Mollie, surprised at her sister's fervor, also falls into step behind her.

THE TRAIL FINISHES ITS CLIMB and opens into a wide amber field. In silence the three siblings cross the field toward the house and barn, moving through the stalks of dead wildflowers and grasses, until the trail forks. To Mollie's surprise, Livia leads them to the right, instead of continuing on straight to the house.

"We can see that last," she tells Mollie. "You'll love it, there's a big garden out back, and a huge pumpkin patch backing up into a pine forest."

"Biggest pumpkins in Tennessee," Hendley adds. "You should see the patch. All tangly and crazy-looking. It's wild."

Mollie opens her mouth, rehearsing what she plans to say: "Why in the world are we talking about pumpkins? Does nobody but me care about what's happening to us?" But they are moving ahead of her fast, and all she can do is struggle to keep up as they lead her down this second trail.

The trail follows a deep stream whose current is moving swiftly past them, downhill. The stream winds its way through thick maple, oak, and hickory forest, and the leaves are falling in droves, often landing on Mollie's head or shoulders. After about a half mile, a rickety wooden bridge spans the stream, and beyond it, another slender path opens to their right, beginning a downhill course.

"That's the West Fork trail," Livia explains. "It goes to a hidden waterfall. Do you want to see it?"

Mollie has to say yes, and they take the short, rocky path down to where a branch of the stream rushes down a rock wall into a deep green pool. The rocks around the water are laced with moss and the mist rising from the falls is opalescent in the light. The three sit down on the rocks and watch the water for a while. Mollie watches the dance of the water but is debating how to bring up the subject again. Maybe, she thinks, it would be best to talk to each of them individually. Maybe then she could get an answer.

They return to the main trail and continue on through the woods. Livia and Hendley talk excitedly, pointing out particular trees. "There's the elephant!" Hendley says triumphantly when they pass a massive stump that does in fact seem to have a trunk and ears. "He's just the same."

"We're coming up on the ginkgo cathedral," Livia narrates as they walk. "That's how you know you're almost to the east bridge."

The gingko cathedral turns out to be a perfect circle of ginkgo trees, their shell-like leaves forming a carpet of soft yellows and greens in the clearing. Mollie follows Livia and Hendley into the clearing, and looks up at the canopy of intertwining branches overhead.

"This was no accident," Livia goes on. "Somebody created this, meaning for it to look like this forever, for whoever came here later."

"The whole place is like that," Hendley murmurs. "Somehow, it stays so perfect."

"What's on the other side of the east bridge?" Mollie asks, impatient.

"You'll see," Livia says.

Mollie starts to say more, but they are already walking again, returning to the main trail. The river seems to be moving faster past them, and they are beginning to climb again, moving toward the summit. Mollie knows the house and barn are in the distance somewhere to their left, but she can't see them, and the forest seems endless, deep and heavy.

Ahead of her, Livia says softly, "We could save up the money to buy it. If we both worked."

"I've thought of that," Hendley admits. "I've been thinking about it for weeks. If we both took on more hours—if we got some more loans for school—"

"What do you want to buy?" Mollie pants, catching up with them.

"Mithland," Livia says.

Mollie says, "Oh." Then, "Why?"

"Here's the dogwood tunnel," Hendley says, his voice taking on the same excitement as before.

Mollie follows his gaze; ahead, the path thins and cuts through a tunnel of dogwoods that are in ferocious bloom—red, pink, and still-green. The dogwoods are thick. It is like stepping into a heavy and fragrant bouquet.

"I want to go ahead a little, make sure the bridge isn't out," Hendley says as they start down the tunnel.

Livia hesitates.

"I'll be okay," Hendley assures her.

"Be careful. There are bears."

"I know." He walks ahead, disappearing around a bend in the path, and Mollie is alone with her sister.

"Isn't it beautiful," Livia says softly. "Look at these colors."

"Livia," Mollie says, struggling to keep apace. "I need to know what you're going to do. You and Hendley."

Livia stops. She does not look at Mollie, but instead reaches up to touch the bark of the closest dogwood. "There are so many breeds up here," she says. "Somebody brought them up here. The seeds, I mean. Wolfeye, Sweetwater Red, Spring Glow, Pollywood. I know every tree."

Mollie is suddenly close to tears. "Why won't you just answer me? What am I supposed to do? How do I know what to do, if I don't know what you and Hendley—"

"That's just it, kiddo," Livia sighs. She squints at Mollie through her glasses, which have cleared in the shade of the trees. "We don't want to be the ones to decide for you. You have to do what you want to do. What you feel right about."

"But how do I know?" Mollie asks hopelessly. She is beginning to cry, but she bites back the tears with a furious effort, and keeps her chin up.

"I don't know. All I can tell you, I think, is how *not* to decide. Don't make your decision based on whose fault you think it is. That isn't fair to them. Don't decide based on who you think needs you the most. You understand? You have to be happy. It has to be for you."

Mollie doesn't understand, and she is caught up on one nagging thought: "They must have favorites."

"Don't think like that. That's not how you should decide this," Livia says firmly.

"What are you going to do?"

"Don't worry about that right now. Let's just worry about you. You know me—I'll be fine whatever I do."

Mollie does know this, and she nods through her gathering tears. "But what about Hendley?"

"Everyone's going to be fine. You just think about yourself and what you want, kiddo. Okay?"

This is not the answer Mollie had hoped for, but she is so relieved to have gotten any response at all from her sister that for the moment she is pacified. When Livia begins walking again, Mollie walks at her side, listening as Livia points out different species of trees.

Hendley is waiting at the east bridge, which is still standing, but swaying a little under his weight. "Come on," he says, his face flushed. "I've already gone ahead a little. Oh, this is the best part."

"Not yet," Livia says. "Let's show her the bunker first."

Hendley concedes and the three of them bypass the bridge and continue on the main trail. The stream forks ahead of them; the main branch is to the left, close the trail, and a second branch wanders off to the right into thick woods. Livia and Hendley surprise Mollie by leading her rock to rock across the water at the point where the streams intersect. She clutches their arms as they make their precarious way over the stream, and when her foot slips on moss, Livia tightens her hold on her and hefts her onto the bank. When everyone is across, they begin hiking through the unmarked forest.

"This is the way to the bunker," Hendley explains. "There's no trail—that's how they kept it hidden. You have to stay on a straight line in the exact middle of the two streams."

Mollie, too fascinated to think about much else for the moment, follows them through the rich understory, and they blaze their way to a small clearing. Hendley and Livia immediately go to work clearing branches and weeds away from what Mollie realizes is a wide wooden door with a latch.

She watches as they work together to lift the hatch. She isn't sure what to expect—she has a crazy idea of old muskets being down there, or bones—but what she finds when they descend the few stairs is a cool, dark room, furnished with wooden bunks, a table and chairs, and rock shelves built into the walls. When the autumn light pours into the underground home, it is lovely—peaceful and hardy, ready to weather anything. Livia rushes off and comes back with a big handful of maple branches, like the one Hendley offered Mollie in the morning. She sets her water bottle on the table and stuffs the little branches in so that it looks like a vase of flowers when she steps back from it.

Hendley blows away dust and wipes accumulated dirt off the other furnishings, and Mollie stands there watching, wondering what will happen next. Livia goes out to find evergreen branches to make the room smell sweet and Mollie waits until she is gone to turn to her brother and ask, "What are you going to do, Hendley? When are you going to make up your mind?"

"I don't want to talk about it," he says simply, not stopping his work. His hands are filthy but he seems unbothered.

"Are you both just okay with everything?" Mollie demands. "It's just not a big deal to you?"

"I never said that. But sometimes you have to just let things go. Accept them. That's what Livia told me. It's not in our control."

"Accept them," Mollie repeats, dazed. "Let it go. Is she crazy?"

"Is who crazy?" Livia wants to know, climbing back down the stairs. She is carrying pine branches and her eyes have a dreamy, faraway look. "Isn't this place something else? Imagine all the people who hid out here. This was their salvation, you know? This may have been the only reason they got to go home, go back to their families."

Mollie pushes past her sister and climbs her way out of the shelter. The cold sun, falling in pink rays as it is filtered through maple, refreshes her. She mutters, "They are both crazy," and wipes at her face. "I don't understand them."

She can just barely hear them, down below: "We could do it. How much could a deposit on the land really be?"

"It might take awhile. But we wouldn't have to lose this place."

It SEEMS LIKE AN ETERNITY before Livia and Hendley are willing to leave the bunker. When they finally do emerge, the three of them retrace their steps back to the east bridge and cross the stream again. Livia and Hendley are still talking, but at this point, Mollie is so caught up in her frustration that she can barely speak. She is beginning to wonder if her brother and sister have actually forgotten what's happening. She envies them. The question that has been making her sick since the day it was put to her feels closer than ever now—it rides on her back, tugs at her shoulders. She is exhausted.

As if reading her mind, Livia says to her, "This is the part that will make you forget everything else in the world."

What Livia is talking about turns out to be a birch grove. Mollie can see immediately that there is nothing ordinary about the grove. The birches seem to be planted in perfect lines, close together and arranged like dominoes stretching out into an infinite distance. Their leaves have fallen and the forest floor plays its own kind of music as the three of them move quietly beneath the trees. Mollie has never seen birches so white; their dark patches are like weak little efforts to eclipse a much greater light. As they move deeper into the grove, Mollie feels as though her own limbs are entwined with the birches'; their perfection seems to invite her in, rather than expel her, and for the first time since this hike began, Mollie has a flash of understanding. She has an idea of why her brother and sister are so in love with this place, so determined to keep it.

"Do you see the lanterns?" Hendley whispers.

"What?"

He and Livia point them out: little oil lanterns hanging off low branches. Almost too many to count. In an instant, Mollie can see how these woods would look at night, with all these tiny flames lit in the darkness: a village right out of a storybook, fireflies dancing around the glass, the path glowing gold. She stops.

"They put them there? Our—the ones who lived here first?"

"We did," Livia says, reaching out to touch Mollie's shoulder. Her eyes lift and a shaft of sunlight drops down between the trees and ignites the auburn in her hair. "We put them up. Hendley and me."

These last three words undo Mollie. In her mind, she sees the two of them, moving through the world together, magically untouched, impossibly strong. She sees herself alone in her little bedroom at home, hugging her stuffed cat, left behind. Lost. She feels a sob rising up in her throat and she drops down into the leaves. Hendley has his arms around her before she can say anything, and Livia, leaning over her, looks so strong and sure in the cool sunlight that Mollie wants to climb into her bones and stay there forever.

"I'm not like you," she chokes out. "I can't do it like you can. I don't want to. I don't want to choose—"

"I know, honey," Livia keeps saying. "I know you're scared. I know you think it's the end of everything." Her voice catches a little, but she clears her throat: "It isn't, though. Everything will be fine. We're all going to be okay."

Mollie finally quiets and stands up with Hendley and Livia holding either arm. With stinging eyes she takes in the birches one last time as they pass out of the wood. What she sees later—the old house, even the wild pumpkin patch—does not stay with her as this birch grove does. In the car on the way back, she listens to Livia and Hendley plotting out ways to gather together the money for Mithland. She falls asleep. In that sleep, she dreams about the birches, and almost believes what they seem to be telling her: there are no decisions to be made, and nothing in the world is wrong.

September Dance

She shot her husband point-blank between the eyes fifteen minutes after she found their four-year-old son drowned in a tub full of tepid water. He seemed to stagger backwards and hit the floor all at once, landing in a heap in the tiny hallway. She didn't look at the blood, or look at his face, or touch his wrist. He had already slammed her head into the sink once, and everything was spiraling away from her, the walls quivering before her vision. She fell back against the still-full tub and let her head rest on its rim. One hand trailed in the chilly water as she hunched there with her eyes closed. Raven Rock, Tennessee was a tiny town, a tattered bouquet of houses and gas stations and churches gathered in the mountains along the Doe River. She knew some neighbor would have heard the shot and called the police. She knew it wouldn't be long before she was arrested. She had been battered long enough to know that the law is never on the side of the innocent.

She had come home from her overnight shift at the factory so that she could switch places with her husband, as she always did. He would leave at four in the morning just as she was getting back; their son would be sleeping. For months there had been a warning bell clanging, telling her it was no longer safe to leave her son alone with her husband, but what other choice was there? She could not go to her family. Ever since the first bruise, the first black eye, she had been unable to go back to the farm upriver. She had made her bed and had no idea how to escape it.

But she had come home in the dark and had turned on the bathroom light to find her son face down in the bathtub, his hair spooled out around his head in an auburn halo and his rubber toys bobbing on the water. Her husband had already left, or so she thought. She did not scream. She did not think. She pulled the child out of the water, wrapped him in a terry cloth robe and carried him into his bedroom. She set him on the bed and in the movement caught sight of herself in a mirror: a woman with scars all along her face and arms, holding a dead child wrapped in a robe. The horror of it sank through her as though she had swallowed a stone. When the stone touched bottom, it stirred sediment and woke fossils. She could almost see the tendrils of sand, fish darting away from the surprise impact of that rock. She turned on her heel and went back into the bathroom.

In the bottom drawer of the cheap vanity was a pink plastic case marked "Spare Lipsticks." It was a zippered, cushioned case that her husband had never seen or at least never bothered to investigate—one of the few possessions of hers he had not commandeered. He regularly went through her purse, her phone, even her locker at work. But not the lipstick case. From it she drew out a small .38 revolver, a relic from her teenage years of target shooting on her parents' farm. Her hands did not shake as she loaded it with the six bullets she kept tucked inside three empty lipstick tubes. She was too late—this much she knew—but with the desperate logic of the ruined, she knew there was nothing else she could do.

She thought she had some time. But her husband was still in the house. As she loaded the last bullet she heard him coming up from their tiny basement, where he kept his guns and his liquor. His steps were quick, light, and sure—not the heavy and meandering steps that often meant regret or drunkenness. He was in the bathroom before she could move. He took one look at the empty tub and reached down for her; she was still crouched beside the open drawer. He did not see the pistol, but she had it in her hand, partly concealed in the drawer, when he grabbed the side of her head and bashed it into the sink. The room glittered for a moment -- then she shook herself and her vision cleared. Her husband had stepped back as if to survey what he'd done, and her right arm came up straight and steady. Her left hand rose to meet it, providing a shelf for the gun. There was only a fragment of second before she shot him, during which he simply gaped at her.

Now she sits huddled against the tub, her head hung on its rim, her hand limp in the water. Her body shakes with the aftermath. She knows it's over, her life shattered. Two funerals, her little boy gone. Prison. Solitude. Suicide. She can see the road ahead as clearly as though the map is seared inside her eyelids. Her head sinks lower; her shoulders slump. The gun is cool now, lying at her knees.

But the water against her hand is cool as well, and in place of that map, she sees the Doe River, the water she grew up loving. She wonders if she has time to see the river once more—not here, in Raven Rock, but upstream, in the farm country—before her time is up. Her head lifts and she pushes herself off the bathroom floor. She steps over the body of her husband and does not look down. She only vaguely registers the nebula of blood on the far wall.

In her room, she hurriedly changes out of her work clothes. She reaches for another heavy shirt, thick work pants, then stops and shoves all of her hangers to one side of the closet. Way in the back are the dresses her husband would never let her wear: remnants from her college days, summery, lightweight, colorful dresses she wore to dances and parties. She selects a white knee-length dress and zips herself into it. It is looser than it was when she was twenty; she is bone-thin now, fear having burned any extra weight from her body and thinned the hair that used to fall in thick auburn waves to her waist. She finds an old cardigan to protect her shoulders against the early autumn wind and pulls her hair out of its tight knot.

For a moment she hovers in her son's doorway, wanting to carry him with her, but the sight of the back of his neck, already a pallid blue, sends her reeling. And so she leaves, not looking back, moving quickly through the scrabble of yard behind the house and then through dense forest down toward the Doe. She is deep in the woods before she realizes she is clutching one of her son's toys, a rubber tugboat that had been floating in the bathwater with him. She stows it in the pocket of her sweater and pushes on.

It is still dark. She moves upstream as quickly as she can, over rocks and occasionally along fishermen's paths, toward farm country. It is a three-mile walk but she is a powerful hiker even in her thinness and she reaches the broad green valleys before the sun is up. A playful blue light flirts with the river, competing with the moon's waning rays, and the stones of the rapids spark lilac and rose. As she moves she realizes her aim was not merely to see the river again; she is in search of a more particular spot. A wide green clearing, just beyond a stippling of rapids called The Applause for the sound they made, where a September dance was once held. She had been twenty years old then, in her second year of college, with no idea that she would have to drop out very soon to care for a dying mother. She had no idea about anything, really; she was not like the others, with grand plans for the future. She had always been a person who lived one day at a time. Maybe, she reflects now, that had been the beginning of her failing—her inability to look ahead. Maybe it all started there.

It amazes her that she still knows the way to the clearing. It has been ten years since that September dance. She thinks of the salmon that make their way through the ocean to a single rivermouth in Alaska, where they race against bears and eagles and ferocious currents so that they might return to their birthplace. She once read that those salmon have magnets inside of them, guiding them to the precise patch of gravel from which they came. In college she lived for these stories. Now she wonders if the compass is inside her as well. She knows where to cross the river—remembers the pattern of stones and ancient logs. Running along the opposite side, she can feel the trees changing—there is the tri-color birch grove, there is the little forest of rock cairns left by some settler long-ago, or a Cherokee on the run—and she knows the clearing is not far.

A diamond mist has fallen over the water and is held captive there by the overhanging trees. Rocks rising from the silvery green current are clothed in moss that drinks up the mist and breathes it gently back out in tiny puffs. The mountains that loom above the river are entirely concealed. Only a faint glimmer of sunrise red seeps through the trees, and she moves quietly from patch of light to patch of light, watching as her feet—bare, muddied—turn golden. There is complete silence save for the current and she does not look up until she has nearly stumbled over an old boat, banked at the edge of the clearing she has been seeking.

Her breath stops and she looks left and right. She sees no one; the boat is empty except for a rusted tackle box, and there is only the clearing, emerald green as she remembered it to be, stretching from the river into a forest of poplars and oak that will give way to black pine at the higher elevations, and wind-stripped white pine at the summits. For a moment, she can see herself as she was then: a girl of twenty, dancing here on the wild grass with the other girls, whirling about in search of a partner. The men—no, boys, really—wore their church jackets and were gentlemen for a day, no longer the rough-limbed farmers' sons who would try to kiss the girls in the backs of their trucks. She cannot remember whose idea it was to hold this dance, or who she danced with.

She knew nothing that day about her mother dying, or about the man who would enter her life when she was at her weakest and most vulnerable; she couldn't know that this man would move her into a house that was like a casket, give her a child he did not want, and then slowly teach her what hell was. Back then, she had an innocent faith in her own future happiness.

She finishes her walk along the tree line, moving slowly to delay her return. Back at the riverbank, she is startled to see someone bending over the abandoned boat.

"Hello?" she ventures anxiously, hanging back.

A man stands up beside the boat and mist falls from him. "Oh. Good God, you scared me half to death. I didn't know anyone else was here."

She moves closer and when she can see his face clearly, she stops.

"You all right?" the man asks. "You look like you've seen a ghost."

She thinks that maybe she has. She knows this man, remembers him with startling abruptness. His is a face she can remember from that September dance, because he was the one she did *not* dance with—his name was Otto, a name that Elisa had brooded over, and he hadn't come from Tennessee but from up north, Minnesota or maybe it was Michigan. The last she'd heard of him, he'd been studying agriculture somewhere out West. She remembers his face perfectly: the fine bones of his jaw, his pale skin, blue eyes fringed with gold-tinted lashes. He was in an art history class with her and whenever he spoke, the room fell silent. He was quiet and never played sports; there were rumors he'd had some illness before college. Once, in the dead of winter, he'd appeared seemingly out of nowhere to help her up from an icy sidewalk on campus where she'd fallen. She knew he was too good for her but it didn't stop her from hoping. All that afternoon, in her fluttering dress with her hair down, she tried to catch his eye, even managed to catch his arm in the middle of a dance, but he did not choose her as his partner, not once.

"I can't believe this," she says.

He smiles uncertainly at her, looking down at himself; he's wearing a button-down khaki shirt and knee-high boots, clearly here to fish, but still he seems out of place. He says, "What can't you believe?"

She says, "I think we might know each other. I mean, from college—Hayworth Valley? My name was—is—Elisa Dunworth."

He shifts a little, taking her in. "I guess I don't remember. That was awhile back for me."

"Oh—oh, sure," she agrees quickly. "I mean we hardly knew each other."

"Were we in the same class?"

"Yes. You're Otto, right?" she presses. She is still in shock, but there is no mistaking his eyes, or the way he tugs at his hair when he speaks.

Now his eyebrows come up. "You remember my name?"

Something in his tone worries her—perhaps he thinks she's crazy—and she rushes to explain: "It's just, I was thinking about college while I was walking here. We had a dance here once—maybe you don't re-member it—but I was thinking about that, and when I recognized you, I remembered you being here."

"A dance," he repeats. He smiles lopsidedly. "I do remember those, quite a few of them. I never could dance for anything, though." Then he ges-tures at her. "Why are you in that dress, in this cold? It's almost fall, and it's six o'clock in the morning. And what happened to your shoes?"

"I walked from downriver," she explains. "I just—wanted to get out-side. I do that sometimes. I live really close to the water." Seeing another question surfacing in Otto's eyes, she continues quickly, "Are you living out here now? You never went back north?"

He nods and shifts his weight. "I studied agriculture in Montana. I thought I wanted to work out there but I changed my mind, and my father helped me buy a small farm out here. It had been in the family for awhile. There was something about this place—I got attached back in college. Now I'm addicted to early-morning fishing, too," he adds, giving the boat a fond rub. "Every day of the week, I'm out here before sunup."

"It's a beautiful time to be on the water," Elisa agrees. "I wish I had learned. I grew up on a farm but that was one of the only things I never really did as a kid."

"Never too late." He seems to consider her for a moment, and then says, "Would you like to come downriver with me? Take a ride in the boat? We'll have to be quiet, for the fish, but you can watch and learn. I can give you a lift back to your place and then you won't have to hike it back. Unless you were going to keep heading upriver in those bare feet of yours." There is kindness in his voice, and he steps back as if to let her inspect the boat before making her decision.

Abruptly Elisa thinks of the scars on her face, the bruises that she knows must be showing on the side of her head, and wonders why Otto has not asked about them. As inconspicuously as possible she draws her hair out from behind her shoulders and lets it fall against her face, down her chest. Then she registers what he has proposed, and something swells deep within her.

"I would love that," she tells him breathlessly.

"Are you in a hurry to get back?"

"No."

"We'll take our time, then. This is the best time to be out here, like you said. Got to enjoy the river before the sun comes out full-force."

Otto helps her into the boat, and Elisa stares down at his hands when they clasp hers. She glances up at him just in time to see him blink in what looks like confusion or surprise. Then he moves away from her, and as gracefully as he has moved in her memories, Otto coaxes the boat into the river and makes a quick jump into the stern behind her. The boat leaps from the water when he begins to row, and they begin their gentle course downriver.

As Otto maneuvers them over The Applause, she listens for their encouragement—the lively staccato she once knew by heart—and smiles. It is, she thinks, the most lighthearted stretch of the Doe. She reaches into her sweater pocket for the little tugboat and then releases it over the side, watching it careen jauntily downstream.

"What was that?" Otto asks from behind her, but she does not answer.

Their boat gradually moves into calmer waters, and though the mountains remain hidden, she can hear wildlife rustling above them. Deer break brambles and birds awaken to search out food and each other. Elisa peers into the water and sees the green glint of trout passing beneath them.

She turns her head every so often, expecting to see Otto threading bait, casting lines, but he does not touch the tackle box between them. Twice he gives her a small and sheepish grin as if to say, *The truth is, I'm happy just rowing.* She wants to watch him, but resolutely faces forward as they travel.

The river begins to transform under the nascent light. It is what her father used to call the wooden time, when all of the colors are not really colors of the sky, but colors of the forest's heartwoods. There is the faintest pink of mountain laurel, the rich violet of purpleheart, the pewter-blue and amber-brown of walnut; and the grain of it all is spalted, continually in motion but never uniform, uncoiling in all directions, cavorting like dancers. Where the river narrows, the woods curve protectively around the boat; where the river widens, the mist spreads and the paling moon shows herself from behind a veil of clouds. And all around them are the mountains, rising up shrouded in blue-green smoke. Elisa takes in a breath. Then she turns to Otto.

"Isn't it--?" she begins.

He holds up one hand, not to silence her, but to preserve the moment: "I know."

He rows them on. And in the boat's steady course over the water is a momentum to feed Elisa's own dreaming. Her house, her child and husband, are light years from this place; quite suddenly she feels closer in time to the day of that September dance than to the events of this morning. She looks down at her white dress. In the young light it appears fresh and unworn. She thinks of telling Otto everything, of running away with him, changing her name. They are moving so fast downriver. At this pace they could be out of the county within hours, out of the state by nightfall. She turns again.

"Otto," she says, fighting to keep her voice steady, "why did you let me into your boat, if you didn't remember me?"

"You looked a little lost, to tell you the truth," he responds, his shoulders thrown back with the oars. "I thought I should at least help you get home. But who says I don't know you? When I helped you into the boat, I remembered."

The words tumble from her lips: "Because you helped me when I fell in the snow that time."

"Yes," he says, astonished. "I remembered that."

For a moment they simply hold each other's gazes, the boat swaying beneath them.

"You wouldn't dance with me, that day," Elisa tells him finally, surprising herself with the words. "At that dance in autumn? We were both there, but you never danced with me."

"I'm sorry, then."

"I am too."

"How far would you like to go?"

She takes in a breath. "As far as we can."

"The sun is coming up."

"Does it matter?"

He smiles at her; their eyes lock. Now, in the strengthening light, she feels certain he will ask about her scars, but still he says nothing. She wonders what marks of his own he bears, what pain he has suffered in these ten years. He wears no wedding ring; there are deep wrinkles at the corners of his eyes, for a man of just thirty or so. She wonders how she looks to him now—if he sees the change in her as well.

As if reading her mind, Otto says, "You look beautiful there, in the boat. Like a woman out of a very old story."

"Let's keep going, can't we?" she pleads, facing forward again, her heart hammering.

"I don't have to get back, really. I have all the time in the world."

She turns; the boat is flushed with crimson light, and she blinks into the glare of the newly-bared sun. She cannot see Otto. She grips the side of the boat, starts to rise. The boat pitches. For a moment, Otto seems to have vanished. Then she thinks she sees him pull back the oars once more—a single stroke—and she exhales in relief. She drops her hand into the river to feel the water. The chill startles her and she opens her eyes.

SHE WAS RIGHT THAT SOMEONE HEARD THE SHOT and called the police. As she regains consciousness, she hears sirens, someone pounding on her front door and shouting. Her head throbs, her body aches, the old bruises scream out at her as she tries to pick herself up off the bathroom floor. But her hand is still trailing in the tepid bath, as is the little tugboat. She falls back against the porcelain, staggered at the sight of it there. The door is opening. There are voices, sirens pealing into the house, a scream as someone finds her husband in the hall and her child in the bedroom. But there is still time, in the moment before they take her away, to perceive the gentle lapping of the water, and the quick flash of something beneath the surface, like a salmon darting through a shaft of sun. It is there and then gone.

Us vs. They

The summer my brother Tommy got divorced was the last time all four of us guys were together. Tommy was twenty-six, I was eighteen, and our little brother Josh was eleven. Dad and Josh and I were still living in the old house in Oak Ridge, a ramshackle place constructed in the forties and left over from the Manhattan Project, when they built the atomic bomb there. I had just finished high school and my girlfriend Christa and I were spending every night together, plotting our life together in Louisiana, where we'd be moving for college in a couple of months. My dad came home from the paper mill every evening and collapsed in front of the TV with a cigarette and a microwaved meal. Tommy had been the first to get out, but he only moved to the other side of town, to one of the nice apartments near the golf course, and he was already back, using our house as a base while he hunted around for what he called a new situation. His wife, Ashley, had gotten into drugs and was a lost cause. I didn't tell Tommy that I'd seen it coming—what else did people in Oak Ridge do, unless they had plans, like me?—but I couldn't help but feel a little smug about the fact that I was eight years younger than he was and I knew more about the way the world worked than he did.

"Tommy's a dreamer, he's got sugar plums in his head," my dad used to tell us. But how much of a dreamer could he be, I thought, if the best he can do is be an assistant manager at a Knoxville Best Buy, and settle down in an apartment in Oak Ridge? Who cares if the place was near the golf course?

I hated that town all my life. There's a story that when I was nine, I said to my aunt that my mother had died after Josh was born because she just didn't want to live here anymore. I got slapped for that, but I meant it. For one, I'm one of those people who can't ignore an elephant in the room, and the elephant in Oak Ridge was the nuke plant. I would look at my classmates during some mindless activity and be thinking, *did you ever see pictures from Hiroshima? Do you know that mushroom cloud from hell came together right here, right behind that ridge?* For another, I can tell you that growing up around a lot of crime does not make you immune to it, or tolerant of it. The house next door, and the one next to that, was a revolving door for drug dealers and prostitutes for as long as I can remember, and I never stopped feeling disgusted at the sight of them—the pasty, smoked-out girls with their floppy breasts, or their scumbag boyfriends who used idiotic symbols like garden gnomes on the front porch to indicate when they were open for business. Three times our house was broken into by our own neighbors, and the cops were useless, since most of them were in on the drug deals to begin with. That was another thing about Oak Ridge—a famously corrupt police force, and traffic cameras on every corner that snapped photos of anything the town could steal your money for. The town was a sinking ship, drowning in its own trash, and as I told my girlfriend, these people brought it all on themselves.

So when Tommy came home with his dog, Levi, and settled back in our old bedroom, I was as disgusted with him as I was sorry. He looked bad. We all had the same dirty blond hair but his was falling into his eyes all the time like he wanted to hide his face, and his hands shook a lot. That first breakfast we all ate together, at five in the morning because my dad had to get to the plant, he just listened to us talk and barely touched his eggs.

"Wilder here is going to college in August," my dad said, between forkfuls. "Got an academic scholarship. New Orleans, Louisiana. What do you make of that."

"He knows that, Dad," I reminded him. "I told him that."

"New Orleans," my dad said again, drawing out the words. "Can't get my head around it. That's the ocean, you know."

"The Gulf," Josh supplied, looking at me for approval.

"And Josh is playing baseball," my dad continued. "He's got my arm. Or what used to be my arm."

"No football, kid?" Tommy asked, finally opening his mouth. "I thought for sure. All those games we played, all the times Us beat They. Good times."

My dad smiled at his plate. Those football games had been his invention. My dad was quite the inventor. He was always insisting that stuff that was really popular, like dinner-at-the-movies or Frisbee golf, had originally been his idea. He loved to come up with games, and his crowning achievement was Us vs. They, a version of football that allowed us to literally play against ourselves, since there really wasn't anyone else around to be our opposing team. We'd be out in the yard moving up the field as Us, and then eventually turning around to be They. If the points went to Us, we cheered and jumped around; if They scored, we jeered and swore revenge. Sometimes we'd come inside almost in pain from laughing so hard. It never got old, though we hadn't played in ages; my dad was getting a little heavy, and lacked the energy on those rare occasions when we were all at home at the same time.

"I'm too shrimpy for football," Josh was saying, grinning. "Wilder says I'll get my head cracked open."

"Aw, come on," Tommy said, ruffling Josh's hair. "It might be worth a try."

"Better he plays baseball and gets a scholarship with it or something," I pointed out. "He could get the hell out of this place after high school on an athletic grant."

"It's all Wilder thinks about," my dad muttered.

There was a long silence and we all went back to eating. Josh gulped down his orange juice and finally said, "Where's Levi?"

"In my room. I mean, Wilder's room," Tommy said. "I put a plastic gate up. He won't bother you."

"He's never bothered anybody," my dad said. "That's one special dog."

"I'm selling him," Tommy said, just audibly. "Just so you guys know."

My younger brother was upset. "Levi? What? No way."

"Can't afford to keep him. He ought to be on a farm somewhere, anyway. He's not gonna be happy in some tiny apartment." Tommy pushed his eggs around and didn't look at any of us. "I already found a buyer. I used Craigslist. This guy's gonna pick him up here this afternoon and take him out to LaFollette. He's got a big house, big piece of land. Levi can run all over the place."

"Don't let him take him," Josh said, leaning forward. "Come on, Tommy. You should call that guy and tell him you changed your mind."

"Lay off," Tommy said, and rose. He left the room.

Levi was a special dog -- a big golden retriever, strong and sleek with a distinctly noble bearing. I had never especially liked dogs, but even I had to admit that my brother had made a good choice. Levi would sit there and look at you so calmly, it made you think of somebody in a history book, Socrates or Abe Lincoln or someone like that who made big decisions and thought them out pretty carefully before doing so. Tommy'd had him since he was twenty-two.

"We should play a round," my dad said. "Us vs. They. Since we're all together, you know? What do you say, how about when I get home? There'll still be plenty of light."

"Sure," Josh said. "I'm in."

"Fine by me," I told them. "For old times' sake."

"Get your brother to say yes." My dad rose and went for his summer jacket, where his cigarettes were. He put it on and filled up his thermos with coffee and dumped four sugar packets in. He always got ready for work like it was winter, even in the heat of a Tennessee June.

"Dad?" Josh said. "Will Tommy stay with us? Since Wilder's going?"

I looked at him. My dad said slowly, "I don't know how long he'll stay,

Josh. Maybe just a month, maybe a long time. I wouldn't ask him. Just let him be a little. He's had a rough go of it. And don't you worry, just because Wilder's going to college doesn't mean he's never coming back."

He was always a man of few words, and this was quite a speech to us. I watched my brother take the words in. I wanted to correct what my father had said about me—it was my dream to never set foot in this town again—but I didn't.

We watched our father leave, and then Josh announced that he was meeting his friends for baseball practice and then to get ice cream. He took off with his mitt, climbing on his Goodwill bicycle to pedal out to Wilder Park (which, as a little kid, he bragged to his friends was named after me). I stood on the porch for awhile. I watched a drug deal go down and watched a couple of other neighbors drink their Pepsi and smoke their pot on the porch across the street. One of them held up his middle finger at me, and I shrugged and went back inside. These people were on my suspect list for our most recent break-in; I had even spotted one of them wearing one of my dad's shirts. *Fuckers*, I thought. *I can't leave you in the dust fast enough.*

WHEN I CAME BACK INSIDE, I found Tommy sitting on the floor in the hallway, next to the dog gate that blocked my bedroom door. Levi sat on the other side of the gate, and they were looking intently at each other in a way that embarrassed me. It seemed to embarrass Tommy, too, because he cleared his throat when he saw me and said, "Hey man. What're you up to today?"

"Nothing, really. Going to see Christa later, probably. I've got the day off from work." I was delivering pizzas then, and also tutoring wealthy people's high schoolers on the weekends and banking with it. "Dad wants to play Us vs. They when he gets back."

Tommy smiled faintly. "Oh, Dad."

"Will you?"

"Sure, I guess. Whatever the old man wants."

I sat down across from him. Levi tilted his head toward me and I reached over the gate to rub his head. "Why not let him out?" I asked.

Tommy grunted a little. "Ugh, I don't know. I want him to get used to the idea. You know? That I won't really be with him too much longer. It's, uh, kind of a big day for him. He's never even met this guy who's coming."

My brother's throat was visibly tight. I didn't know what to say—I never saw him like that before—so I just sat there.

"Things pretty serious with Christa?" Tommy asked me after a moment.

"Yeah. We're going to New Orleans together. She got into the same school."

"That's great, man. It really sounds great."

"She's majoring in English. I'm going to get a business degree, like I told you. We figure we've got a good chance at making decent money down there once we both get started. And we visited last month—it was a hell of a road trip—and it's just an awesome city. I wish you could see the bridge over Lake Pontchartrain. It's like crossing over the ocean. And the way the Gulf looks from a distance. It looks like it's on fire when the sun's out." I stopped, seeing my brother's face.

"It really sounds great," Tommy repeated. He looked back at Levi, who eyed him quietly.

"What are you going to do?" I asked.

"I don't know. Get an apartment in Knox, close to work. It's all I can think of right now. I'm—I'm sort of broke."

"Broke? What about your job?"

"Ashley…" His voice trailed off. "Ashley sort of emptied out my account. It was about a month ago. I didn't know what was happening. She just—couldn't stop. There's no way to get it back. I didn't even get my deposit back on the apartment, because of some shit she did to the house." He saw my face and waved off my questions. He finished, "So, I'm sort of playing catch-up right now."

"Christ." I sat back and stared at him. "She is a fucking loser, Tommy. She really is."

He didn't say anything, just reached out to stroke Levi over the gate.

"At least you guys didn't have any brats," I went on. I was thinking of all the people I knew—probably a dozen of them—who were my age and already strapped down in their miserable duplexes with babies and factory jobs.

"You're an ass, you know that," Tommy finally said. "Kind of an arrogant mother."

"How's that, exactly?" I wanted to know.

"You act like you're above it all. That's all."

"I sure hope to God I am," I said hotly. "You think I want to be like these morons I go to school with? Have you looked up and down our block?"

"It's not that simple, kid."

The word *kid* bit at me. "I'm eighteen years old," I muttered.

"Exactly."

I stood up and brushed myself off. I decided to ignore the conversation entirely. I didn't want to fight with my brother, especially when he was like this, more hangdog that Levi was. "Is there anything you want to do today?" I asked. "Before Dad gets back?"

"I'm just gonna wait for this guy to show," Tommy said. He stood also, and unlocked the dog gate. Levi sat there, waiting patiently, until Tommy gestured at him, and then the two went off down the hall. "Gonna take him for a walk," my brother said over his shoulder, and I nodded. I went into the bedroom we now shared, and it smelled like Tommy. Cigarettes and golden retriever and Axe deodorant and total failure.

I SAT DOWN ON MY BED with my phone, and called Christa while Tommy was out.

"How's your brother?" she wanted to know. "Is he handling things okay?"

"I guess." I glanced around the room. "I don't know. Look, my dad wants us all to hang out tonight, so I think maybe we shouldn't get together. Is that okay?"

"Of course. You should spend time with them while you can."

I laughed. "I've seen them all plenty, believe me." Then, lowering my voice, "Are you getting excited, or what? Last night I was up for hours looking at photos online. I just can't wait to get down there."

"Me too. My mom's starting to get used to the idea, thank God. She keeps telling me how hot it'll be, but that's about it."

"My dad says that, too. Not like he's ever been out of Tennessee, but he keeps saying we're going to roast."

"What are you guys going to do tonight?"

"Play football in the backyard."

She laughed. "Us vs. They?"

"When did I tell you about that?"

"You didn't. Josh did, that time I was helping him with his homework. Remember?"

"Huh. Well, it's a tradition." I peered out the window; no sign of Tommy on the street. "I guess I'd better let you go. I'll call you tomorrow?"

"Sounds good."

I hesitated; the words were still new, both thrilling and terrifying: "I love you."

"I love you, too."

She broke the connection, and I looked around the room again. I got up and went to my dresser. In the bottom drawer, stuffed into an old knit hat, I had rolls and rolls of cash, money I'd saved up from the tutoring gigs. My pizza delivery money always went into my checking account; the tutoring cash was set aside. I had the idea that it was smart to have your eggs in two baskets. And I just liked feeling the cash, knowing the possibilities it represented. I had nine hundred dollars in there. I planned to use it to fund our first few weeks in New Orleans: textbooks, grocery trips, gas. But as I fingered the cash, kneeling there on the floor, I heard Levi and Tommy out on the front porch, and wondered how much Tommy was asking for the dog. The idea occurred to me that I could give Tommy whatever amount he'd been planning to take from this buyer, and that if I did this, he could keep Levi.

The two of them were in the kitchen now; I could hear Tommy pouring Levi's food into the metal bowl he'd brought with. "Here ya go, bud," I heard Tommy say.

I stuffed the cash back into the hat. I needed that money, I reminded myself. Tommy's situation was his own fault. I wasn't going to start sacrificing my own chances before I'd even left.

When he came back into the room with Levi, I was nowhere near the dresser. I was messing with the clothes in my closet, and I told my brother I was looking for the old UT tee shirt I used to wear for Us vs. They. Then I really did try to find it, but I couldn't.

THE NEXT FEW HOURS WERE QUIET, but the house was tense, and at times, I imagined the walls were trembling. Levi was very still, lying on my bedroom floor, while Tommy paced the house, occasionally flipping the TV on only to turn it off with a snap a few minutes later. He probably smoked ten cigarettes, going out on the porch each time. I spent most of the early afternoon in my room, reading, but whenever I emerged to get a snack or a drink, Tommy was always hovering by the kitchen window, staring out at the street.

"What time is this guy coming?" I asked him once.

He started, as if only then noticing me. "Um, about three. It's a long drive from LaFollette."

"I know where it is." I should have asked him if he wanted to do something—anything—to get his mind off Levi's going, but I couldn't think of what to ask, and I wanted to get back to my book. It was making me nervous watching my brother pace around. I felt sorry for him, but already, I wanted him to leave. I wanted to see Christa, I wanted to get ahead in my first semester's classes, I wanted not to be around to watch him say goodbye to his dog, or to mope about his addict wife the rest of the summer.

I was deep into the textbook for my fall Political Economy class—

I'd ordered it ahead of time—when I heard Tommy moving very fast through the front of the house. I heard the gravel in our driveway crunching and looked out my window. It was a forest green pickup truck that had pulled in, and as I watched, a husky-looking guy jumped out of the driver's side and strode up the gravel. He was wearing a uniform like the guys at the Jiffy Lube wore and I thought I could see a name tag patched onto his shirt. I got up and went into the hall.

Tommy was at the front door, but it was closed, and he was peering out the little window there, just barely lifting my mother's ancient pink curtain from the glass. Levi sat quietly beside him, looking up. They both seemed to jump when the doorbell rang.

I hadn't moved, and I held still, waiting. Tommy, instead of opening the door, slowly knelt down beside Levi and murmured something I couldn't hear. He got his hands around the dog's lifted head, rubbed at his ears, said something else. Levi simply looked at him. The doorbell rang again.

"Want me to get it?" I said, and Tommy jumped. He looked at me with something so close to hatred that I stepped back.

"Leave us alone, kay?" he said hoarsely. "Go read your fucking books."

I stood there, wavering, as my brother opened the front door and let in this man whose nametag I could now see read *Frank*. He had dark crew-cut hair and even from the hall I could smell motor oil and something else, something that reminded me of my mother—pine? Cedar?— even from where I stood.

"Frank," the guy said heartily. He shook Tommy's hand. Tommy said nothing as Frank bent down over Levi. "Can I get a paw, fellow?" Frank asked. He held out one hand.

Levi's paw, trained to do this, came up and landed in the stranger's hand almost immediately.

Tommy turned away.

"He's a good dog, as beautiful as you said," Frank told him. He was stroking Levi's back now, his big hand moving slowly over the golden coat. "Very healthy. He's going to love it out there. I've got fifty acres for him to run on."

Tommy nodded. His hands were shoved deep in his pockets. Frank looked up and noticed me.

"Hi there," he said.

"I'm Wilder, Tommy's brother." I walked up to them and also shook Frank's hand. I had the impulse to ask how much he was paying for Levi, to offer my brother the money right then and there, but as before, I choked it back, and stepped aside.

Frank dug around in his enormous pants pockets and came out with a checkbook. "I can do cash, if you prefer," he told Tommy, who winced.

"Naw, check is fine," he said. "Somethin' I don't like about taking cash for my dog."

Frank nodded. "Sure, I get that." He pressed his checkbook to the wall beside the front door and used a chewed-up plastic pen to fill it out. I couldn't see what number he wrote down; they'd obviously agreed upon it ahead of time.

"That's ready to go through, anytime you like," Frank promised as he handed the check over. "You want my license number on there or anything?"

"It's okay. I'll trust you." Tommy took the check, folded it, and slid it into his shirt pocket. "Thanks."

"Thank you. I can't tell you how long I've been wanting a dog like this. Levi," and he looked down at the retriever, "we've got a bit of a drive back, but I like the windows open."

This seemed to cheer my brother.

Frank asked, "He got a leash? I didn't bring one."

Then Tommy's face fell just perceptibly, and I realized it hadn't really hit home yet for him what was going on. After a moment he said with forced casualness, "He don't usually need one, but yeah, I've got one. Hang on a second." And he passed by me without a look, going down the hall to our old room.

He came back with a blue leash and handed it to Frank, who expertly clipped the collar around Levi's neck and then looked at Tommy. "Well," he said, shifting his weight a little. "I expect you want to say goodbye? I know you said you've had him a long time."

Tommy cleared his throat and didn't look at either of us. He dropped down and crouched in front of his dog. I knew he'd already said his words, before he'd let Frank in, and sure enough, he said nothing at all. He just gave Levi a few hard rubs against his chest and then gripped the dog's forehead for a moment, looking in the animal's deep brown eyes, before he stood up again.

"Take good care of the guy," Tommy said.

"You bet."

Tommy opened the door and watched as Frank led Levi out. Levi, probably thinking this was just an adventure and that he'd be back with Tommy by nightfall, trotted out after Frank and did not resist when the man encouraged him up into the truck's passenger seat. I came and stood beside my brother to watch the truck drive off. I was afraid to look at him.

After a long silence, Tommy said to the window, "It'll pay the deposit on an apartment."

Then, as though the matter were closed, he turned sharply and went down the hall. I heard the bathroom door snap shut and the shower come on after a minute. I stayed where I was.

I DIDN'T SEE MUCH OF TOMMY until just before my father and Josh came home, around five. Josh got on the phone and ordered pizza, holding my dad's debit card and reading off the numbers since nobody had cash. Tommy took a second shower and emerged wearing a Chicago Bears shirt that he sheepishly explained he got at the Salvation Army shop for a dollar. My dad put out paper plates and found a liter of Mountain Dew in the back of the fridge. For awhile there, things felt normal, like we were all kids again. Then, after the food, we went in the yard for Us vs. They.

Some of our old routines came back to us. I was almost always the quarterback, because I could throw well but as Tommy said I couldn't catch a medicine ball if it were thrown to me. Josh mostly hiked the ball; Tommy ran hard for passes, which he almost always caught, and my father, the genius behind this game, did fake-outs and complicated short runs, as though we really were trying to trick the players on the opposing team. Josh, always clumsy, tripped over himself a lot. My father, always more talkative while moving than while still, made jokes, called us names. When Tommy dropped the ball or when I misplaced a throw, and when we had to turn around as They and ended up scoring (which hurt Us), we swore and moaned and slapped our foreheads. "We're fucked," Josh groaned when Tommy made a touchdown (we were They for this) and my father, predictably, said, "No F-word and no Jesus Christ or God damn on this field please," and I, as I always did, said, "But you just said it!" And when They ended up winning, Josh insisted They had cheated, and Tommy agreed They were dirty rats who never played by the rules. It wasn't our fault, he said. We did our best. We all agreed on this as we went sweating back into the house, not knowing it was our last game ever.

The game looks different to me now, looking back on it, than it did that evening as we played it. Now, I can see that my father was panting, stopping for breath far more often than I ever remember him doing. I can see that he was making up excuses to stop—his shoes kept coming untied, he thought he heard the phone in the house, he had something stuck in his eye. I can see my little brother and how closely he followed my movements and Tommy's; I know now that the kid was scared that his family was about to come apart. I understand how lonely he must have been growing up without a mother and how it must have panicked him to think that both his brothers would soon be gone. And Tommy. I remember that he kept pulling out his cell phone and toying with it, just opening it and staring at it for a few seconds before putting it away, and at the time, I thought with disgust that he was thinking of calling Ashley. Now, of course, I know he wanted to call Frank, and ask for his dog back. That check was probably still in his pocket, untouched.

I see myself differently, too. That day, I thought I was doing them all a favor by playing this game. I was on my way out, but I still had it in me to have fun with my brothers and my father. Really, I was condescending to them all, patronizing them with my participation as I would later patronize them with the occasional phone call updating them on my life. That night, I had all the anticipation of an ancient seafarer about to set sail in the morning for a new continent. I had already left them behind.

I know this to be true, because I can't even remember what happened that night after the game was over.

THINGS WENT WELL ENOUGH IN LOUISIANA. After a year in the dorms, Christa and I got a small apartment and took out loans for what we couldn't cover. We made rare trips back home to visit our families, claiming we had too much work to do, and did well in our classes.

In our third year, Christa turned up pregnant. I knew right away we couldn't go through with it. I told her, we'll end up just like all the scumbags we grew up with. I told her our lives would go downhill and never stop rolling if she had that baby. And she listened. She had the abortion and was at home, eating ice cream, that same night. She seemed to handle it okay even though she'd fought with me about it. Sometimes I'd wake up to hear her crying, or I'd find her gone in the middle of the night and she'd be in the bathroom just staring at herself in the mirror. But I thought we'd be okay.

I was wrong. It took a long time, but eventually I understood that something was in ruins and couldn't be rebuilt. We rarely talked when we ate meals together. I found myself smoking cigarettes like my father and brother, using it as an excuse to go outside when our silence was too much for me. In our fourth year out there, I started picking up beer once or twice a week and putting it in the fridge. I started having one after work each day. Then, while we were washing dishes one night, Christa told me she had a job offer in Nebraska. A girl friend from our college had parents who ran an academy out there, and they wanted Christa to teach for them. I just stood there with my hands in the soapy water and looked at our reflections in the dirty kitchen window until she dried the dish she was holding and left the room.

I had hoped to go to graduate school but didn't get into the programs I applied for. I took a job in sales just to keep things going, so that I wouldn't have to move back home, and found an even smaller place that was closer to the Gulf but a long way from the parts of the city I had come to love. Not too long after that, Tommy called me to tell me our dad had had a massive heart attack and died, right there at the paper mill. I flew home for the funeral, but they let me leave before I learned that Josh was going to live with our aunt in Chattanooga, because no one else had the means to take care of him. Tommy was still supporting his ex-wife, and he was keeping the old house because in my father's will he'd asked him to do this. It was, Dad had written, "our house with Mom." Over the phone, Tommy told me I shouldn't even think about coming back to live there. He said this like he wanted the best for me, but I could tell it was because he just didn't want me around, and I didn't blame him at that point. He'd had to take care of everything, and admitting to our aunt that he couldn't support Josh must have about killed him.

For a long time, it's been my routine to take a beer or a couple of shots out onto the tiny balcony outside my apartment after work and think about what I could have done differently. More often, I've caught myself thinking about how unfair it all was, and is. And I wonder a lot about Christa. To the best of my knowledge, she's still out there in Nebraska. When I think of those endless plains, I get so lonely I almost can't breathe. I stand on my balcony and drink, staring out at a sliver of the Gulf. The water doesn't sparkle as I once described it to my brother. It's brown, and it's filled with the skeletal remains of the hurricanes I once thought of as romantic, back before I understood first-hand what they leave in their wakes.

I think about how, when Christa and I moved into our apartment back by the college, we had a sign made for our kitchen that read, *Anywhere but There.* Though our families never saw it, it was a childish thing to do, and cruel. But after all, a child is what I was, thinking that I was different from those people who got addicted and hurt their families and robbed homes and dropped bombs that killed soldiers and babies alike. A child living on his own six hundred miles from his backyard, not realizing that all his inarticulate anger, all his resentment for the way the world spins, was just disappointment in discovering the truth about the game: if They win, there is no rematch for Us. And however it was They cheated at the game, the truth is that we only play against ourselves, and have only ourselves to blame.

THREE TO THE VINE

MIDNIGHT FINDS MILL STRETCHED OUT on the couch in front of the living room window, her .22 perfectly balanced against her shoulder, the barrel of the rifle peeking out between two slats of the blinds she has been meaning to change for months.

"Mill. For God's sake." Martin is standing behind her, half-asleep and wearing only his camouflage boxers, scattered tattoos, and the long scars that mark his arms and shoulders. "There's nobody trying to get in here."

She pulls back the bolt. "Like hell there isn't. This is the third time, Martin. I know what I heard, and I know what I saw."

"That same shadow? How do you know it wasn't just some dog?"

Slowly her eyes float over the barrel to his, and he backs up a step, throwing up both hands. "OK. You know what, do what you feel you need to do." He disappears into their bedroom, but a moment later, returns with a cartridge box—50 shells—and sets it gently on the floor beside the couch. On his way back to bed, he stops to look into Mill's son's room. She hears him touching things in there, knows the sound of Charles' closet being opened. After what seems like a long pause, Martin goes back to bed.

When she first moved from Chicago to Oak Ridge, Tennessee, Mill was fooled by the sound of Cecil's tractor engine at her front door; she always thought it was UPS. In time, though, she learned that Cecil preferred to drive his tractor directly to his neighbors' doorsteps, even if it meant demolishing a flower or two, and she knew when he was coming.

Now, Martin having left for work at the Jiffy Lube, Mill gets up from Charles' bed at the familiar rumble. "Goddam sun," she mutters, blocking the light with one hand as she opens the front door.

On his tractor, Cecil is haloed in the fresh sun, and the graying blond of his beard looks like it's on fire. He has a plastic bottle of Canadian Superior between his knees, and a cantaloupe in the other. "Motherfucker," he yells at her over the engine. "I been waiting three days to give you this melon and I keep forgetting. You doin' alright?"

Mill reaches for it, hefts its cool, pale weight. The watery smell of the fruit washes over her and she presses her nose to the cantaloupe's skin. "How many to the vine this year?"

"Three! I thought for sure there'd be just two again, but this vine, she surprised me. She had more in her than I thought." Cecil is triumphant. He offers her the whiskey, but Mill shakes her head.

"So I heard your dumbass husband and his tramp are coming down." Cecil is still yelling.

"Ex," she reminds him. "Ex-husband. But that first part is right."

"What time they gettin' here? You gonna share this with them?"

Mill hugs the melon to her chest. "Hell no. He said around eight. They're getting a hotel in Knoxville."

"Probably the best fucking hotel in town."

"Cecil, you noticed anyone creeping around my house at night? Anything strange lately?"

Cecil scratches at his beard with the same hand that grips the whiskey. "Not that I can think of. I'm usually out in the yard pretty late and I ain't seen anyone. You got somebody messing with you?"

"I don't know," she says, still squinting into the daylight. "I keep seeing shadows and hearing things by the porch. I keep thinking someone's trying to get in."

"Don't know about that, but I'll keep two eyes open." Cecil has already started rolling down the lawn, and he waves back at her as he starts across the street. Mill closes the door. The rifle is still on the couch, and she considers leaving it there for when her ex-husband and his wife arrive.

She waters her son's bonsai tree, marks this down on a sheet of paper beside it. She is determined to keep it green—for years if she can. The phone rings and she ignores it until the fifth ring. "Hello?" She is still holding her tiny watering can, or rather, Charles' watering can.

"This is Sandra at the Oak Ridge Public Library." The woman's voice is crisp. "I'm calling about a set of overdue items? We've tried to reach you several times."

"I'm sorry, I don't know what you mean," Mill says sweetly. She sets down the can, wanders over to a stack of books, ten or twelve, with glossy covers and titles involving pirates, gemstones, and the Loch Ness.

"Your son has several books checked out in his name, ma'am," the woman goes on, now clearly irritated. "Those books are more than three months overdue. You will need to return them, or pay for them. We have this documented—if you really don't have the books, he may have lost them or misplaced them without you knowing—"

"My son," Mill says calmly, "never lost a library book in his life."

"Ma'am—"

"Tell you what. I'll check around for them, and if I find them …I'll pay for them."

"Ma'am?"

Mill drops the phone into its cradle and rests her hand on the pile of books for a moment before moving into the kitchen. She investigates the refrigerator—she has already made up her mind that she will not go out and purchase a single thing for this dinner with her ex-husband and his wife. The possibilities then are: toast; cereal with no milk; yogurt; macaroni and cheese from a box (why is this in the fridge? she wants to know); grilled cheese sandwiches. She checks the cabinets, which are equally drab, filled only with tomato paste, scattered half-used pasta boxes, old saltines, and tea bags. There is also Martin's stash of cigarettes, which he only began smoking again a few weeks ago. There is nothing else save for a little pile of fruit snacks, Teddy Grahams, and gummy bears, set carefully to one side.

"Well they can have pizza from Venice," she mutters. Venice's pizza is terrible and it's a local joke that the residents always tell strangers to eat there.

She goes back to the fridge, pulls out some rotting apples and a couple of questionable-looking oranges. Cecil's melon fills the space they occupied, and Mill opens the back door onto her deck porch and flings the apples and oranges into the jungle below. The house stands on a steeply-sloping hill, and the backyard isn't really a backyard, but a mass of trees and shrubbery behind which, out of sight, are more houses downhill. Beyond the trees is the ridgeline, very blue at night, but becoming more and more difficult to make out as the weeks pass and the growth behind the house rises. Martin calls it their Compost Heap because they have gotten into the inexplicable habit of throwing things back there— old fruit, meat gone bad, coffee they don't finish. It seems that the ferns and leaves reach higher every morning.

The village has called them several times about the Compost Heap, demanding that they clear it all out, but Martin usually fords the calls, and he won't have it. "Fucking right we're leaving it the way it is," he'll say. "It's our property and we'll turn it into a goddam Amazon if we want to! I'm paying taxes, aren't I?"

The kitchen phone rings, and Mill hesitates: at this hour, it will either be the village again, or her ex.

It's her ex, Paul. "Millicent?"

She cringes but doesn't bother to correct him. "Yes, Paul. Are you in town?"

"Not quite—still on 75. We've had a bit of a rough drive. Accidents everywhere, and Amanda got so hungry that we had to stop. That, and—"

"Sorry it's been so difficult," Mill says dryly.

"Oh, not at all, we're just fine. We'll be in by eight-thirty."

There is a pause, and Paul says, "Will he be there?"

Mill laughs, a short bark. "Martin? No, Paul, I'm going to kick him out for the night so that you won't be offended."

"Jesus, Millicent, I'm just asking."

"Will Amanda be there?"

Paul sighs. "OK, OK. I just wondered. I just think it's a little—strange, that's all."

"Strange for the man Charles and I have been living with for three years to be at the house for dinner?"

"Well—Charlie wasn't his son."

Mill's hand tightens around the phone and she envisions the receiver slamming through the window that overlooks the Heap.

"Are you still there?"

"I'm sorry," she says, in the same tone she used with the librarian. "How was Charles your son, exactly?"

"Millicent—"

"When's his birthday, Paul?"

"Oh for Pete's sake—"

"When did he learn to ride a bike? Who was his best friend in pre-school? What was the name of his first pet?"

"Stop this, will you?"

"That's probably a good idea, before you start guessing dog names, and then I have to tell you it was a fucking snail that he chose. A snail named Horace. 'Your' son named his snail after Horace Kephart? The guy who trailblazed the Smokies? Only *my* son would have a grasp of irony at the age of seven."

"Millicent, what in God's name are you talking about?"

"Forget it. Eight-thirty?"

"Eight-thirty."

She hangs up and checks on Horace, whose brown feelers wave up at her from under a pebble.

AFTER SHE'D DISCOVERED that Paul had been sleeping with the same woman he'd dated before he and Mill got married, Mill decided it was time to go back south. She got custody of Charles, then two years old, without much of a fight from Paul, and went down to Knoxville, where she'd visited as a girl. The dream of going back had been there for years, she realized—it had been an intermittent pull, a soft calling, all through high school and college, and even during her marriage. At the time she didn't know why. Her memory of the place was comprised of a few bright but random splices of time: there were two hiking trails in the Smokies she'd taken with her cousins; a sculptor with a roadside shop who let her take home chunks of spalted maple wood; a woman who sold her strawberries from a wooden cart and invited Mill and her cousins to come out to her farm anytime to pick berries themselves. There was a blue cross, afire with tiny bulbs, perched high on a forested hill. There was an inn—the Old Mill—that she walked by one night and found herself staring at for a good hour. It had a lit gate, big windows reflecting the mountains above, a wheel churning water, the smell of baking apples wafting out from an open door. A nebulous garden filled the space between the inn and the next house. The place, she thought then, looked like it was made of something that could weather anything.

It wasn't long after finding a job in Oak Ridge that she found Martin. Like so many other men she met in the area, he didn't go by his first name—Martin was his middle name, Jeremiah his first. "You can see why I don't go with that one," he'd drawled to her the day they met. He gestured across his own body. "It don't fit." He was right—he had tattoos across his swollen biceps, untamed hair that wasn't exactly Biblical, and a way of standing that made it seem like he was about to take a swing at someone. But he couldn't help that—"It's this accident I was in, my posture's all fucked up"—and when he first kissed her, he was so gentle she had to keep her eyes open to make sure it was happening.

They camped. Martin showed her what boots to buy, how to compress a sleeping bag, how to strap on a 65-liter backpack ("don't let it overwhelm you; think of it as a little spider monkey who wants to come along for the ride"). He showed her how to choose a good walking stick from a woodworker just outside Gatlinburg. The first trail they hit was the Kephart Prong south of Newfound Gap. They got a late start and in the blue-green twilight passed the ruins of old chimneys and cairns, broken walls, water pipes, railroad ties. In the shelter at the trail's end Martin laid her on his sleeping pad, deftly undid the three buttons on her khakis, put one hand under her back and wrapped the other around her wrist, and made it clear to her that his gentleness extended only as far as she wanted it to.

He thrilled her. Paul had been the only one before him, and Paul had always been so unresponsive, so unlikely to initiate any kind of touch, that she'd always thought of sex as something labored and leading only to more frustration. When she explained to Martin, he said with disgust, "The pansy ass. I know his ilk."

Mill wasn't sure what ilk Paul was, but the man surely lacked spirit. Even little Charles seemed hardly to remember him. Martin had never laughed so hard as when Mill asked Charles one Christmas, "Do you miss your Dad, honey?" and Charles, looking up from a plastic tugboat, simply cocked his head at her, baffled.

Paul, still a faithful Catholic, and Mill's parents, also Catholic, had asked her literally hundreds of times, "Why aren't you getting married to Martin?"

Mill's response: "Once was overkill."

She didn't mean it. She was just happy with Martin and Charles, knew that Martin wasn't going anywhere, and saw no reason to ask the world to prove it on paper. It was only six months ago that Martin had told her over dinner that he wanted to formally adopt Charles and so they needed to get married. "I mean I know we already are," he'd said, his face burning a little—which amazed her—"We don't need no papers. But for him I think maybe we should."

She loved him for saying it. But Charles was killed before Martin could adopt him, and so that beautiful dinner, at the Flatwater Grill on Melton Lake, was all for nothing.

BY EIGHT O'CLOCK, the pizza has been ordered, and Charles' room secured: Mill has hidden away everything small enough to hide, every book and toy, and has even folded up his bedclothes, the Thomas the Tank Engine pillows he was just beginning to be embarrassed about. She doesn't want Paul looking at any of it, doesn't think he's earned it.

The rest of the house is still in disorder, though, and she feels hopeless to change it. She has spent so much time in Charles' room that the other rooms surprise her a little each time she steps into them. There is the pile of dishrags, folded differently than usual because Martin folded them; her bottles of lotions and soaps in the bathroom are misaligned. She keeps losing things: her calculator for the bills, her little pestle for making herb tea, her backup pair of boots. This morning she couldn't find her birth control pills. She half expects to discover pieces of furniture missing in the living room—their house, their world, has seemed so off kilter.

In the hallway she makes a half-hearted attempt to straighten the line of framed photographs from the many trails she has taken in the Smokies and in the Bald River Gorge south of here. The bees are from Andrews Bald, where she once stumbled upon a couple making love in the tall grass. She smiles at the memory, but the smile dies quickly. She closes the door to Charles' room, makes sure it clicks.

The front door swings open simultaneously. "Mill-li-cent," Martin sings out.

She stands, arms crossed, in the hallway. "That's not even funny."

Martin is unbuttoning his uniform smock and heeling off his boots. "I know—sorry." He kicks his boots over to the closet door and rubs at his hair. "I can't tell if I'm nervous, or if I'm just getting ready for a fight," he admits.

Something unidentifiable tumbles out of his hair onto the floor, and

Mill laughs. "Could you time something like that during dinner? But make sure it's a bug or something worse?"

Martin rakes his hair upwards. "It could be arranged. What are we eating?"

"Venice."

He grins. "Show no mercy."

"I hope they meet Cecil."

"I hope he forces them to meet him."

"I got Charles' room ready," Mill says, looking over her shoulder at the closed door.

"Ready?"

"I hid everything."

Martin moves carefully, not looking at her as he sets all their shoes in careful disarray near the door. She notes that he perches his dirtiest boot up against the coffee table.

"I dragged the mower out and a bunch of other crap from the garage and left it in the lawn this morning on purpose," Martin confesses.

"I threw more shit into the Compost Heap."

"Should I put the couch out there in the yard?"

She kisses him, tasting sweat, his long day. "They will be here any minute."

While Martin showers, twilight falls. Mill paces the house. She is listening hard—first, for the sound of the water shutting off, and second, for sounds on the porch. There is a soft clunk as if in answer to her thoughts, and instead of going for the .22, Mill strides to the door and throws it open.

Outside is only the darkening sky, already showing thousands of stars, and the scattered soft porch lights on Robertsville Road. When her eyes adjust, she can see a deer standing in her neighbor Rusty's lawn. Her breath catches.

Headlights swing over the top of the hill that is her block, and a Range Rover slows down in front of her house. She watches as the driver, her ex-husband, hesitates at the choices: parking on the street, or parking on the lawn. He chooses the street.

Mill peeks backward into the living room; the rifle is still lying on the sofa, and she grins, leaving it there. After a moment Martin joins her at the door, clad in a fresh shirt, and then Paul and Amanda are climbing out of their car and coming up the broken walkway arm-in-arm.

"Well, you made it," Mill says. The words come out dry.

"We did," says Paul, glancing around at the street. He starts up the porch steps with Amanda, and then stops for a moment, staring; Mill follows his gaze to the tricycle that is parked next to the house.

"He outgrew that ages ago," is all she can think of to say. Paul blinks hard and steps up onto the landing, taking a quick look around as Mill gestures him into the living room. Amanda follows, and in the porch light, she is very much the same as Mill remembers her: silky hair dyed black, thick eye makeup, tight jeans, spilling out of a black blouse that probably cost seventy dollars. Mill has an unexpected rush of pride: not too long ago, she would have felt inferior somehow, embarrassed beside this refined femininity, but not anymore. Long miles on trails and the sight of her own flushed skin and hazel eyes in mirrors after her hikes have taught her something about her own beauty.

Martin often reads her mind: "You guys want to sit down? We ordered pizza and it should be here any minute," he says, ushering them into the kitchen where he has rolled in Mill's swivel chair to add a fourth place to their table. "Don't worry, I'll take the office chair," he adds.

Mill hears little of the small talk that begins their night; she is studying Paul, his perfectly-cut hair, clean hands, faultless clothes. She is trying to imagine him when they first met when she catches the word "ritual" and breaks out of her haze.

"What was that?" she asks.

It is Amanda who is speaking; she turns her thickly-lashed eyes on Mill and says earnestly, "I was saying to Martin, that this is really important to both of us, it's a ritual experience if that makes sense."

Mill frowns. "What is?"

Paul squints at her. "Have you not been listening? Being here, saying goodbye to Charlie."

"You could have come to the funeral and the wake," Mill points out.

Paul cringes. "You know we couldn't make it. It nearly killed me to not be able to come. My job doesn't allow for spontaneous disappearances."

Mill kicks Martin under the table—she can tell he's getting fired up—and he drums his fingers on the tabletop. "I understand," Mill says. "I guess neither of us has to worry about that too much."

Martin snorts. "That's the truth. We don't make enough money."

Amanda looks confused. "Enough money to do what?"

"To care all that much about our jobs," Mill explains.

Paul says, "Wouldn't you care more if you weren't making much money? Not to press the point."

"Paul." Amanda reaches over, smoothes his hair. "Honey."

Martin's nose crinkles. "Was that the pizza guy?"

Mill stands. "I think I heard something too."

They all pause, listening, but there is nothing. "Maybe it's that guy again," Mill says uneasily, glancing at Martin. She wants to go to the living room window, to peer out onto the street for the shadow she has been seeing, but wills herself to sit back down.

Amanda says, "What guy?"

"Nothing. Anyhow…have you been out here before, Amanda?" Mill asks the question as lightly as she can, trying to look at Amanda without really looking at her, the woman her husband betrayed her with.

Amanda, clearly undergoing the same struggle, avoids Mill's eyes, but her voice is sweet: "No, I haven't. It's beautiful country. I've never seen hills like this. It's so bucolic. I can see why you'd want to move out here."

"Charles loved it," Martin breaks in. "He was a born-and-bred Southerner, don't matter where he came from originally. That kid read more about the mountains than I ever did and I been here my whole life."

Mill looks at him in surprise, but Martin goes on: "He was like a freaking encyclopedia. His latest thing was ice ages. He would give us these reports at night by the TV. Like he was a reporter. Did you know," and he leans forward, toward Amanda, "that the Smokies stayed standing, one ice age after another? Nothing could touch 'em. Everything else was getting changed and they somehow got through every one."

Amanda is polite; she smiles and nods along with his words, but Paul is blinking as though Martin is speaking a foreign language.

Paul says, "Well that's something." He glances at Mill. "Millicent, I should have asked when I first came in here—I was hoping you'd let me go into Charlie's room for awhile. I'd just like to see it. I'm sure you understand. Would that be all right?"

His voice is respectful, but he is already standing, sure of himself. Mill looks up at him. "Actually, I would prefer that you didn't," she says softly.

Amanda's eyes widen and she waits. Paul says, "I'm sorry?"

"I would prefer that you didn't go in there." Mill wraps her arm around Martin's chair back. "I don't really feel comfortable with that if you want to know the truth. Isn't it enough to be here and talk about him a little? And besides," she adds, seeing that he is already moving toward the hall, "won't it just be kind of…do you really think it will do something for you?"

Paul opens his mouth, and then the doorbell rings. Amanda says gently, "Why don't you sit down, for now," and he does, not taking his eyes off Mill. She stands up and realizes she is trembling.

MARTIN FOLLOWS MILL TO THE DOOR and hands her a roll of cash for the pizza. "As far as I can tell, even this is just an official duty of some kind," Mill mutters as she makes change for the delivery boy's tip. "Flatliner that he is. I just can't do it; I can't let him take Charles."

"He can't," Martin says quietly. He takes the pizza box in both arms. "You should know that."

"I guess I should. But I can't stop shaking. I don't know why."

Martin looks back toward the kitchen. "If it makes you feel any better—they really don't like our house." He grins. "Did you notice I've been letting the mail pile up? They had to have seen it on the way in. Isn't that a total white trash thing to do?"

Mill smiles and they reenter the kitchen together. "Food's on," Martin announces, and unceremoniously dumps the pizza box on the center of the table. He flips the lid, revealing Venice's largest pizza, a monstrosity of greasy cheese dotted with crumbly bits of sausage and limp vegetables. Amanda purses her lips and glances at Paul.

Mill doles out the slices, two to a plate, and passes them around. Amanda asks for a fork. Martin pours Coke from a two-liter bottle in the fridge. They chew in silence for a few minutes, Mill struggling not to laugh as Amanda picks at her slice, until Paul says, "Just out of curiosity—do you always keep a rifle in the living room? It was kind of impossible not to see it on our way in."

"Not usually," Martin says. He folds his pizza in half and takes a huge bite. Around the bite he adds, "Lately Mill's been keeping it out for safety's sake. We think somebody's been creeping around our house at night."

Amanda looks at Mill. "Is there a lot of crime in the area?"

"Not really. Everybody here knows everybody else, so I think that's sort of a natural deterrent, you know? People know that if they do something to one house, there are probably five neighbors watching who are going to take it personally."

"But you're still worried," Amanda points out.

Mill says, "Just taking precautions. I know we're not exactly a gated community here, but it's safer than you'd think."

Paul sets down his pizza, clearly disgusted with it. He pushes his plate a little to one side and says, "Really, Mill, I don't want to make too much of this, but the gun is just ridiculous. I can't believe you keep it lying around the house that way. It's bad enough that you own one to begin with." Martin's jaw goes hard and Mill says rapidly, "I had the gun long before Martin moved in, in case you were wondering."

"I still don't understand why you have it."

"How about you tell me why not?"

Amanda shifts in her seat, touches Paul lightly on the arm. "Honey, maybe we should change the subject, OK?" She looks at Mill, then Martin. "Once he gets started . . . ," she says, rolling her eyes a little, trying to smile.

Paul ignores her entirely. "I'll tell you why not. Because it's immoral. It's not up to you to decide who gets hurt or killed if someone breaks into your house."

Martin's jaw drops. "You want to explain that maybe?"

Paul leans back, crosses his arms. "Well," he says slowly, "say somebody breaks in here in the middle of the night. Are you willing to possibly take his life, in self-defense? Who says you get to be the one to decide who gets hurt or killed? You've put yourself in the position of God when you pick up that gun."

Mill starts to speak, but Martin leans forward, putting both arms on the table. "Nobody here is going to shoot a man without good reason," he says. "But let's say this man comes in armed. Let's say he's after my wife or child." His voice breaks on "child" and he clears his throat. "Let's say that. You're telling me I should stand there and let whatever happens happen? You're telling me I can't even pop this guy in the leg to get him to back off my family? That is some amazing bullshit."

Mill leans toward Paul. "So you're saying," she murmurs, "that it's wrong to make an active choice about who lives or dies."

Paul says, "Yes."

"But you're making a choice either way," she says excitedly. "If you stand by and let the guy hurt your family, you are still making a choice. You are sacrificing someone else for the sake of your own morality. You're the good guy because you transfer the responsibility onto the criminal? That makes no sense."

Paul's mouth opens and closes, and Mill presses on: "You've just chosen the criminal over the husband or wife or child. If you want to sacrifice yourself, that's one thing, but if you stand by and watch, you've surrendered the innocent to the malicious. And then you get to feel good about yourself for being so—so what? So forgiving? So nonjudgmental? That's just cowardice if you ask me. So explain how that's moral, Paul. Explain how it's moral not to fight for what you love."

Martin says through gritted teeth, "I'll bet you'd just be too scared to draw his fire on you. You pick up a gun to defend someone, now you're the one being aimed at. You get to go unnoticed even by God. You get to stand there with your hands folded." He shakes a cigarette out of the packet in his shirt pocket, doesn't light it. "Somebody or something has got you gutted."

Amanda says sharply, "I think that's enough." She reaches for the bottle of Coke and noisily unscrews the cap, refills her cup. "Honestly, I don't know why we're having this conversation of all things," she goes on, her voice pleading, eyes flickering over to her husband. "Can we please drop it? Paul? Please? We're here because of your son, remember?"

Mill says, "His son?" and Martin sucks in a breath.

Paul stands up. "I've had about enough talk, too," he says. "I've had enough of all of this, actually. I'd like to see Charlie's room now if you're over whatever your issue was an hour ago."

"Don't you go in there," Mill says quietly. "And no one ever called him Charlie. He hates being called Charlie."

"I have every fucking right," Paul says, voice rising. But he stands motionless, and suddenly, Mill realizes that her ex-husband is afraid of Martin. Or maybe of both of them.

She looks at Martin, whose face is beginning to turn red. His hands grip the edges of the table. "Look, man," he says, "I'll be honest, I don't know what you're doing here in the first place. Trying to claim something that ain't yours. It's a crock if you ask me. You show up now, just in time to get all teary-eyed over your kid's old toys? What the fuck is that? Where the hell were you?"

"I don't have to listen to this," Paul says. His voice is steady, but his jaw works in the way Mill remembers from nights when he came home tense and preoccupied with some problem. "I'm going in my son's room now if you don't mind."

Martin gets up fast, and Paul, clearly drawing on every ounce of composure, walks quickly but calmly out of the kitchen and down the hallway. Amanda sits frozen at the table, not looking at anyone. Mill puts her hand over Martin's, and then leaves; Martin sits down again. He looks at Amanda and says, "You all just do not belong here."

MILL PAUSES IN THE HALLWAY, closes her eyes, breathes. She thinks of the story she and Martin told Paul: that the rockslide happened lightning-quick, on a deep curve of 129, the Dragon's Tail, an infamously dangerous road in the North Carolina mountains. They were heading back from a long day in the Joyce Kilmer Forest where the three of them had hiked until twilight. They had driven this way many times, and had never seen so much as a stone in the road. The avalanche crushed the back of the car where Charles sat strapped in and sleeping. They were alone out there; there was no help for hours, and it was pure chance that the front of the car remained intact, that neither Martin nor Mill was killed. At the time, Mill felt there was no way to tell Paul how it had really happened, not without corrupting something she wanted to keep pure.

She thinks of the truth: that there were two other cars, both in front of them, when the boulders came exploding from the mountainside and rained down around them. The rocks completely demolished the car in front of them; the second car was difficult to see but there was smoke rising from it after the first sudden silence. Martin knew about rockslides, knew that they stopped and then started again in waves, and he screamed at Charles as Charles unbuckled his seatbelt and went flying from the backseat out into the road. Charles ran straight for the third car, seeming to understand that there was nothing they could do for the other one. In a mad chase Martin followed, Mill close behind, and then the second avalanche showered them. Charles was on the ground within seconds, Martin's arms and shoulders cut to ribbons, Mill somehow untouched except by dust. She knelt there screaming over her motionless son and over Martin, who was knocked unconscious and bleeding fast into the pavement, until someone from the third car came scrambling to her side with a cell phone.

The question later was, of course, what made him do it? Mill never once believed she had been that good of a parent, that it was her own instruction that led to the choice Charles made after the first rockslide. Half-dreaming and dazed from painkillers, Martin said to her in the hospital, "He did it because he grew up out here," and passed out again.

She feels that there are some questions which cannot be answered; they go too far beyond her. But these mountains, she knows, are as old as death, as old as love. It is something she has no way of communicating to Paul; it is something that her son somehow understood before she did. And she knows she has to keep it safe, hidden from unknowing eyes and clumsy hands. She is afraid of this thing dying. Afraid that the world she fell in love with as a girl in Knoxville is the last of its kind.

SHE FINDS HER EX-HUSBAND sitting on Charles' bed, holding a DVD in his hands—March of the Penguins. Paul is staring dumbly down at it, rubbing his thumb over the picture on the front.

Paul looks up, and his eyes are red. "I always pictured him on Power Wheels and racing remote-control trucks through the house. Playing video games."

"He wasn't like that at all. One of our neighbors gave him a Power Wheel car their kid outgrew, and Charles just took it apart and put it back together until it got too easy for him."

"What else did he do?"

Mill lets out a long breath. "It's almost impossible to answer that question, you know that. You could have easily found out for yourself ages ago."

"I know."

"Paul." She steps closer and stops. "I need to know why you are doing this. I don't want to be callous, but I have to ask. You never cared before. None of this feels genuine to me."

Paul looks at the ceiling, then closes his eyes. "I remembered this time when Charlie wanted to go to sleep with one of my shirts and I told him no. All he wanted was—I don't know." He opens his eyes, and he is abruptly his old self again, shrugging and standing up with complete composure. "Well. In any case. I suppose it's just a matter of closure. You took a psychology class or two."

Mill laughs softly. "You know, I almost had you for a minute there—I almost saw something different. But you disappeared right away. I wonder if you are going to live your whole life like this, in the mode you are in now."

He looks confusedly at her. "What are you talking about?"

"Nothing. Forget it."

For a long moment he circles the room, looks at the few things she has left out—Charles' lighthouse lamp, a giant poster picturing a fossilized mastodon, a wooden chest Martin built, with figures of deer and elk carved into the oak. But he looks at everything blindly, and she sees his arms go limp with a kind of helplessness: Charles can't be known this way. Paul, too, is on the brink of answers that are too much to face. Mill leans against the doorframe, feeling the anger drain from her.

"Paul," she sighs, "I think maybe you should go home."

He says nothing, just pushes past her through the hallway and back to the kitchen where Amanda is already standing up, setting her purse on her shoulder. Martin has boxed the pizza and put it out of sight, and the plates are stacked in the sink.

Amanda looks at Paul. "Are you ready to go? Are you okay?"

"I'm fine."

Martin hangs back and Mill follows them to the door. She watches as they make their way back to their Range Rover. From across the street,

Cecil, bathed in the light from his toolshed, yells at them: "Hey ya'll! Hope ya have a great drive back! Shame I didn't get to meet ya!"

Amanda grabs Paul's arm and looks back at Mill in alarm. Mill looks past her and just waves at Cecil, who waves back; he's holding what looks like a trowel. He has a habit of gardening late at night. Gardening and drinking, switching back and forth between the two.

Paul and Amanda climb quickly into their car and in a moment the Range Rover glides back onto the road. The taillights vanish over the top of the hill and Mill lets out her breath.

WHEN MILL REENTERS THE HOUSE, Martin is sitting at the kitchen table under the soft light, slicing into Cecil's cantaloupe with a steak knife. Mill sits down across from him and takes the half-moon of fruit Martin holds out to her. Rivers of juice run from the opened melon and seeds tumble out and scatter all over the tabletop.

Mill takes a bite, chews. She says, "Did you hide my birth control pills?"

He grins around a mouthful. "I'm not confessing to it in writing."

She finishes her slice, reaches out and picks up the knife. "I want more of this."

They eat in silence, making a bowl of the fruit, until Martin leans back in his chair. "I think we're set, huh?"

"Cecil would be proud."

"We shouldn't waste the rest, though. It'll be rotten by morning."

They rise from the table, and Mill opens the back door. Night behind the Compost Heap is blue-black and afire with stars. Something rustles in the trees. Martin steps out next to Mill and heaves the rest of the melon into the glowing wilderness below.

Parachutes

Niles has walked in Cades Cove nearly every Saturday morning since his wife died eight years ago. He is forty-four years old and ashamed of the fact that his sanity seems to rely so heavily on his routines. On the few weekends he has missed this hike, he has felt off, his world tilted. There are eight hundred miles of hiking trails in this national park, but Niles prefers to walk through the sweeping valley that is Cades Cove, because the place reminds him of the days when he and his wife were field gleaners, working for a charity that sent them out to east Tennessee farms to collect produce for shelters. It was the kind of thing Niles only had the courage to do when Hannah was with him.

It is not only his memories that draw him to the cove. It is also his belief that he truly knows this place—that nothing unexpected can happen to him here. He imagines that, from above, this cove is a bright peridot blank amidst the chaos of the surrounding mountains, and that anyone flying a plane would be tempted to land here. Niles imagines that at night, the sky gathers itself together and sleeps here, settling gently into a ball of cobalt-blue and of stars, and dozing on the soft grass.

It is April, and the valley's fringe of woods is beginning to brighten with the first dogwood blooms. Niles moves slowly. As he does every Saturday morning, he focuses on keeping his mind as blank as possible, on stilling his nerves. He is constantly tempted to look up and around, to see if anyone is staring at him—this lone, awkward figure in the middle of the field—but stops himself.

Don't worry what other people think. Just walk. Just look at this place.

For long while, he does just this. He is only interrupted in his determined blankness when he steps on something that bites into the sole of his shoe. Niles squints and pushes his glasses up higher on his nose. Bending low, he sinks his fingers into the grass and finds something dark and waxy—a child's toy, a brown plastic soldier with a tiny orange parachute attached to his back with string. The toy is filthy and the soldier is almost unrecognizable, the body caked with dirt and caved in at the torso, probably from Niles' own foot. He holds it in his palm for a minute, staring, and then scrubs at it with his shirttail until the soldier is clean, the parachute shiny. He stares at it a long time before putting it into his pants pocket and turning around to go home.

HE BREATHES A DEEP SIGH OF RELIEF upon discovering the house to be empty. His daughter, Kara, and her best friend, Ilsabeth, are staying with him during the University of Tennessee's spring break, and he has been anxious and sleepless since they arrived five days ago. The girls are in their senior year; Kara has been accepted into a business school in Florida, and Ilsabeth will start a master's degree in English in Michigan in the fall. They are tense and excitable, plowing through their last weeks of young adulthood, and even Ilsabeth, who has always been so calm, has seemed on edge.

It is hard enough for Niles to feel comfortable in his own home with them there; it is a thousand times worse when he is not the only basket case, as Kara would call him, in the house. He is grateful that his study, where his piano is, is located at the back of the house, as far from Kara's bedroom as possible. In there, he at least has some peace.

He decides to tidy up the kitchen before going to his piano. First he refills his glass salt shaker; he has to do this often to keep it even with the pepper shaker, since his wife is no longer here to use the pepper as she often had. It comforts Niles to see the glass jars filled always to the same line. Then he starts on the breakfast dishes. He notices that his coffee mug has been washed and set beside the coffeemaker, complete with his little silver sugar spoon and jar of creamer lined up neatly beside it, and he smiles to himself. This is one of Kara's rare kindnesses, a thing she does for him whenever she and Ilsabeth come home for a visit, and what makes it so charming to Niles is that she never acknowledges having done it.

As Niles' hands move in the soapy water, he eyes the counter with all its Kara-created disorder that stands in direct contrast to his cup and spoon: half-filled glasses, a forgotten chapstick, a Heath bar, and what looks like a bracelet made out of a neon glow-stick.

Kara baffles him and always has. Where her genes came from, Niles can't fathom, but she is nothing like her mother was, and even less like Niles. Where Niles is stooped, awkward, and self-conscious, Kara is loud, unabashedly sexual, and so confident that even the way she eats cereal expresses surety. Her highlighted hair dances on her shoulders when she talks and her clothes flaunt a voluptuous figure that Niles wishes she would take more care to cover.

Last night, Niles got up at two in the morning for milk. Halfway down the long hall to the kitchen, he heard the girls' voices, and realized they were already in there. He was about to turn around when he heard Kara say, "Even his *walk* is embarrassing. He's pathetic, moping all the time like his puppy just died. Come on, admit it. Look, I'm Niles Willet!"

Niles stopped and took a couple of steps toward the kitchen until his daughter wove her way into sight. She was in her pajamas and had flipped her hair over her face so it hung over her eyes the way Niles' hair did. She was shuffling across the linoleum, hands deep in imaginary pockets, her nose down. Clearly, she was expecting Ilsabeth to laugh, but the girl just sat there at the kitchen counter, her head in her hand. She only glanced at Kara and then looked back down at the countertop, tracing her fingers over it as though a map were drawn there. Niles suddenly felt guilty for resenting all the holidays Ilsabeth had spent at this house. Her parents, after all, had been divorced for years, and she had nowhere she could really call home, from what Kara had told him.

Niles made a mental promise to do something kind for Ilsabeth the next day. Then he turned and went quietly back to his bed, lying as always on the left side. He lay awake a long time, listening to their voices, before clamping a pillow over his head and finally drifting off.

"And the ridiculous part is, he thought he had a *chance* with me." Kara's voice drifts into the house from the front door, and in a moment, she has keyed her way in with Ilsabeth close behind. "That loser. Like I'd make his dinners and have his kids instead of going to grad school."

Ilsabeth says, "Hi, Mr. Willett."

Niles smiles at her; she has never been able to use his first name. "Who's this loser you're talking about?" he asks Kara from the sink, drying off his hands.

Kara waves him off. "Just some idiot from back at school who keeps calling me. How was the walk, Dad?" She rubs his shoulder, but rolls her eyes. "See anything new out there?"

"Not really, no." He clears his throat and glances at Ilsabeth, who is hovering on the other side of the counter, just as she did last night. "What are you ladies up to today?"

"This one here," Kara says, pointing at her friend, "is being a stick in the mud. Says she wants to write. Me, I'm heading back out in a minute here. I've got to do some serious shopping for graduation. And I want to look at some laptops. Can I take your car out again?"

"Sure. I'm not going anywhere." Niles stacks the clean dishes and smiles at Ilsabeth. "What are you working on? Another short story?"

"I'm trying," she says, shrugging. She pulls at her dark hair, which falls in uncombed waves down her back. "I'm just not really getting anywhere right now. I was thinking that a change of scenery might help." She clears her throat, the sound almost a match for Niles', and adds, "I was wondering if I could write in your studio."

"Study," Niles corrects, at the exact same time Kara says, *"Study,* Ilsa. *Studio* sounds too professional. Right, Dad?"

"Right," he says sheepishly. "I'm not a pianist. Not anymore."

"That's not true," Ilsabeth begins, but Kara speaks over her: "Dad hasn't written anything in years. Teaching piano does not make you a pianist. That's what he always says."

"Use it whenever you want," Niles says to Ilsabeth, though it hurts to say it. He can see his last remaining hours of peace and solitude slipping out of his reach. But, he reminds himself, he did promise the night before to do something for her.

"Thank you so much," Ilsabeth says, brightening.

"Just give me an hour or so in there first. I have to get some things ready for some students tomorrow, and I need to do some practicing. Try not to listen. I'm sure it will sound terrible." He is down the hall before she can respond.

HE RUNS THROUGH HIS USUAL PRACTICE ROUTINE and then waits for the front door to slam—the sound of Kara departing—to begin working on the next segment of the song he has been composing for nearly a year now. He remembers when the first bars came to him—it was actually at this time last April, when Kara first brought Ilsabeth home for the spring break of their junior year. He wasn't sure what lit the fire, but he could not get the melody out of his head, nor could he shake the intimidating suspicion that it might be something good enough to invest real time in. He hadn't written anything worth two measures in years.

The song has no title, but it has a clear feeling, an identity as real as a person. Niles presses the left pedal down to quiet the keys as much as possible, and plays the finished segments lightly, his long pale fingers dancing over the keys. The bass is gently insistent, almost stubbornly predictable, but the treble is a whole other story, careening in from the heavens like a windstorm and tracing wild circles all across the landscape the bass has created. Niles loses himself for a long time in the treble, closing his eyes. He knows he should be working on a new segment, but he is afraid to. To his thinking, if he goes any further, he might ruin it, or find out it was never going anywhere in the first place.

He plays on uninterrupted until the house phone's shrill call startles him. Annoyed, Niles waits for Ilsabeth to pick it up, but she doesn't, and so he has to leave his study and go into the hallway. He picks up the hall phone from its little table and answers irritably: "Yes?"

"Niles? It's Gregory."

Gregory is the vice president of Maryville College, where Niles works as an adjunct music teacher, and Niles winces. "What can I do for you?"

"Niles, I already know what you're going to say, but I have to ask anyway. I think you know what I'm going to ask?"

"Well, no, I don't."

"The faculty benefit concert is almost here again."

Niles is silent.

"Niles? The concert is the second week of May."

Niles swallows. "I'm not interested. I mean I really can't."

"You said that last year."

"And you convinced me to play anyway. And remember what happened?" He is a little sick just thinking about it, and his hand drifts to his belly, remembering how he'd thrown up that night, after tearing his way out of the college theater.

"It happened. But it doesn't have to happen again, Niles. Anyone can have a—anyone can experience that, even the best musicians. But you're too gifted not to be on that stage. I was hoping you would give it another go."

"No."

"Niles."

"I can't. I'm sorry. I'm just not the person you want up there. There are plenty of other faculty who are better performers. You can't possibly need me."

Gregory lets out a gust of a sigh. "We don't need you. We want you. Please, just consider it, all right? Think about it and get back to me.

Sleep on it. You could play whatever you like. Something of your own, if you have anything new."

"I don't write music anymore. I just teach."

There is a pause, and then Gregory responds, "You know what, I don't believe that for a minute. You've got the spark, Niles. You could maybe share it with some people out there, too. Let's not forget: you were the most exceptional performer we had not that long ago."

"That was a longer time ago than you think." What Niles really wants to say is, *That was when Hannah was alive and in the audience.*

"Just think about it and call me."

To end it, Niles says, "Fine. I'll think about it."

"Good." Gregory says goodbye, and then Niles sets the phone down and stares at it. His hands are shaking. Last year's recital had been the humiliation of his life. The previous year had been bad enough—he'd had a panic attack hours before the concert, and had had to call the department chair to say he was too ill to play. Last year, he'd made it onto the stage, and this had been a far worse mistake. He got ten bars into his piece before fumbling, and then he began to count his mistakes: two, five, seven, ten, fourteen . . . until the piece literally came apart right there on the piano, its notes blowing away from him the way the fragile skeleton of a dead dandelion scatters in a quick puff of wind. The piece was so thoroughly ruined, its essence so brutalized by Niles' mistakes, that he simply stopped playing, rose, gave the audience a quick bow, and rushed off the stage. He vomited into a trash can behind the theater before rushing to his car and driving home. His heart was hammering so hard he thought he might have some kind of attack, and his hands shook violently so that the car seemed too big a thing for him to control. Reaching his little studio and closing the door behind him was the greatest relief he had ever known.

The faculty at Maryville had a nickname for him after that disaster—Nervous Niles—and though nobody said it to his face, it got around to him pretty quickly via some wily students and one very talkative department secretary. He started eating his lunches in the bathroom, or in his car, between student lessons, and came up with illnesses to excuse him from faculty meetings. He thanked God that most of his students had not attended the recital, but he felt like a fraud teaching them to play the piano and preparing them for student recitals when he himself could not even play in front of a crowd.

He fights now to still his hands and to reassure himself that he does not have to participate in this concert. Regardless of his position, Gregory cannot force him to do it, and Niles never has to touch a piano in front of anyone again.

"Mr. Willett?" Ilsabeth, who always moves quietly, surprises him at his side. "Are you all right? You look a little green."

He tries to laugh. "That's probably pretty accurate."

"Are you okay?"

"I'm fine. Did you want to use my study now? I'm done with my practicing."

"Oh. Well, yeah, I do. I was kind of hoping though that you wouldn't stop working just because of me. We could work in there at the same time, right?"

Niles frowns. "I think my playing would distract you. I think it's probably not the best help for someone with writer's block."

Ilsabeth laughs. "How would you know? I actually write best to music." She moves down the hall and disappears into Kara's room for a moment, then comes back with her computer bag. From the bag's depths she removes a pair of headphones. "See?" she says. "I'll be listening to my own music on my laptop. You can work on yours. I won't even be able to hear you. You know how my generation is. We all love to blast our eardrums apart with our abominable excuses for music." She is quoting something Niles said long ago, and they both smile.

"Well," Niles says, scratching at his hair. "I suppose so. But if it's bothering you, I want the truth. Right away."

"It's a deal."

It is painfully awkward for the first half an hour or so, with Ilsabeth typing hesitantly on her keyboard and Niles plunking out scales and other meaningless bits on the piano, and each pretending to believe that the other is deaf. After awhile, though, they fall into a rhythm, their bodies taking on almost identical poses: both hunched over, shoulders scrunched up, hands extended and moving fast as water.

It is water Niles is thinking of as he listens to Ilsabeth type over the sound of his scales. He thinks she must be reaching her stride in her story, because quite suddenly her typing has sped up, the letters falling into line and only rarely interrupted by the staccato of the backspace key. Her keys sound to him like a strong rain, and he closes his eyes. Without realizing it right away, he plays the first few bars of his composition, and then, startled, glances sidelong at Ilsabeth. She seems entirely engrossed, her eyes fixed on her screen, and so he closes his eyes again and continues playing.

First he sees rain falling on a field. Then leaves fluttering down from the great heights of poplars; jellyfish drifting in the thousands in a wide turquoise sea. His right hand is flying; the treble is descending over the base like a heron skimming to a landing over a marsh. In a flash of insight, Niles knows how the next few bars should go, and he improvises, testing out the sounds. It only takes a few tries before he has it. In jubilation, he opens his eyes and smiles.

Ilsabeth has stopped typing. Though her headphones are still on, she is just staring at his hands, her mouth open.

"Sorry," Niles says automatically. "Sorry."

She pulls the headphones off. "Are you crazy? My God. Could you play that again?"

A tiny tremor rises in Niles—the old familiar anxiety—but Ilsabeth, hunched there at her computer, holds out clasped hands in a self-mocking little prayer, and so he turns back to the keys. He manages to repeat the new chords, and cannot help smiling yet again at his discovery.

"Not just that part. The whole thing. What *is* that?"

"It's nothing," Niles tells her. But he goes back to the beginning and plays, feeling rather than seeing Ilsabeth leaning forward in his desk chair.

"It has no name? You wrote it, didn't you." She shakes her head when he stops playing. "Has Kara heard this? Jesus."

"Oh, no. It's not anything, believe me. I've made pretty much no progress on it. I don't think it's ever going to leave this room."

"That would be a shame. It's stunning."

To cover his embarrassment, Niles nods at her laptop. "So how is the story coming? What's it about?"

Ilsabeth glances at the screen. "It's crap."

"I'll bet it isn't. Who are your characters?"

She grins at him. "Mr. Willett, thank you so much for buying us lotions and razors and all that and leaving them in the bathroom. We both always forget to bring them."

He is temporarily flustered—buying those items does in fact make him incredibly uncomfortable at the drugstore—but he says, "Don't change the subject. Come on, what's the story?"

She tugs at her hair. "It's sort of based on something that really happened to me. Back when I was working in home care to make money for college? I was working for this old woman who lived alone for about six months. Honestly, she drove me kind of crazy. She just had all these weird habits and would get lost in the moment all the time, like she had to be reminded of where she was. Then this one day I had just made her lunch, and we heard this huge crash from the back of the house. I thought somebody had broken in and I ran back there. The sound came from her room, from this walk-in-closet she had. What happened was that a shelf in the closet collapsed from too much weight. It was holding up these huge boxes full of old letters. I sat on the floor and tried to reorganize them but there were too many. I was getting frustrated until it hit me what I was looking at. I mean, those were all letters from one person, her husband. I was literally sitting in this snowstorm of somebody's love. It was like all of a sudden this woman made sense to me. She came alive to me."

It is the most Ilsabeth has ever said to Niles in one sitting, and he is quiet, taking it in. "And the story," he finally asks, "is it about her, or you?"

"Her," Ilsabeth says. Then she points at the piano. "Now tell me once and for all the name of that song."

Niles looks at the keys, his mind racing. For some reason, he feels the need to dredge up a name for her, anything. Just when he thinks the task is hopeless, he feels the toy soldier in his pants pocket, its plastic edges poking at him.

"*Parachutes*," he tells Ilsabeth.

Her eyes widen.

"Bad name?"

"Absolutely not." She considers him for a long moment, then turns back to her laptop. "You shouldn't be afraid to work on it with me here. I promise, I won't listen if it really bothers you that much." She reaches for her headphones.

"No—it's all right. Just do what you feel like doing."

Ilsabeth smiles. She rises, excusing herself to use the restroom, and Niles turns back to his piano.

They work for the next few hours, with no sign of Kara. Pizza arrives at the door around six o'clock and Ilsabeth confesses to have ordered it when she said she was going to the restroom. Niles, finding himself oddly delighted in this food he would never have ordered for himself, eats more than half the pizza.

Whether it is the sugar and carbohydrates from the pizza, or the exhilaration of having made some progress in their creative efforts, both are talkative and laughing when Kara finally comes home. Niles, stuffed with pizza, is playing a version of "Heart and Soul" that he calls "Misery and Rage," an atonal, staggered mess of a song that sends Ilsabeth into shrieks of laughter every time he hits an off key. He complements the performance by pairing expressions of mock horror with each hideous chord, and when Kara walks in, Ilsabeth is doubled over in her chair.

Niles immediately stops playing and pushes his glasses up. "Hi, honey. Where've you been all day?"

"Good Lord. What are you guys, drunk?" Kara drops her purse on the floor and puts her hands on her hips. "And you had pizza? I missed a party." She looks at Ilsabeth. "I didn't even know my dad *could* party."

"I got a lot of work done," Ilsabeth insists, turning her laptop toward Kara.

Kara barely glances at the screen. "That's great. What the hell were you playing, Dad?"

Niles launches into the Barcarolle. "Just some classical."

"Oh, God. Not the Barcalounger!" It is one of their oldest jokes, and for a moment, Niles basks in his daughter's grin before Kara turns back to Ilsabeth. "We have a double date tomorrow," she announces. "Tomorrow night. Ready to meet somebody new? I promise, you'll like this one."

"You could have asked me first. How many new somebodies can one person meet? What is this, your tenth date this month?"

Kara shrugs. "Who knows. Are you coming or what?"

"I'm your guest. Whatever you want."

"Oh, that's the spirit." Kara rolls her eyes. "Come on, I want to show you my graduation dress. You don't want to spend the night in this closet."

"There's clean towels I just put in the bathroom for you," Niles calls after them as they walk out.

NILES HAS TO TEACH all the following day—three classes and six private lessons—and he does not see the girls until he gets home at seven o'clock. His head is brimming; he has been piecing together the next bit of his composition even as he taught his students scales and fingering techniques. He cannot wait to sit at his own piano.

Kara strides into the kitchen as soon as he enters, wearing tight blue jeans and an animal-print top that has a large swath cut out across her chest. "Dad, we need the car. We're meeting our dates in like half an hour."

"I know. Here." He hands her his keys. "Will you be back pretty late, then?"

"I have no idea."

"Okay." He hesitates. "That's what you're wearing?"

Kara laughs. "When you start dating, Dad, we'll talk about clubbing outfits."

"Dating?"

Kara is still laughing when Ilsabeth walks into the kitchen in khakis and a blue tee shirt.

"That's what *you're* wearing?" Kara yelps. "I am not going clubbing with Emily Dickinson. Christ."

Ilsabeth shrugs. "Take it or leave it."

"Oh, whatever. We don't have time to worry about it. We'll see you later," Kara says to Niles.

"You're leaving tomorrow morning, right? What time should I plan on getting up to take you back to campus?"

"There's no rush. Maybe ten."

"All right."

The girls go out the door, and when the door clicks softly shut, Niles goes to his coffeemaker. The clean cup, the spoon and creamer jar, is set and ready for him, only today, there is something new: a tiny glass jar of raspberry preserves, bright as rubies, with a deep pink ribbon tied around its neck. Niles shakes his head. He cups the jar in both hands and recognizes it as the only love language his daughter is capable of. He wonders whether it is his fault somehow that she feels the need to pretend to feel nothing, for anyone.

He's pathetic, Kara had said. *He mopes around like his puppy just died.*

Niles is sure that this is false; he does not mope. And as far as Niles knows, Kara has never moped, either. The only sign of her distress after her mother died was that for nearly six months, she wore Hannah's perfume to school every day. Niles would often come home to the sensation that his wife had only recently passed through the kitchen or the living room. It saddened him when Kara stopped doing that, and when she stopped talking about her mother altogether, as though that part of her life had never existed at all.

The phone rings and Niles checks the I.D.: Gregory again, still waiting for an answer about the recital. Niles just lets it ring.

THE GIRLS STILL AREN'T HOME when Niles goes to bed at ten-thirty. He tosses in his sleep, his mind wrestling with the next few bars, and wakes to see 2:45 AM on his digital clock.

"Who are you to criticize me? Jesus, you're a guest in my house." It is his daughter, her voice ringing down the hall.

"So you keep reminding me." Ilsabeth's voice, considerably quieter. Niles sits up.

"You ruined the whole night. Sometimes I don't know why I even try to get you to come out with me. You're like a ninety-year-old woman, you know that? Just sit back and have some fun for once in your life."

"That's what it's all about for you, right? Just having fun? Maybe I graduated out of that school a little early. You want the truth? It's fucking boring. There's nothing for me in it."

Niles rises as quietly as he can and moves to his door. He cracks it, and sees light coming from Kara's room down the hall. He steps into the hall and just stands there.

"That's what I mean about being ninety years old."

"At least I'm not a whore. Throwing myself at everyone like it doesn't matter. God, you led him on like he was just a toy. Did you see the way he looked at you? You told me you were friends when you were kids. He *cared* about you, Kara."

"Now you're calling me a whore." Kara says something else Niles can't hear.

Ilsabeth's voice rises: "You know what's crazy? Is that you just pretend to be one. Everything is pretend, every last fucking comment you make to whatever guy you're playing with. It's all a scheme to make everyone around you think you don't need a soul. But in the end, nobody's going to buy that lie."

"It's no lie. I'm not you, Ilsabeth. I *don't* need anyone. Some of us—"

"Don't start that again. Don't you get it? I'm not trying to insult you. I'm trying to help you."

Kara's laugh is hard-edged; she sounds cornered. "Look who's talking. What's going to happen to you when you leave college? You aren't going to know a damn soul out there. And you're not going to have the guts to meet anyone, either."

"I feel like I've done a pretty good job taking care of myself, all things considered," Ilsabeth responds. "But what I wanted to say was, I am trying to help you not miss out on things. You will miss out if you pretend like you don't need anybody. You'll end up even more alone than the rest of us."

"No, I don't think so. People like my father? Look at him. That's the definition of alone. He's such a half-baked sop of a man without my mother, he can barely walk straight."

Niles sinks down to the floor and sits with his back against the wall. *I am not. It isn't true,* he thinks. His hands clench into fists and he imagines getting up and striding into the room to say this. But of course, he cannot.

"Would you feel better if he'd just forgotten all about your mom? Would you want *your* husband to do that to you?"

"I hope he would. I hope he'd move on."

"I wouldn't," Ilsabeth says with feeling.

"Well, that's you."

"You're just scared you'll end up alone as he is," Ilsabeth says, so quietly Niles can barely hear her. "I know how it feels. I never really had anyone until I met you."

There is a long, pregnant silence. Niles leans forward to hear what comes next, but there are only the faint sounds of Kara settling into her bed and Ilsabeth spreading out her bedding on the floor. At last Niles rises and moves carefully back to his own room.

He watches the bright green digits change on his clock. It has never occurred to him that Kara might hold it against him for not leaving her mother's memory behind. He is insisting to himself, *I am not the way she says, I am not* ... when he drifts back into his fitful sleep.

IN THE MORNING, the three of them load up Niles' battered sedan with the girls' duffel bags, and Kara places herself in the backseat without a word to either of them. She is silent and sulky the whole way to Knoxville, giving one-word answers when Niles asks if they forgot anything or if anyone wants to stop for food. He glances occasionally at Ilsabeth, who stares out of her window. Her profile is pale. He wonders if their friendship is over.

Driving around UT's campus makes Niles jittery, with the throngs of students and hundreds of other cars unloading bags and post-spring-breakers, most of them tanned and hung-over-looking. Impatiently, Kara directs him to a parking space down the street from the house she shares with Ilsabeth and three other girls. Niles starts to open his door, but Kara says, "I've got it, Dad, just pop the trunk," so he obeys.

He is deeply disheartened, thinking of how many times this has happened: he does not know how to say goodbye to his own daughter, and feels that any words he might come up with will be inadequate, stupid. He simply lacks the strength to meet the boldness—and now, he realizes, the resentment—in her eyes. He is thinking so hard about this that it startles him to discover that Ilsabeth is still in the car.

"Do you need help with your bags?" he asks, shifting in his seat. "Let me grab them."

Ilsabeth waves him off. "No. I'll get them in a second."

Niles follows her gaze—she is watching Kara, who is at the curb, shuffling through a bag, probably already discovering that she's forgotten something. When Ilsabeth faces him, her face is paler than ever, but resolute. Her hands are folded in her lap as though in prayer.

"Niles?" she says.

His name coming from her mouth is electric, making him sit up straight. "What's the matter?"

"I need to tell you that you ruined college for me. And probably grad school, too." She gives a tiny laugh, and a sudden rush of color flushes her cheeks. Niles stares at her in confusion.

"Look," she says, "I know you must have heard what happened between Kara and me last night. I don't know if she'll ever talk to me again. Even if she did, we're going our separate ways, and chances are we'll never see each other again after graduation. Which means I'll never see you again, either." She clears her throat. "Do you know, that listening to you play is like being in a conversation with someone? It's always a better kind of conversation, too. I kept coming back with Kara, just thinking I'd get to talk to you that way."

"I'm not sure I understand," Niles says.

"I know you don't. Do you remember that first winter when I stayed with you guys for Christmas? And I asked to borrow your old afghan? Did you even notice that I never gave it back, that I took it with me to school? Did you know I used to record your piano playing on that little tape recorder that I told you was for a speech class? And when you said that *Parachutes* was the name of that song you were writing, it made the most perfect sense to me, because I could feel what you were trying to do with the music, and it amazed me that two people could understand a thing like that without even talking about it." She stops, out of breath, and Niles is amazed to see tears.

"What are you trying to say?" he gets out.

"Don't you know? I never wanted anyone else. Nobody I met was you. I couldn't get interested in anybody here. Because I think I understand you. You're one of those people who was only meant to be one half of somebody else. It doesn't make you anything less, it just makes you different. I know because I'm the same way. I'm always just one half. And it's like I can feel that missing half, all ghostlike over to one side, and when I'm lonely, it's the way you feel when you're coming down stairs and you think there's going to be one more step but there isn't. You just kind of drop."

From the sidewalk, Kara is staring at them, her hand on one hip. Then she throws both hands in the air in exasperation and points to her watch. Niles reaches for the steering wheel, bracing himself. "Are you the one who always washes my coffee cup?"

Ilsabeth smiles faintly. "Of course."

"I—I had no idea," Niles stammers. "I honestly had no idea you—"

"I know. It's okay. I'm not asking for anything. I only need you to know. Not for me but because I think you should know. What you are, I mean. You should know it."

He is struggling for words, and then she is out of the car, moving up the walk behind Kara. She bends for her bag and does not look back. Niles rolls down his window and calls out to Kara: "See you soon, honey," in a voice he hardly recognizes as his own. Kara gives him a little wave and then she too has turned away, back to her life.

NILES TAKES HIS TIME driving home. Somewhere between the university and his house, he passes a park where a Little League game is being played. On impulse, he pulls into the parking lot. He does not normally do things like this—detours, sudden moves—especially among strangers, but he climbs out of the car and moves up the bleachers, finding a seat high up.

The boys play on. As he watches, Niles realizes that this was the last thing he did before he and Hannah lost their virginity to each other. He'd known it was going to happen. He had covered the ceiling above his bed with hundreds of tiny wildflowers, painstakingly securing each one by the stem with bits of invisible tape so that she could look up into a sky-garden of every imaginable color. Then, waiting for her to arrive, he'd walked to the local park and watched some kids play baseball. Sitting there in the bleachers, he knew that night was going to be the night. And neither he nor she was ashamed of the fact that they were twenty-four years old and new to all of this. That was what Hannah did for him: made him sure of his choices, even when all those around them seemed to think so little, or nothing at all, about them. There was meaning in what they did, and there was a promise in it. There had never been anything casual in what they'd had, from the first winter night they had coffee in a warmly-lit shop that was like the sparkling inside of a snow-globe, to the night Hannah died, also in the snow, when her car skidded into a guardrail near the Tennessee River.

Niles watches a tall boy go to bat. He is clearly gifted, the small crowd of parents and siblings going quiet as he approaches the plate. Tense and wary, yet utterly liquid, his body sways with the rhythm of the pitch before it even comes. The boy lifts the bat, squints, and then pivots, drawing a half-circle in the air with his slowly-straightening arms and then letting his right hand drop and drift at the finish of the swing. The moment of contact with the ball feels as preordained as a planet dropping into its orbit. As the boy sprints off, Niles has the sense that he did not simply hit the ball; he set it exactly where it was always meant to be.

This, Niles knows, was what Hannah's love did for him. And for a moment, watching the ball sail over the field, Niles is right there with it, once again secured in the arc he was meant to follow. He is himself; he is complete.

He will not pretend to be a brazen soul, bold and fearless as light. He is not the treble and never will be. He is the bass, needing wind to move across his face to bring out the truth of his features. To be loved, he is sure, is the truest way to learn one's own name, maybe the only way, and Ilsabeth's words have left him no longer ashamed to admit it.

The team with the talented player wins the game. When the families stand and cheer, Niles stands up with them, clapping hard and loud. A few heads turn, and he hears one father say something like, "Who the hell's *his* kid?" Nobody else is clapping, Niles realizes, because that is what you do at a concert; it is not what you do at a baseball game. At a baseball game, you cheer and whoop. He hurries back to his car, his face burning, but finds himself laughing as he pulls back onto the road.

When he gets home, there are three new messages from Gregory, waiting for his answer about the faculty recital. Niles listens to them all and then sits down beside the machine, pulling the phone into his lap, to listen to them once more.

THE FOLLOWING SATURDAY, Niles goes back to Cades Cove in the early morning.

It has grown warmer, and the national park is quiet as Niles drives along Laurel Creek Road to the valley. So he is surprised to see two buses parked at Cades Cove, and to find the valley swarming with kids. They look like Boy Scouts, or some kind of boys' troop; they wear matching uniforms, and there are just a few adults milling about, watching them. At first, Niles isn't sure what he's seeing, so he climbs out of his car and moves to the rickety fence that borders the field. He stands there, staring, squinting, until he understands: they are flying kites, kites of all shapes and sizes, and there are so many of them it reminds him of autumn, the leaves spiraling down in droves.

He enters the field. A couple of the adults glance his way but they don't speak to him. Niles moves past a boy who is struggling with a kite shaped like a giant caterpillar and then nearly stumbles over two smaller boys who are stringing something to their own kite. Niles walks on a few steps before stopping and going back to them. He can't stop himself.

"What is that?" he asks.

"A paratrooper," one of the boys tells him, holding up the toy. It is a match for the one Niles found two weeks ago.

"You kids bring those out here a lot?"

"Sometimes." The boys go back to their work, ignoring him, and Niles backs away. He turns and scans the field, wondering how many of the other kites will go up this way, with the plastic men attached, the flimsy soldiers with their futile parachutes made out of cheap plastic sheeting. He starts to walk again, moving faster now, his arms swinging at his sides.

They are in the air, rising and falling. He can just make out their tiny frames. He can see their fate: some will end up crushed into the wet autumn ground, lost, and some will be taken home, to be flown again on another day. Niles makes a huge circle around the group, keeping his eye on them all the while, and the morning shimmers into the blue afternoon, warmth seeping into him and into the field. The forest's edge is alive with color; a distant storm is breaking apart at the valley's edge, the clouds gently releasing their hold on each other to allow streams of topaz sunlight through the gaps.

The boys break up for lunch, and Niles can hear their leaders calling them to the buses. It feels like it takes forever for them to board the bus and finally leave. A faint dust rises in the buses' wake. Niles turns back to the valley. It occurs to him how enormous the cove must seem to a child, to someone smaller than he is. For the first time, he too is overwhelmed by the valley, realizing that while the circle he walks every Saturday is small, these fields tumble on and on, and even those wide-open plains are no match for the hundreds of miles of forest that peer over the cove's shoulder. Anything, any danger and any beauty, could lie within those wild woods.

He starts his search, moving slowly, meticulously, through the tall grass, his eyes on the ground. Surely, he thinks, there is a soldier here, his parachute torn from his back. His voice might be weak, but it is not too small to be heard, even in the hugeness of this place.

INCLUSIONS

THERE WAS SOME DEBATE over whether to let my son, Boyd, play with his Little League team tonight at the field in Elizabethton, which happens to be about fifty feet from the prison where his uncle is incarcerated. Boyd loves his Uncle Casey, my husband Graham's older brother, and was heartbroken when Casey was hauled off. Boyd is only eight, and though my father-in-law insisted we sugar-coat the whole situation, I couldn't help but wish we could tell him the truth: "Boyd," I'd tell him if he were older, "your uncle is a loser. He sells drugs, he uses drugs, and he belongs exactly where he is."

But Clint, my father-in-law, sincerely believes that his boys can do no wrong, and so he tells my son it was all a silly mix-up and that Casey will be out in no time. Though when he heard about where tonight's game was, he cursed: "What kind of shitbird town builds a kids' baseball field next to a prison? You can practically see though the windows from home plate."

Boyd is eating a late lunch in his treehouse and I am working my way through a tower of dirty dishes when Clint, who has been living with us for the last month, thumps his way downstairs and comes muttering through the kitchen doorway. "This place is a pit," he says.

"It's always like this after Graham leaves," I say. "He's got more important things to do than clean up after his meals."

"Graham is called," Clint says simply. "That's what God asked him to do, and he has no other choice in the matter." Then, "Did you wash Boyd's uniform? I saw it lying on the floor last night, still grungy from last week's game."

"No, I didn't, not yet."

"Want him to look like a damn orphan? Get it washed."

Clint helps himself to orange juice from the fridge and leaves his dirty glass on the counter next to me when he continues on to my little deck for a cigarette. He leaves the sliding glass door open as if to say, "I can still see you."

Clint has been living here for a month because he caught wind of a rumor that I've got a lover. He thinks the man is another teacher at the college prep academy where I work, and he showed up there every day last month before the semester ended, loitering in the parking lot like a private eye.

He is a man who lives for his sons, though he has no idea who they are, and wasn't around for them much when they were young. His oldest, Dakota, was killed while driving drunk about five years ago; you would think he died a martyr. Next in line is Casey, and then there is my husband, who is gold to Clint, something close to a god. Graham has never touched a drink or lit up a joint in his life. Instead, he's gone from teacher to missionary in the last ten years, and now spends the majority of his time in countries like Ecuador and Nigeria with his church group. He comes home every few months, as he did about a week ago, stays long enough to leave a mess for me to clean up and to torment Boyd who does not understand why Graham chooses strangers over him, and then vanishes again, back up to Mount Sinai. When he returns, he has that Moses-glow, everything about him luminous with a kind of triumph. He seems to know things the rest of us do not, and to treat us with a gentle condescension, like a saint dealing with bumbling but well-meaning sinners.

This, I think as I scrub the dishes Graham ate on two nights ago before leaving again, is how holiness must work: like heat, lengthening a man's reach, his goals, his ego. If Graham is ever-expanding, like a galaxy, I am spinning myself into a denser and denser nucleus, becoming more of my own world with each journey he takes.

The phone rings and immediately Clint returns to the kitchen. He seats himself at the breakfast table and watches expectantly, still smoking, as I pick up the phone.

"Please take the cigarette outside," I tell him as I lift the receiver. He takes another drag.

"Hello?" I say.

"Norah? Are you alone?"

"No."

"Shit. Doesn't he ever leave? Look, we have to talk, Norah. I'm waiting for an answer from you and I'm this close to signing off on that house. You can't keep using him as an excuse to keep avoiding this conversation."

"Thanks for explaining, but I'm not interested. We're very happy with our cable service right now," I say brightly, and I can hear Danny's frustrated sigh as I hang up. I'm pretty sure I hear his fist hitting a wall, too.

"You don't have cable," Clint says gruffly.

"Well, I had to get rid of him. You know these people."

"Mm-hm. Get Boyd's uniform washed." And he's gone, moving back upstairs to the guest room he's taken over. I think about my lover's ultimatum, as I have every minute for the last week: leave Graham and move with my son into the house Danny has chosen for us, or watch him walk.

I FINISH THE LAST DISH. There was a time—years ago—when right now, I'd be crying bitterly to myself, drying the last dish he used and setting it in the cupboard the way you might stow away a memento. At the beginning, it was just the loneliness of Graham leaving. Later, it was resentment, and a deeper sadness. I hate the fact that if you turn your back on a bud, it will have bloomed the next time you look. I want to see a thing in the act of growing. Whenever Graham left, I knew I'd be blind to whatever discoveries he might make, and I felt I was losing him.

Then came Danny. My mother used to tell me I couldn't do a casual thing if I tried. She was right. It took me five years to admit I had fallen in love with Danny, and it took us three more years to evolve from two friends to two people unable to let each other go. Like me, he has the ability to hold onto a thing longer than what most people would call reasonable, though I know he is about to reach his limit with me.

There is nothing reasonable about Danny, in fact. Though the mountain town we're living in, Pine Haven, has been coming apart at the seams for years, turning into a mess of crime and failing business-es, Danny's on a one-man crusade to salvage it, one recovered building at a time. He renovates the abandoned homes he buys, and tries to market them to people who remind him of his parents—hard-working and clean-living. I moved here for Graham after we graduated college together, but this is where Danny grew up, and he loves every tree and the whole glimmering shoreline of Watauga Lake. I sometimes think Danny imagines he can resurrect even the ancient town that's buried under that lake—a tiny city the government drowned when it decided to build the reservoir.

In a trusting moment after sex, many years ago, I once asked Graham what he would do if I died. What I gathered from his answer is that Graham would be reasonable. He would carry on with his life and shed very quickly, and very economically, any nostalgia or longing that might hold him back. Not Danny.

I put Boyd's uniform in with a load of laundry and slam the washer closed. Then I pour a tall glass of orange juice and take it out to the treehouse—a work of art Danny built for Boyd last year. When I first met Danny, I had hired him to fix a leak in our roof. I picked his business number out of the white pages. I had no idea that when he held out his hand to shake mine, it would feel like that hand was under my clothes, against my rib cage and then further in, to where I housed secrets and memories and wants that never saw the light of day. While he was shaking my hand he was turning over tables in there, ransacking closets, and when he let go, I ached like he had bruised me in his search. We made the smallest of small talk, both of us on edge as though we already knew what was going to happen—even though it would be years before we made any move toward each other. Graham has never looked at me the way Danny does: intent as a thief planning a heist. I found something else for Danny to fix just two weeks later, his phone number pinned to my refrigerator door with "Repair Man" written under it.

Since his early childhood, Boyd has known Danny as the Repair Man, and Danny has repaired plenty: the rotting boards on the front porch, the collapsing section of wooden fence out back, a broken air conditioner. Each time he comes around to fix something, Boyd demands to be there for it, and Danny teaches him how to do whatever it is he's doing. I told Graham and Clint that I hired someone to build the treehouse, but that wasn't exactly true. Danny built it of his own volition, with Boyd supervising every step, looking like a tiny version of Danny with Danny's spare tool belt cinched tight around his little waist.

I look up and smile through the sunlight at the address plaque my son asked for: *1518 Oak Avenue*, a number that has a secret meaning for him.

"May I come up?" I call out.

Boyd's small sunburned face appears in one of the windows and he grins, doffing his cap. "The place is presentable," he says.

I climb the ladder, careful not to spill his juice, and then I'm in his little world, where he keeps everything in perfect order. His shelf of books, his sturdy little pieces of furniture, his box of "emergency supplies" which includes a flashlight, first-aid kit, a pop-gun, and a lot of candy. On one windowsill is a line of tea lights; behind them, the distant mountains. I sit cross-legged on the throw-rug Boyd stole from Graham's study. He sits down across from me and slurps the juice, his eyes very blue in the sunlight that steals in through the window.

"Excited for your game tonight?" I ask.

He wipes his mouth. "I guess."

"You guess? I thought you were going to get some extra chances to bat."

"Yeah." He shrugs, hides his face behind the upturned glass.

"Are you nervous, kiddo? You shouldn't be. You'll do great."

He hesitates; the glass comes down. "Do they let them watch the game?"

"Who?"

"The people in the prison by the baseball field."

I sigh. "Who told you about the prison?"

"Tommy. He told me his mom said that's the one Uncle Casey is in. She told him it's right there by our field."

I think, *that witch*, and I say, "Your friend is right, that is where Uncle Casey is. But you don't need to worry about that, okay? This is your game. Don't worry about Uncle Casey." I spit out Clint's lie: "He'll be out soon, and whatever Tommy says, is just made-up."

"But they might let him watch," Boyd persists.

"I honestly don't know, hon. I don't think so."

"He was really good back when he played, wasn't he. Uncle Casey."

"I guess so, yeah. Granddad used to tell a lot of stories about his high school games. Why?"

Boyd is quiet, staring into the dregs of his juice, lost in his own world. "How long is Dad going to be gone this time?"

"About three months, sweetheart."

Another hesitation. "Does Dad have any other kids? Besides me?"

I blink. "Any other kids?"

He just waits, chewing his lower lip.

"No," I tell him. "He has no other kids. He just has people to take care of. People who need a lot of extra help. We talked about this. Remember?"

Boyd nods. His look is so adult, so forgiving, it hurts. "Granddad said he'd teach me to make a bat. Since Uncle Casey can't do it anymore, and Dad can't do it either. He let me look at the lathe in the garage."

"I'm sure Granddad will take you out to pick out the perfect piece of wood. Maybe next weekend."

Boyd starts to reply, and then we hear Clint from below, his voice gruff from the years of smoking: "The washer just finished."

I call back, "The dryer already has the Bounce in it, just go ahead and toss it all in there."

Clint is halfway up the ladder. "Woman's work," he responds. He winks up at my son. "Not for us."

My son has no response, but still, I imagine shoving Clint off the ladder, imagine him going down on his bad knee and cursing at the top of his lungs. Then I start down the ladder, forcing Clint to move down, and I tell myself this is one small achievement: creating a little distance between them whenever I can.

On the ground, Clint says, "Who did you say was the builder who did this?"

"The treehouse? Why?"

"It's a hell of a fine job, but I could've done better. Still don't understand why you didn't ask me first. Been bugging me since I moved in here with you all."

I shrug and move past him, try to ignore the look of real sadness that darts across Clint's face, quick as the shadow of a bird.

I HIDE MYSELF AWAY IN MY ROOM and listen to the sound of my neighbor's house being roofed. I love the music of nail guns. It makes me think of Danny, and each ping has me glancing over at my cell phone. I have been preparing words with which to meet his ultimatum, but they keep changing. I try to write them out on a notepad, but I keep remembering what my writing instructor used to tell me in college: *Show, don't tell,* and instead of words, I want to show Danny pictures to make him understand my terror of leaving my marriage.

In one picture, my parents lead me down the aisle in the church at the Christian college Graham and I attended in Kentucky. We pass professors, friends, family members, all of them wearing the same expression of approval. In another, Graham skips stones across the Doe River's amber surface, the light catching on his wedding ring and on the cross he wears around his neck. The final one is of me, in a fine jewelry store in Knoxville. I'm alone and I'm looking into a case no one else seems interested in—dark opals with their strange nebulae, onyx, jade—when I run into some old friends from college. They ask me only about Graham and I realize, after they've left, that this is what I am: Graham's wife. That the diamond on my hand is all they need to know about me. A loud peal from my laptop announces an incoming Skype call from Graham. I stare at the flickering screen, listen to the bubbly tune for a long moment before crossing the room and clicking *Accept Call.* There is no video; the connection must be poor there. Only my husband's voice fills the room: "Norah? I'm all settled in. Just wanted to check in with you all."

"How was the trip?"

"Fantastic. Everyone's in great spirits. How is Dad? How's Boyd?"

Graham thinks that his father is here because he's lonely for company, and I have no choice but to help him believe what Clint told him. "Your dad seems thrilled to get to see so much of Boyd. Boyd's got that big game tonight. He's supposed to get some extra chances to bat. I think he's nervous."

"Oh, he'll knock it out of the park." There is a pause; I hear other voices. Then Graham returns. "Sorry," he says with a laugh. "Kind of chaotic around here. Everyone's so excited. Even though we're all exhausted."

"Sure. So what is tomorrow going to be like for you?" I always ask him this when he makes his check-in call. I used to listen to the answer. Now I don't. As he talks, my gaze wanders around the room to our wedding photos and a button-down shirt he left lying on the floor. I can't remember seeing him wear it, though I know it's his.

"A complete stranger," I mutter. "Jesus Christ."

"Sorry, what?"

"Nothing. What was that last? I didn't catch it."

"I was talking about the idea of mystery." Graham's voice, even over

Skype, is charged. Though I can't see his face, I know how he looks: incandescent. "We were talking about it on the way here, and then I sort of got lost thinking about it when just about everyone else had gone to sleep. I was looking out the plane windows and the clouds looked like a white ocean—you know? And I was thinking about the prophets. How they took these massive risks, climbing summits, I mean not just literally but to places other people wouldn't dare to go. And they saw things nobody else saw, and when they came back, they must have sounded like they were speaking in tongues."

I start to interrupt, but he goes on: "But really, they should have been speaking the easiest language to understand of all. I mean, Christ's language. Something so old we've just forgotten it." He laughs, and the static makes the laugh sound shaky. "I feel like every time I do this, I learn more of the vocabulary. It's not hieroglyphics on the wall anymore for me, you know?"

I never know what to say when Graham talks like this. Maybe he doesn't want or need a reply. As if reading my mind, he abruptly changes the subject: "I found a strange note in my bag from my father. On your stationery."

"A note?" I sit bolt upright; my stomach turns over. "What do you mean? What did he say?"

"It doesn't make much sense. It says he's sorry about Dakota and about Casey. That's it. Has he said anything to you?"

I exhale. "No, nothing. What do you think he meant?"

"I have no idea. He never talks about Dakota."

"I can't imagine he'd feel responsible for Casey. Casey of the magic high school years, Casey of the precious good looks. He's still pretending to Boyd that it's all a mix-up that Casey got arrested."

"Yeah." There is some scuffling, and a woman's voice saying something about food.

"Norah? I've got to log off. There are other people waiting and we've got a prayer service to start after we eat here. You take care."

"Thanks for checking in. Have a great night, Graham."

"You—" The end of his sentence vanishes, and Skype lets out its tragic little moan: *Call Ended.*

I look at the blank screen and stand up. I think of Danny's fist hitting the wall when I ended our phone call earlier. I can see his deep-tanned skin and the way his eyes glint turquoise when he is angry, the bits of dark blond hair poking out from under his ball cap, the way he always puts his hands on his hips and rocks forward when he laughs. I know he's angry now, sick with the waiting, and I want all this to stop. But I still don't know what to say to him, and I wonder if by the time Boyd's game is over, I will have the words.

I put on a long white sundress, and pluck my favorite necklace out of my jewelry box—a gorgeous dendritic opal Danny gave me two years ago. The moon-white stone with its dark inclusions, ebony flecks branching all across its surface, is cool against my skin, and I look at myself in the mirror for a long moment. The night Danny gave this to me, I met him at Roan Mountain, driving the dangerous winding road all the way up to Carvers Gap, to the place where the mountains suddenly look like Scotland. In the twilight we hiked up the balds, through lush emerald grass and past savagely pink rhododendron, until Danny pulled me off the trail into one of the endless fields and told me he wanted to stop. I had been thinking of saying the same to him: *We need to stop this, Danny. I'm married. Think about Boyd. This could never be.* I was thinking of saying, *I don't understand how happiness can be possible for us, when nobody else sees anything right in any of this.*

But what he said next was, "I want to stop meeting for one night at a time. We're past that. Way past. I want to move you and Boyd into a house, any house you want. I'll rebuild it from the ground for you." He clasped the opal around my neck and stood back, looking at it in the rose-blue light. He smiled. "And when you're free, we'll get married, and you can both have the life you ought to have."

I was too startled, too terrified of the possibilities his words dangled in front of me, to really respond. So I looked down at the pendant and said, "What is this?"

He explained that his father had been a gemologist, that the man had taught him all about gemstones and had passed on his most beloved pieces to Danny, including the pendant. He taught me a great deal that night—about rocks, about the way the earth moves—before we realized how late it was, and had to rush back down the mountain to our cars.

There is an aggressive knock on my door, and then Clint is filling the doorframe, frowning. "Kind of fancy for a baseball game, ain't it?" he asks, looking me up and down. "Somebody special coming to this game?"

I walk over to the laptop and slap it shut, just to make some noise. "No, Clint, nobody special is coming to the game. I just don't feel like sweating on those bleachers, okay? It's going to be hot."

"No it isn't. It's a night game. Are you ready? Boyd says he wants to go early. He's already waiting outside."

"That's fine. I'll be just a minute, if you'll wait downstairs."

Clint doesn't move, and I sigh and grab my purse. "Okay. Let's just go."

I EXPECT TO FIND BOYD already in the car, but he's nowhere to be found, and I send Clint around back to check for him. In a moment, I hear Clint yelling something unintelligible, and I leave my purse on the hood and rush around to the back of the house.

Clint and Boyd are up on the deck, Boyd standing there with his head hung, his baseball bat limp in one hand.

"What is going on?" I demand, and then I see the damage—one of the deck rails is battered, almost to the point of snapping, and there are woodchips everywhere.

"I was just practicing my swing," Boyd whines. "I swear I didn't mean to do it."

"Didn't mean to, my ass," Clint says. "How close were you standing to that? You know how much it costs to fix things like that?"

I touch Boyd's shoulder and bend over to look at the rail. "This is a mess.

I don't get it, Boyd. Since when do you practice your swing on the deck?" I look at my watch. "We can talk about this later. We need to get going."

Clint is shaking his head. "Graham will have to fix it when he gets back. I'm getting too old for this."

Boyd looks quickly at me. "You should call the repair man, Mom. He could get it fixed right away." He gestures with the bat at the rail. "If it breaks, someone could fall through."

I study him until he looks away. I glance at Clint, who is too irritated to pay attention to what Boyd is saying. "Sure we can call him," I say. "We'll call in the morning."

"Maybe we should call now."

"It's too short notice, hon. Besides, we have to get to your game. He's not going to work here alone while we're away."

"He could just come to the game with us," Boyd persists, "and fix it after."

I say, "Tomorrow." I pat his back. "Let's just get going, okay?"

He nods, casts one backward glance at the rail, and then follows Clint and me out front.

Clint climbs into the passenger seat and Boyd finds his Discman—an ancient machine Graham gave him—and claps on his headphones. It's his way of gearing up, and the music is loud enough to be piping out of the headphones. I drive in silence, cracking the window to air out the smell of smoke that clings to Clint's clothes. Just when I am thanking God for a chance to think, Clint says quietly, "I know what it means, you know."

My heart jumps. "What?"

"The treehouse address. 1518. He told me."

"No he didn't."

"The fifteen is because Graham promised to teach him to drive at fifteen. The eighteen is because Graham promised to take him on a mission trip at eighteen. To show him the world."

I drive. The highway seems suddenly blurry. Clint's raspy voice is soft: "I promised the first one to Graham, too, when he was about Boyd's age. That's the first thing I thought of, when he told me."

"I don't know why he'd confide in you." The words fly out: "You haven't exactly been a father to him. You just got here."

"Better late than never," Clint snaps. Then he sags in his seat. "Just how many stories have you heard about Casey and all those baseball games?"

"Plenty, between you and Graham . . . why?"

"I never saw a single one. Did you know that?" He fishes a cigarette from his shirt pocket and ignores the look I give him as he lights it. "Never a one."

"What are you talking about?"

"I got the stories from Casey. Or from Graham. I never went. Know where I was? Knoxville. Or Bristol, or Chattanooga. Getting drunk out of my mind and spending the night in motels with women who didn't care I had a tan line on my ring finger. You know?"

My hands tighten on the wheel and I glance in the rearview mirror at my sleeping son. "Put the cigarette out. Why are you telling me this now?"

"Let's call it a cautionary tale. Let's say I don't want you to end up like me. Screwing around while your kid is growing up. Missing everything."

My laugh is painful in my throat. "Oh? What do you call what Graham is doing? Who supports Boyd, Clint? Who's there every day of his life? You only take Graham's side because he's your son."

"You know what I'm talking about."

"I don't. You have no proof," I start, and he cuts in: "I don't need it. I just know." He finishes the cigarette and tosses the butt out the window.

I wait for more, but he says nothing, and we are nearly to Elizabethton anyway. Boyd wakes just as I pull into the little parking lot behind the baseball field at the edge of town, and I see his eyes cut immediately to the immense prison building—unmistakable—to our left.

"There's lights on," he murmurs.

"Let's go, kiddo," I say. We climb out of the car and I kiss Boyd's baseball-capped head before he goes to the dugout to meet his teammates.

Twilight is descending as Clint and I pick out seats on our side's bleachers. Clint leaves his seat cushion behind to make a run to the concession stand, and comes back with a bag full of hot dogs. Other parents fill in the spaces around us and then the game is beginning, Boyd's team batting first. I watch as his friend Curtis steps up to bat, and I try to look interested, but my mind is working, thinking of what to say to Danny. I am going to have to call him tomorrow.

Clint's chewing is audible. I turn slightly away from him, and in the movement, catch sight of Danny, sitting high up in the opposing team's bleachers. I freeze. He doesn't see me, and for a long moment, I just watch him: he is with another man about our age, and they are talking together, Danny sitting with his body hunched over a little and his hands clasped together. I don't dare glance at Clint. Then Danny looks up and finds me.

My hands tighten on the bleacher seat's edge and I shake my head ever so slightly, though I know he can't possibly see that from where he is. He rises, and starts down the bleachers, forcing parents to make room for his descent. I say to Clint, "I'm going to get a Coke."

"Since when do you drink Coke?"

I ignore him and scramble down the bleachers, my dress catching as I jump down. I smooth it down and hurry toward the concession stand, hoping to head Danny off. We nearly trample each other behind the little booth and he catches both my wrists.

"What are you doing here?" he says, and I say, "Are you kidding me? What are *you* doing here?"

"I'm here for my cousin's kid," Danny says, not letting go of me though I am pulling back. "He's playing. I said I'd go. I had no idea they'd be playing Boyd's team."

"Oh, right." I am choking a little; I keep glancing over my shoulder. "I'm here with my father-in-law and you didn't know I'd be here?"

"Jesus. Clint's here? I had no idea, Norah, I swear to God." But his grip tightens on me and he leans in. "You know what, though, I don't care. I can't take this distance anymore. You can talk to me here good as anyplace else." His gaze drifts down to my pendant, then back up to my face; his expression softens. "Norah," he says.

"We can't talk about this now," I hiss, looking around. "Let go of me, Danny."

He lets go. I step back. At that moment, little Pete Corbin's mother comes bouncing up to us, and says, "Boyd's up."

"Thanks, Leigh," I say, forcing a smile, and she continues on in the near-dark, hurrying toward the restrooms. I look back at Danny.

"These people know me," I remind him. "They know Graham."

"Do they? When was the last time he came to a game?"

I step away from the shadows behind the stand and watch my son step up to the plate. I can feel Danny behind me, though he says nothing. Boyd doesn't see me, though I wave to get his attention; his eyes are on the prison to his left. He keeps turning toward it as he taps the dirt with his bat, and when the first pitch comes, he misses it because he is looking the other way.

"Come on, Boyd," I yell, and I hear other parents echo me.

Boyd glances briefly at me and then back at the prison. He swings; he misses. The third time around, he makes contact with the ball, but it drops right into the hands of an infielder, and he's out. I shout with the other parents that it's okay, he'll get 'em next time, but Boyd is in another world, looking only at that prison. He walks back to the dugout with both hands on his head as if to keep his hat from blowing away.

"Poor kid. He'll get another shot," Danny says softly from behind me. "He's got good form."

"His uncle's in that prison. His uncle Casey," I explain. "I told you about that, right?"

"Yes."

"Some kid made a comment about it. I think it's bothering Boyd. I think he's embarrassed."

"Who can blame him?"

I am still in front of him, barely moving my mouth as I speak: "My father-in-law is watching every move I make at the house, Danny."

"Your husband should be watching."

"He's away. Saving the world," I say, and though the words are sarcastic, I mean them; I can see Graham in that faraway place, cradling half-starved children in his arms and teaching English on a chalkboard to young mothers desperately taking notes.

"You don't have to get on a plane or even leave the state to save the world," Danny says quietly. "The last time we were together, you picked up a box turtle off the road so you could put him back in the trees. Is that any less of a thing?"

Still resolutely facing forward, I say, "Please, Danny. Not here. I can't do this right now."

"Fine. But I don't know what we're waiting for anymore. As for your question: the woman who was going to sell me that house? She got killed this weekend in a car wreck. Her son called me asking if I still wanted the place. And I was sick thinking that I still didn't know if I could get you to live there with me, and sicker knowing that that kind of thing could happen to anyone, at any time, and if it happens to us, we'll have missed out on just about everything."

The Fleenors walk by arm-in-arm, both sipping sodas, and Ashley gives me a look of frank curiosity as they pass. Beautiful Ashley, with a husband who loves her, and a bedroom with a huge crucifix above the bed—I've seen it, at her kid's birthday party. A chill moves through me and I turn to Danny, but he is already gone, walking back to the bleachers.

I watch him walk and then my hand comes up to my mouth when I realize Clint is directly in his path. Danny stops and Clint says something to him that I can't hear. I start toward them and stop. Danny's right hand comes up to adjust his cap, which means he's angry or nervous, and Clint leans forward dangerously. I think he is going to strike Danny, and at the last moment, Clint glances my way, and our eyes meet. Behind me, somebody hits a ball, and I hear small feet kicking up dirt. A man shouts, "That's how we get 'em, Connor!"

Clint's maneuver around Danny is one of such open disgust that I ache for Danny, who turns to watch Clint go and then looks briefly at me before continuing on to his bleachers. I am trembling when Clint reaches me. He seems huge, towering over me with the field lights burning orange around his silhouette. "Sit back down," he says calmly. "Let's go. Back to our seats so we can watch Boyd."

Numbly, I follow him. I wonder if things are not as bad as they seem; maybe Danny knew just what to say. But as soon as we sit down, Clint faces the field and says softly, "You fucking whore."

I take small, measured breaths and just sit there, facing forward. The other team is at bat. Boyd is in the outfield, pacing, visibly nervous.

"Boyd ain't his, is he," Clint goes on.

Now I do look at him. "Excuse me?"

"Boyd. He ain't Graham's."

I open my mouth, and Clint says in the same monotone, "I got a good look at the man. The one who was all over you back there. He's just like him. Here I thought you had some trashy two-month fling going. Now I find out my son's been raising a kid who ain't even his."

My God, I wish, I find myself thinking with sudden violence, and then I realize I've said it aloud.

"Excuse me?" Clint hisses.

"I wish," I repeat. My throat is tight and I try to clear it. "Clint, do you think I would have stayed with Graham all this time, if Boyd wasn't his? You think I don't wish he were Danny's son?"

"Danny." He breathes out the name, makes it sound like a curse. "I don't believe you."

"It's true, but I don't care whether you believe it."

"You're no decent kind of mother."

"Graham is no kind of father." I have never said it aloud, and my stomach quakes. "He is no kind of husband, either."

Clint smiles tightly, eyes on the field. "You will not talk about my son that way again."

"He is married to Jesus and he's father to children I will never meet. If that counts in somebody's eyes, then fine, but he is no father to Boyd, Clint."

"He is too good for you."

"Maybe he is. Maybe he just made a bad choice. He should have found a woman just like him. Some woman who doesn't need anything but God."

"Keep your voice down. Wipe your goddam face, people are staring at you."

I realize my face is soaked in tears and I do as he says, trying to avoid the other parents' looks. I bend over with my head in my hands and murmur, "What do you expect me to do? I can only do it alone for so long."

Clint waits until I look up, then jabs his finger toward the field. "Watch the game and pull yourself together. And when this is over, we're going to talk about how you're going to make things right for my son."

I watch, and hold my hands clasped, the way Danny does. I can see him—he is pacing along the opposite fence, hands in his pants pockets. I force myself to look away. Boyd is up to bat again, his small body illuminated under the lights. He taps the plate with his bat, takes a few practice swings, and once again looks hard at the prison, whose windows are still lit. I follow his gaze and wonder what he thinks he sees there. I wonder what cruel things the other children have said to him.

The first pitch is fast and Boyd swings; too late. Strike. Clint nearly blasts my eardrum, hollering, "You got the next one, Boyd!" But he doesn't; he misses the next pitch as well. Boyd looks at us and then repositions himself; he is a lefty, and he is turned almost completely toward the prison, so that when he swings, his whole body spins with the movement, and the ball flies. But once again, the ball is caught, and Boyd is out. The next boy is waiting for the plate, but Boyd just stands there, not moving, and then suddenly he is yanking off his helmet and throwing it into the dirt, and I can see that my son is crying. Sobbing.

"What the hell," Clint starts, but I am halfway down the bleachers, rushing toward him, thinking he's been hit and I didn't see it. His coach is bending over him but Boyd won't face him; he's got his hands over his face. I push past the assistant coach, who tells me to hold on, and hurry to my son.

"What happened, kiddo? What's wrong?" I ask, reaching to touch his face. With my shoulder, I block the coach, who is still hovering.

His eyes find mine; they are drowning. "Now he'll never come out," he says, choking on the words. "He's never going to want to come over by us or teach me anything. That was my last chance."

"Who, Boyd? What are you talking about?"

"Uncle Casey." He gestures hopelessly at the prison. "He saw how bad I was and now why would he want to come back?"

Stunned, I take his hands and lead him off the field, past the coach and the wide-eyed parents and the already-snickering boys in the dugout. I kneel in the grass in front of him. "Honey," I say, "Uncle Casey is not in there by choice. He doesn't get to just leave when he wants to. It's got nothing to do with you. It's not his choice to be there."

Boyd says, "Yes it is. It is his choice."

I am sitting on my heels, staring up at my son, when I feel both Clint and Danny behind me. Clint, to my left, also kneels, coming down hard on his bad knee. "She's right," he tells Boyd. "Casey made a choice. It's his own damn fault. So don't you worry what he thinks. You did fine out there."

Danny moves a step closer, and when Boyd sees him, his face brightens. He says, "You came to my game." Then, "Are you going to fix our deck?"

I look at Clint, who is fixated on Boyd. Before Danny can respond, Clint says, "Is that what you want, son?"

"I broke it," Boyd says by way of answer, confessing directly to Danny. "Someone could fall through if you don't fix it up. Will you fix it?"

Clint lets out a breath from between his teeth and makes a move to rise, struggling for a moment with his knee. Danny puts out a hand to help him, but Clint holds up his palm and says gruffly, "No need." When he's on his feet, he looks down at me and says, "So he's the builder, then. The treehouse?"

I nod, and Danny stands up a little straighter.

"He going to fix this, too?" Clint's voice is heavy, full of question, and I hold his gaze. For a moment, it is as though we are alone.

"He always has," I tell him. "But it's up to him if he still wants to."

Boyd is still looking at Danny, who crouches down with us. One hand goes to my back, balled into a fist, the other to Boyd's shoulder, and in a moment, Boyd drops his head against Danny's and holds it there. Danny closes his eyes. I can feel Clint hovering behind us,.

"Yeah," Danny says at last, "I'm gonna fix your deck. Whatever's wrong with it. However many times it takes to get it fixed." His eyes stay closed, but his hand opens on my back like a bird's wings spreading.

It hits me finally that Boyd really is Danny's son, if fatherhood means loving a child, being willing to wait and to sacrifice anything for that child and for his mother. It hits me that this has been my true family all along, as different as it all is from what I thought I was supposed to have.

The light from the field must be catching on my pendant, because Boyd reaches out and touches it. I look down at it, and I think of all that Danny taught me about the stone after he clasped it around my neck that night.

A dendritic opal is not really an opal at all. It's chalcedony, a much less valued stone, and it is scarred with inclusions, imperfections that would render many gemstones worthless to a jeweler. But these marks are wild with mystery, black like spindly trees against a winter landscape, or like flocks of birds sweeping across a silent field. Sometimes cumulus clouds drift across the surface of these stones; sometimes lilac light suffuses the snow. As I kneel under the light of the baseball field with my lover and our son, I am amazed to find that this strange landscape could be my home. I wonder if this is what my husband feels every day, among strangers on the other side of the world, or if it is a mystery yet to be revealed to him.

Winter Renaissance

Tonight, the last night of January, the Shoney's in Caryville, Tennessee is brimming with customers, the regulars tucked in and anonymous among the travelers, the waitstaff overrun. The restaurant sits on an I-75 exit deep in the Cumberland Mountains, and today, this region of Tennessee has had a record snowfall. Instead of staying home, like sensible people would, it seems that everyone has bolted to this restaurant, in search of warm lights or soup or sound.

"I don't care what it is," Marla, who has waitressed here for five years, says to one of the new employees. "Nobody should be out on the highway in this snow."

"Enough chat," their boss, Terry, says in passing. "Have you seen the family who just walked in? There's ten or twelve of them. Push some tables together."

Marla curses under her breath and goes into the dining room. To get the tables arranged, she has to shove her way through this family, the members of which are knocking against each other like farm animals fighting to be first in line at the trough. Marla knows what she can expect here: a sticky mess on the floor when they leave, kids crying and throwing food, parents making trip after trip to the buffet and getting the corn into the mashed potatoes and vice versa. When she gets them set up, she takes their drink orders—also predictable, all Cokes—and hurries away.

"Trash," Marla mutters.

The family taking up the four pushed-together tables along the front windows would seem to fit her stereotype exactly. Within minutes, one of the children is shrieking about needing to use the bathroom, and the mother barks at one of her other kids—"Lizzy, wake up, hand me that menu," or something like that. The father begins talking loudly on his cell phone and the mother complains to no one in particular about her ankles bothering her. Marla passes them off to another waitress, Kelly, and breathes a sigh of relief that she has only to attend to the couples and the solitary diners, who she knows are far less trouble, working at their plates in contented silence.

In a booth wedged tightly against the window on the opposite end of the room sits Wesley, whose eighteen-wheeler is parked within view. From the side of his truck where they are painted in bright colors, the Keebler Elves grin maniacally at him, and he tries to look only at the inside of the restaurant or at his salad. Wesley is trying to diet. He has been trucking for ten years and it has been hell on his body, but over time, he's put an end to the fast food and the Swedish Fish he used to be addicted to. Now he goes to places like Shoney's or Perkins and piles vegetables and egg and cheese on lettuce, and tries to use only the light salad dressings. He wonders sometimes if people are making fun of him—the fat trucker eating his dainty dinner—but he is usually so lost in his own thoughts that this worry doesn't linger long. Tonight he sits with his cell phone positioned in the exact center of his table and he is eyeing it as he forks spinach and carrot shavings into his mouth.

He purses his lips around the mouthful as he imagines how he would explain his situation to a stranger: "Today is the anniversary of the day I ran into a girl at a rest stop, a girl who never returns my messages, and I text her every year even though she never responds." The salad as a source of humiliation would pale in comparison to this.

But it's all true. It was three years ago that Wesley stopped at an oasis on I-40 just over the North Carolina border, where the mountains rose up massive and wild, and found himself perched on a plastic mesh picnic table talking to the most radiant young woman he had never met. He had been standing around smoking a cigarette when she appeared; she was wearing hiking clothes, tall boots and a thick polypropylene shirt, and had a nebulous bun of heavy brown hair that looked clean but unbrushed. She hopped onto a picnic table and stretched out there with her arms spread wide as if to hug the sky. Wesley could not help himself. He rarely tried to strike up conversations with women, with anyone really, but he had to do this. He walked slowly to the picnic table and said, as neutrally as he could, "Kind of cold today, isn't it? Where are you coming from?"

She surprised him by sitting right up and engaging him in lively conversation for nearly half an hour. They introduced themselves—her name was Havilah, a name he could not stop turning over on his tongue for months afterward—and she told him she had just finished hiking the entire Art Loeb Trail in Pisgah National Forest.

"Up there," she told him, pointing across the highway at the Appalachian summits, which were blue-black in the late afternoon winter haze. "Way at the top. You can see to the ends of the earth up there. You should have seen the snow I trudged through."

She was agoraphobic, she told him. Or used to be. She had been fighting this battle all her life, she explained. She believed she was finally over it. She could go anywhere now, and not be ruled by fear. As she told him all this, she pulled her hair out of her bun and he saw it wasn't simply brown, but an unlikely blend of auburn, dark blonde, and red. It was like wildflowers in a field. No order, no plan, but it worked; the effect was stunning. Her cheeks were bright red from windburn. He told her he was a trucker for Keebler, and she laughed and told him they made a cookie she had eaten obsessively as a little girl.

"Which one?" he prodded.

"I don't remember the name. Elves with chocolate inside of them? Like a sandwich?"

Then he did a crazy thing he could have lost his job for. He went to his truck and climbed into the back and found the cookies and pried a package out of a box. He knew exactly which cookie she was talking about. He brought them back to her and she fairly squeaked with delight. They ate several of them together, and Wesley, who had been professing his hatred of all things cookie-or-cracker since his first year working this job, had never tasted anything so satisfyingly sweet.

They exchanged numbers and he wondered if her number was real. After all, he was a trucker, a random encounter on the road, and pretty overweight to boot. But when he texted her on the road the next day, something like, "I hope you are finishing off the cookies," she texted back a photograph of the empty plastic container, and his heart soared.

But that was the last he heard from her. He texted her often over the next several months, but never got an answer. He worried that she thought he was a stalker, or that he seemed like he had no life. So he decided he would limit himself to these anniversary texts, although he was not even sure if she understood the significance of the date.

Now, finishing his salad and watching the other diners, Wesley comes to an abrupt understanding: her interest in their conversation, her smiles that day, had nothing to do with him at all. She had won a victory over herself; she was just happy to be who she was, where she was. Her happiness was spilling over, and anyone who had spoken to her that day was within range of it. She was like a waterfall whose beauty is indifferent to its admirers. If he stood too close and got wet, it was his own fault. She was diamond-beautiful, but she needed him no more than cascades need their photographers.

Still. He looks around, basks for a moment in the restaurant's warmth, and imagines the possibilities. He is a shy man, a deeply reserved man. But he spoke to her once and such a thing could happen again. He drives through North Carolina all the time. He picks up the cell phone and composes his message.

Hi Havilah. I hope you are well and still hiking in those mountains. —Wesley.

FRANCES, WHO IS SITTING in the partly-partitioned section of the dining area—a room that is really too cold to eat in, but has the best view of the mountains—sips her third cup of coffee and has not touched her plate of chocolate pudding and strawberries. She feels guilty about eating this sweet treat, not because she worries about calories but because this is celebration food for her and she should not be celebrating at a time like this. Her father just died two weeks ago; the funeral and wake are behind her, but she knows she should still be grieving for him. Though she hardly knew him, had grown up with her mother in another town, she feels it is wrong to be sitting here with excited chills moving up and down her spine and a dish of what her mother would call "giggly food" in front of her.

But during all the exhausting chaos of planning the funeral and wake, Frances met a man. She didn't meet him exactly, as she had in fact known him before—thirty years ago. They went to preschool together here in Caryville. How she remembered this when she heard his name—Hank Ennis—she doesn't know. Hank ran the funeral home in Caryville, a business he had inherited from his father, and he handled most of the details of Frances' father's arrangements. She worked with him daily, since her mother had died years ago and her father had had few friends and no immediate family besides her.

It baffled her, that someone could work a job like this—planning funerals, laying out bodies, helping people choose headstones. She wished her mother were still alive so she could ask her what she thought about it. Men who work with the dead: what sort of men were they? At first she was put off by Hank, feeling that his surprisingly good looks at thirty-five years old were incongruous with his somber surroundings. He had the bright blue eyes she remembered him having as a child, and instead of being fragile and weedy as she would imagine a mortician to be, he looked strong, with powerful arms and a confident way of moving things around. Even the way he bent over a document exuded a kind of calm power, a certainty. Was this what happened, Frances wondered, when you faced death every day of your life? Did you take on this calmness because you came to the understanding that all of this was just temporary, that we were all headed elsewhere when the chaos was over?

She asked herself questions like this as they worked together on the funeral and wake. She tried not to watch him or to be stirred when he occasionally touched her shoulder or smiled at something she said. But Lord, she found the man lovelier than any man she had encountered all these years on her own. Kinder. Wiser. She had lived in three states, had gone as far away as Texas for work, but she always found herself back here in Tennessee. A wild thought flies at her as she finishes this cup of coffee: maybe she kept coming back because something in her knew Hank was here.

Crazy. But a week after the funeral, Hank called her. He said, "I know this is strange. But I was wondering, would you like to, would you be interested in, having dinner with me on Saturday evening? If you're still in town."

He had knocked down her cardboard brick buildings in preschool, stuck gum to her shoe. Pulled her hair. Once, at a Halloween party, he gave her a plastic ring with a pumpkin on it. She remembers all of this. She can't believe it, that after everything she's been though, a divorce, a miscarriage, four jobs, the loss of both her parents, the first little nosegay of gray hairs sprouting up near her right temple, this man who works with the dead might be the one for her. She can't believe that this snow falling past the windows is not a nuisance to her, but something romantic, infused with possibility. She thought she was long past those years when snowflakes swirling on a stray wind could startle her with their ethereal beauty.

She shakes her head and presses her hand against her mouth in an effort to hold in a laugh. Her father, after all, has just died.

But she looks around the restaurant, overhears others' laughter and the murmur of their talk, and picks up her fork. The strawberries, coated in chocolate, taste like redemption.

JAMES HATES IT when they seat him in the middle of the dining area, at a free-standing table. He prefers to be half-hidden in a booth along one of the walls. He has filled his plate with his usual—fried chicken, slabs of meatloaf, mashed potatoes, and a biscuit. Usually he wolfs down his food, starving after his workday, but the fried chicken is starting to shine with cold grease and his biscuit is huddled in an igloo of forgotten potato. He is wondering how he can go about adopting or maybe just stealing his brother's daughter. He can't bear it anymore—that child, living in that house, seeing what she sees.

James works for a company called Floranet and he delivers their floral arrangements to homes all over the Knoxville region, six days a week. He likes his job. After all, the "shoot the messenger" reaction works the opposite way in his case, as he is always the deliverer of something beautiful. Girlfriends receive their boyfriends' Valentines bouquets, and love James for carrying it; the grieving receive the consolation of bright daisies or tulips, and they look at James as though he's resurrected their dead. James has a habit of rearranging the bouquets to better taste and secretly believes himself to have a talent for it. Floranet doesn't advertise on their website that their arrangements are only one-sided. James fixes this. When the bouquets arrive, they are round and full, geometric wonders with a bit of James' own personal flair.

This morning, he squinted hard at the first address on his list and realized it was his brother Mitchell's. Why Mitchell would order flowers, he could not imagine; he had dozens of trampy girlfriends, but he was the last kind of man to give a gift like that. It was only at the front porch, when Mitchell's eight-year-old daughter, Meg, answered, that James knew what had happened. Meg had ordered the arrangement off her father's computer, knowing it would be James to deliver them.

"You're here," she said happily, her small, round face turned up like a sunflower.

"You ordered these, kiddo?" he asked, holding out the arrangement Floranet called "Winter Renaissance."

"I just wanted to see you, Uncle James. I need you to take me somewhere," she told him seriously, pushing her hair back behind her ears.

And then Mitchell was there, behind Meg, dressed for a date. At his heels was a woman James hadn't seen before, with cropped blonde hair and thick, black eye makeup that gave her cat eyes.

"Little bro," Mitchell called out merrily. He was drunk again. "Your timing is perfect. We were just figuring out how we were going to do this."

"Do what?" James asked faintly.

"Well, see, here's what happened. I promised I'd take Meggy here to the aquarium for this penguin thing she wanted to do. And I forgot about it, and now Sara's here, and I promised I'd take *her* out. Do you think you could take Meg into Gatlinburg? I mean, you're here."

"Mitch," James said, "what would you have done if I hadn't shown up?"

"Well, you're here, right? So could you take her?"

James decided he could probably get his deliveries done on the way to Gatlinburg with nobody the wiser. He just wanted to get Meg out of there. Mitchell's eyes were unfocused, barely taking him in, and Sara was eyeing Meg with open distaste.

"You'd better get ready," James sighed, looking at Meg. "We've got to get on the road pronto."

They left quickly, and James listened to his niece talk as he did his deliveries. She told him about her Penguin Encounter, what it involved, and she was practically trembling with excitement.

"So why penguins?" he asked. "It seems like you really love them."

"I do. They're just different. They're not like people."

"How's that?"

"Did you ever watch *March of the Penguins?*"

"I did. I remember them—Emperor penguins." He could see them—great beauties, with swan-like heads and formidable bodies. Their astonishing grace in water, contrasted with their endearing clumsiness on the ice. Their long and taxing journeys—lives of endless, focused labor.

From her little purse Meg pulled out her ticket to the Encounter and sat there holding it. "Sometimes one gets separated and people find it someplace weird like New Zealand and have to bring it back."

"What do they do? The people who find the penguin?"

"They bring it back," Meg repeated firmly. Then, earnestly, "How could they *live*, away from all that? What would *happen* to a penguin stuck on some beach somewhere on the wrong continent?"

"I don't know," James said, surprised by the question.

They just barely made it to the Penguin Encounter in time to meet Tails, a chubby penguin who posed with Meg for a photo and sat in a little wagon while Meg and the other children there petted her and learned about her life from two guides who stood over them. It all lasted just twenty minutes, and then suddenly they were released into the aquarium's crowds, left to their own devices. James suggested they take a walk around; Meg agreed, but was oddly silent, her mood having shifted when he wasn't paying attention.

She was only following James' lead, not showing an interest in anything, until they stopped at a jellyfish tank. Classical music was piping out of hidden speakers and the jellyfish, fluttering through the deep blue waters of their tank, emitted a fantastical orange light. At first glance, the tank seemed enormous, its depth and breadth impossible to measure. But when James leaned in a little closer, he could make out a faint smudge on the far wall, and it startled him to realize just how thin the space really was. It was a mere rivet between two walls—just wide enough for the jellyfish to swim in, far too narrow for anything to carry out a life in. And then he understood why Meg's mood had shifted.

"You want to get them out, don't you," he said to her. "These guys. And the penguins."

She tore her eyes away from the nettles and looked at James. "It isn't fair. They shouldn't be here. And you know what the worst part is? They probably don't even know it. I'll bet they don't even remember what they're supposed to be."

James said, "I hope not. They must know, somehow, even if they were born in a place like this."

"How do they? Do you think they dream about it?"

He wasn't sure how to answer. They didn't talk much as he drove her home, until she said, to the dashboard, "I wish I could do what you do. You're like Moses, but for flowers."

"What? Moses?"

"I read about it in a book. They called him "The Deliverer." He saved all those people and took them where they belonged. That's what you do for the flowers. You're- you're the Deliverer of Roses."

Speechless, James simply drove on, and kissed her goodbye when Mitchell opened the door for her. He went straight to Shoney's like he normally would after work. Coming through the door and seeing the children seated all through the dining room, he began to wonder if raising this little girl was what he had always been meant to do. He felt certain he could do it. He has loved many people in the twenty-six years of his life—his brother, even in all his self-destructiveness, the women he'd dated, his friends—but what good has he ever really done anyone, with his meandering life and his ordinary job and his not-so-good-looks and his solo Saturday nights? And yet he feels that he has it in him to do this.

Marla, his waitress, stops to ask him if he needs anything more. He almost smiles, realizing that for once, he has an answer. He asks for the check. As Marla walks away, she wonders what's gotten into him. He has always been remote and impassive, and tonight he is so animated. Fierce, even, like a man newly converted.

KATHRYN AND HER HUSBAND ROBERT are regulars here and have been for many years. Tonight they sit at their usual booth, close to the cashier's counter because Robert likes to leave in a hurry when he's finished eating. They are a dreary couple even from a distance. Robert hunches over his food, his arms guarding the perimeter of his plate, as though it might be stolen from him at any minute. He rarely glances up at his wife, who eats small spoonfuls of minestrone soup and occasionally a bite of corn muffin. Kathryn's attention is not on her food. Tonight she is watching other people and thinking hard, visiting other worlds even as she sits almost perfectly still across from her husband.

She is trying to conjure up a way to tell her husband that she is planning to take a job in northern Michigan—a job that will mean the end of their marriage. It will come as an incredible shock. It might mean a heart attack, even. Because Kathryn has played the role of the martyr wife for so many years, even she doesn't know how to imagine anything else. The years of her mother and sisters pleading with her to leave Robert, to escape, to follow her children out to the West Coast, weren't enough to spur her into action; Robert's endless affairs, clandestine at the beginning and public as of a few years ago when his fear of losing her caved beneath the weight of his laziness, did not ignite this urgency in her. It was Garth Brooks, the country singer, who finally did. Kathryn wonders if she should tell Robert this. She would have to tell him the whole story, going back to when their son and daughter were still children, to make him understand, and she knows he won't have the patience for it.

"Come out to Oregon," her children, now in their twenties, have often said to her over the phone, or in emails. "We'll find you a place. We'll get you set up. You'll love it here, there is no place in America this gorgeous." Her daughter would describe ancient redwood forests, hiking trails meandering out to cliffs that hung over the ocean, mountains spilling down to bright blue beaches dotted with enormous rock formations like whales suspended in time. And it was true that Kathryn would imagine all of this and would long for it, would feel the pangs of that hunger for days after the call or email, but then she would tell herself it was an insane idea, she was in her fifties, how could she begin her life over now?

Kathryn opens her mouth and closes it. She isn't ready to talk yet. She tries to get interested in her soup again but the floating strands of vegetables turn her stomach. They make her think of the nightmares she has been having lately: she is in their house, and she comes down the stairs into the living room to find that there are worms everywhere, in the carpet and covering the furniture, eating everything away. The house is decaying, rotting before her eyes. She knows what the dreams mean. She herself is rotting away. Her life has been wasted. These dreams have shaken her to her bones and yet they too were not enough to force her hand. It was only three weeks ago, after putting a dusty Garth Brooks CD into the player in the study, that she decided to follow her friend's advice and fill out the application to teach at the college in Marquette, Michigan. Her old roommate, Marian, had become a department chair there and had sought her out while conducting a job search, insisting over the phone that it was something Kathryn might at least consider.

"Marquette," she imagines Robert echoing. "What the hell's in a place like that? It might as well be Siberia, it's so cold." He wouldn't even process what she was telling him.

She plays out more of the conversation in her mind as she watches a woman across the dining room eye a big spoonful of what looks like chocolate pudding: "We were there once, Marian and I, when we were twenty. We took a road trip in spring. We thought it was the most beautiful place on earth. Lake Superior—have you ever seen it? It might as well be an ocean. So clean. So *old*. It feels like the stones on the beaches have been there millions of years. I never even expected an interview -- I haven't taught in so long…. But it's Marian running the department now, and she convinced them to give me a chance. They want me to start in the fall."

Then the final thing, the toughest words: "And I plan on going alone."
He might kill her.

Who would wash his socks and underwear? Who would feed him meals, treat his hangovers, make the tea when he was sick? Who would work to support him when he infuriated another supervisor and lost another job? The women he slept with on the side never did these things.

He would not be able to live without her. The fact of the matter was, he never had.

She would have to explain about Garth Brooks. It started when their kids, Sean and Debbie, were young, maybe nine and eleven. Kathryn was only working part-time and spending the rest of her time caring for the house and for her children. Robert was working at a warehouse and his shifts ended at five, but he was always involved in some affair and so he rarely made it home before eleven at night. Kathryn didn't want her kids to know what their father was doing so she usually told them he had to work late. On one of these desolate nights, knowing her husband was in the back of a car with some woman, Kathryn had a sudden inspiration.

"Pull down all the blinds, and turn off all the lights," she told her kids excitedly.

Surprised, they obeyed, and watched as she dropped one of her Garth Brooks CD's into the player in the living room. They had a great stereo system then, one of Robert's many impulsive purchases, and it was the first time Kathryn was grateful for it. Garth's voice, deep and sexy and soothing all at once, poured into the room, as did a rumble of thunder; she had put on "The Thunder Rolls," a song about a woman who knows her husband is betraying her. Kathryn had always loved Garth Brooks and she had passed his music on to her children, who knew all of his songs to the word. As though reading her mind, they both started to sing, and she piped in with them. Then Debbie, who was always bold and expressive, grabbed Kathryn's hands and began to swing around the room with her. Soon all three of them were dancing. Faster songs came on, and they were sweating, doubled over with laughter, when they finally saw Robert's headlights coming up the driveway.

"Freeze!" Kathryn yelled. "Music off! Blinds up! Act natural!"

Sean killed the music. Debbie set the couch cushions and throw rugs back into place. They all wiped the sweat off their foreheads and set themselves up like wax figures in different parts of the room: Kathryn reading a magazine on the couch, Sean perched in front of the shelf of

DVD's as though in search of a movie, Debbie at her portable keyboard. When Robert walked in, he barely registered them, and said something about wanting a Coke—were there any left? Kathryn winked at her children and they tucked away their grins. It was one of the best nights they'd ever had together, and they began to do this more and more often—three, four nights a week—when Robert was out with his women.

Kathryn had not thought about this in years until three weeks ago when she was going through the piles of books and CD's in the little study, trying to organize the space. Her idea was that she would be happier if she had a room entirely of her own that was clean and neat, conducive to creative thought. But she was getting more and more depressed as she found books she hadn't read since college and mementos from when Robert loved her, before they were married. Then she found the Garth Brooks CD, and on impulse, stuck it in the player that had long ago been moved into a corner of the study.

She sat on the floor and listened to the entire CD. She thought about her children. They loved her—she knew that—and they both possessed a boldness that had always amazed her. Sitting on the floor it occurred to her that this boldness might be in her as well. Robert was a coward; if her children had inherited any of their courage, they must have gotten it from her. She started the CD playing again and got on the computer, going straight to the job posting she had been looking at intermittently.

Now, Kathryn stands up, murmuring that she has to use the restroom. Robert makes no response. She is in a rush to be alone and on her way to the restroom, she bumps into a heavyset man wearing blue coveralls with the name "Wesley" embroidered on the left shoulder. He is on his way out the door when she practically mows him down.

"Oh, I'm sorry," she says, flustered. She reaches out, briefly touches his arm. "My head's just somewhere else tonight."

He grins at her. "I know all about that. Nothing to worry about."

Then he is gone, and she watches out the window as he climbs into his rig under the falling snow. She wonders whether he ever drives that truck as far north as Michigan. Something in his smile has braced her, and she decides to turn around and go back to the table. She will tell her husband what lies ahead, and hope that they both can be big enough for the lives they never saw coming.

SANDIE NEARLY JUMPED OUT OF HER SKIN the first time she saw Emrys, her old lover, sitting in this Shoney's. She never thought she'd see him again. They had been together for two years when they were in their mid-twenties, and then he'd taken off, dropping her so suddenly she thought it was a kind of prank at first. He'd gone to Illinois, or maybe Ohio, somewhere in the Midwest, and she never heard from him again. For months her little boy, Joseph, asked her where Emrys was. And well he should. Sandie was pregnant with Joseph, the child of an ex-boyfriend who had vanished before Sandie even knew about the pregnancy, when she met Emrys. Emrys had been there at the birth and had been Joseph's stand-in father for the first two years of his life. He hadn't lived with them, but he was always there, to the extent that Sandie told her parents she knew Emrys planned to marry her. She brought him to the family farm and showed him how to tend her parents' goats. He was practically a farm hand, and practically their son-in-law, when he left.

She had fallen in love with Emrys the day she met him at Cove Lake State Park, where they were both out for a walk. She loved his strange name and loved that his accent was a blend of Midwestern and Southern. She loved that he walked with a stick carved from aspen; the stick had the face of a woodland spirit carved into it, and Emrys told her it was something that had been passed down to him from his father, who had Cherokee blood. On their second date, Emrys brought her a box of Sandies, shortbread cookies with bits of nut nestled in them, and told her she was as sweet as a Sandie. He told her he didn't mind that she was pregnant and asked her to let him know if she ever got tired or wanted to lie down. This charmed her, and she did what he asked. They did a lot of lying down, on the grass in the park, in Cades Cove, under huge tulip poplars high in the mountains. On her parents' farm, they often lay in the fields talking for hours, even after Joseph was born and they had to bring him out with them in his carrier.

It took much longer to understand that Emrys was not only deceitful and self-aggrandizing, but the victim of chronic depression. The mood swings, the way he would speak so highly of himself one moment but then grovel at her feet the next, the narcissistic poems he would write and leave out for her to read, the way he would compare himself to heroes in classical fiction—it was all so exhausting and so upsetting. She had a baby to care for and didn't know how to care for her lover too. Yet she never wanted him to leave. Emrys had a kind of readiness, a desire to dream and to interpret the world, that Sandie rarely observed in other men. There was actualized poetry to the way he lived his life, from the way he hiked a trail to the way he talked about Nature and interacted with the animals on her parents' farm. She wanted a little of the mythical in her life. She had been drawn to it even as a little girl reading fairytales. Emrys was the type to lie under a night sky with her and fantasize aloud about what went on in those unreachable galaxies. He made her believe they could have those galaxies if they wanted them.

Now Sandie sits at her usual table, watching Emrys who is seated on the other side of the room. She has told no one that she has gotten into the habit of coming here in hopes of seeing him. She knows what they will say, how they'll misunderstand. She isn't here to get him back. She is here because she is worried for him. In the five years since he disappeared, he has aged fifteen; his eyes are sunken, his clothes hang from his body, and his hair has thinned. He seems desperately alone. She has never seen him walk in here with anyone else. He never goes to the buffet, only orders a baked potato which he eats very slowly before shuffling back out of the restaurant. He always has a silver coffee thermos which Sandie suspects is full of vodka or whiskey. The vibrant man who spoke of starfire now seems to be dying, and though Sandie has hated him all these years, she can't bear to see the flame doused.

He left her so abruptly. He told her he had so much to do in the world; he couldn't stay in one place. He spoke as though he were a great talent, a man whose gifts were so tremendous it would be a crime to withhold them from the world. Sandie almost hit him in the mouth when he compared himself to Doctor Zhivago, a literary character they had fought passionately about months earlier. Emrys loved Zhivago. Sandie thought it was disgusting how the man was able to justify anything he did with the conviction that in order to write poetry, one must live life to the fullest.

"He's saying you can hurt anyone you like, as long as it's in the name of art," Sandie had shouted at Emrys during that first argument. "How can you not see that? It isn't romantic, it isn't sexy. It's a child's logic, put into fancy words."

"You just don't understand it," he'd sighed, a professor fatigued by his student. "He's just not someone you could understand."

She should have known, right then, that the very thing she was attracted to in him was actually what would make him a terrible husband. But she didn't hear the pulse that was beating beneath that conversation, and was shocked when he abandoned her and her son.

Now she pushes pasta salad around her plate and watches as Emrys cleans his glasses and puts them back on his face. They are crooked but he doesn't fix them. He is writing something on his napkin and she makes a mental note of this. He might leave it here and then she could read it and get an idea of what was wrong with him. What, she wonders, is he doing back in Tennessee?

She looks at her watch. Joseph is with her mother and she needs to pick him up soon. But she waits to see what Emrys will do, never sure when it will be the last night she sees him.

ON HIS NAPKIN, Emrys has tried to write down reasons to live. But he is so self-conscious, so worried that the waitress will look at it, that he ends up scrawling out a grocery list instead. The items on the list aren't even things he needs. All he wants, really, is a drink, and he has one, in the coffee thermos he walked in here with. He is not drunk now but will be later. He has been hovering around the edges of this town for months, not sure how he's landed back here and yet aware that he has nowhere else go. Back in Chicago, where he last lived, he had the idea that being back in the mountains would revive him. He could start over. By then he had alienated, ruined, or disappointed so many people that he couldn't stand the sight of himself in a mirror. But in the mountains . . .

He thinks of the lie he has been telling for years: that he has Cherokee blood. Why did he tell it? Under his grocery list, he writes, *to belong to something.* Was that it? It made him feel part of something larger? Or was it just a tawdry desire to seem mysterious to others, attractive in his complicated bond with a distant past? It had made him feel like a poet, just talking about it. That tempestuous blood, that need to speak with the trees and the sky, that love of land. The truth was that there was nothing romantic about the Cherokee. They suffered. They were uprooted and made into hopeless pilgrims. He had no right to claim a connection when his own life was so utterly devoid of commitments.

He writes, *mountains are mountains with or without me.* The hills don't need him or his words. This too has taken him years to learn. Shakily he takes a long gulp of his ice water and when he sets the glass down he thinks of the glass next to his bed and the bottle of pills beside the glass. Last night he had very nearly taken them all. He swallowed three and then stopped, his hand on the bottle. He couldn't do it but he wanted to. It was the realization that he had taken every precious thing he knew of and *used* it somehow. He had set it off like a sparkler on a sidewalk, impressing himself or his women or his friends with that brief glow and then tossing aside what remained when the moment had petered out. If he really had been Cherokee, his ancestors would have been ashamed.

He lifts his head and looks around the restaurant. First at the big family with the fat parents, whose children are engaged in a heated argument; then at a silent couple, the husband's face nearly buried in his food; then at a lone woman near a window, smiling to herself. A family of three sitting at a booth. A teenaged couple holding hands at a table. Two men waiting to be seated. Everyone seems happier than he is. Everyone seems to know something he doesn't. Emptiness swirls through him like a cold wind and he wants his bed and the glass and the bottle of pills. He wants this so badly he can almost taste the tablets in his mouth. His shaking has gotten out of control and he decides to splash water on his face before getting in the car. Bent forward, head down, he walks to the restroom and manages to avoid eye contact with anyone he passes.

While he is in the restroom, Sandie pays his bill. She does this quietly and then passes by his table to pick up the napkin. All she can read on it is *to belong to something* and she knows she'll be turning this over in her mind for a long time. She leaves, hurrying to pick up her son.

When the waitress tells Emrys that his bill has been paid, he just stands there. She has to repeat it a few times before he understands. He goes to his car in a daze, and only when he is on the highway does it occur to him that he should have scanned the parking lot to try and figure out who it was that paid his bill. He almost turns around. But the highway is iced, and turning back, against the wind, would be dangerous. Suddenly, he wants to make it, to wherever he is going next.

AT THE END OF THE TABLE that hosts the large family, the loud and messy family that has been exasperating the waitstaff for the past hour, the little girl called Lizzy sits deep in thought, both hands circling her water glass. Her face is an old-woman face, drawn in severe lines against the pale backdrop of her skin, and her eyes are narrowed, focused on some distant and unseen point. When her brother drops macaroni onto her lap, she simply brushes the sticky mess off her jeans, and barely registers that her sister is kicking her under the table. She is mourning the loss of the Christmas tree they left on the curb last night. The sight of it slumped there, stripped of its decorations and sagging in the snow, was unbearable. As was the shoebox her mother had crammed all the ornaments into—a coffin for those bright orbs and twinkling stars.

For days, Lizzy had lived under that tree, creating complex worlds in its lowest branches. The angel ornaments lived in those pine apartments. Each had her own designated branch and of course colored lights. There was one angel in particular, whose dress was tied with a sapphire blue sash, that Lizzy loved, and she made up endless stories about this angel and what her duties were. Tiny houses and a little train set lay below the tree's branches, and this angel worked her magic all though the day, swooping in graceful curves over the glittering roofs and wishing the occupants well. At night, she returned to her bough and lay down to rest under the blue bulb Lizzy had carefully positioned there. She would sleep while Lizzy slept, but it was understood that with first light, she would be up again, flying down to the houses to protect the souls that were just awakening within.

Tea and Oranges

After my divorce, I started going to the Kroger a lot. I was on staff at the Methodist hospital in West Knoxville, working eighty hours a week, and I got into the habit of stopping at the Kroger every morning around ten A.M., when I had twenty minutes or so to myself. I was conscious of seeming pathetic, so I made it clear that I was there to buy my lunch, and always picked up a ready-made sandwich or a box of chicken that could pass for such. I did need to pick up food, but the truth was that I just liked it in that store. The building itself was set on a hill, high enough that you could see the great blue wave of the Smoky Mountains in the distance, and the store was like a little beacon up there, its warm lights pulsing behind clean windows.

I came to know the staff—one welcoming, if reticent, manager who always murmured hello from behind a heavy beard, and a little regiment of teenagers and college students who stocked the shelves and worked the registers. They seemed unusually happy in their jobs, often joking loudly over the registers and tossing mild insults at each other from across the aisles. I took an interest in their dramas and in their endeavors; when I had the time, I liked to ask them about their plans. I was always in scrubs, and like my colleagues, the employees there developed the habit of calling me Dr. Mary instead of Dr. Preston, and I liked that. Maybe I just liked the noise. After several months of this, I came to recognize other customers, too—mostly elderly folks who had the whole day to themselves and just liked to shop in the morning when it was quiet.

The customer I saw most often, and who interested me the most, was an old woman who went by Mrs. Hansard, though I had never observed a wedding ring, or a tan line, on her finger. She was small, not even 5"2, and had faintly curly hair that fell in white wisps around her head. She wore silver-framed glasses and was fond of thick cardigans in all weather. We were both sorting through a rack of discounted produce when she told me her name. I noticed that she wore a cheap plastic name tag that read, "Irene," and I assumed she worked a retail position some-where, which upset me because she had to have been at least seventy years old. Since she introduced herself as Mrs. Hansard, though, that is what I called her whenever we saw each other.

"Do you work in town?" I once asked her as together we questioned a package of wheat-free brownies.

"At the J.C. Penney," she said. "These have as much sugar as any other brownie. Oh, I don't need them anyway. What do I need sweets for?"

The more I saw her, the more I thought about her. First it was her name that troubled me. I had always thought of Irene as a strong, Irish name, one with an almost belligerent ring to it. On Mrs. Hansard, though, the name was different, the syllables becoming as fragile as the clasp of an an-tique bracelet, two pieces held precariously together by time-worn metal. The woman herself was frail, always a little bent as if carrying a pack no one else could see. She never really smiled; her eyes were always squinting, the muscles of her face tight with some concealed tension. Even when we bantered, talking lightly about the weather and about bruised apples, her face did not relax. I pitied her wasted hands, the long roads of blue vein that led to fingers gnarled with arthritis. I got the sense that she did not take care of herself very well, and the few questions I put to her about her health and her conditions at home did not yield the kind of answers a physician wants to hear. I was careful, though, not to harangue her about any of this, because I wanted her to be comfortable around me.

I suspected right away that she was at the Kroger every day for a reason similar to my own: she was lonely, and liked the warmth of the place. She liked the sound of the vegetables taking their showers and liked it when a stocker dropped an armful of something and cursed under his breath. Anything that sounded like another person in the house, in the next room.

More than once, I caught myself talking about her at the hospital. The nurses listened with barely-restrained impatience and my fellow physicians rubbed my shoulder, offered to buy me a drink when we were free. I was lucky; these people were more supportive than competitive, unlike any hospital staff I had ever known. But I saw that they were worried about me, and so I stopped mentioning Mrs. Hansard at work, even later on when things got strange, and there really was something to tell.

My colleagues were good to me. They seemed to have reached a consensus, on their own, that my divorce was all my husband's fault, and implied as much when the topic arose. They encouraged me to move on, to be happy to be free of it all. I listened and nodded numbly at their suggestions, never bothering to set the story straight, finding it easier to imagine their version to be the true one.

I wanted to believe them, and ignore the suspicion that soon, even the satisfaction of my job, even the mountains and the gorgeous lakes my husband and I had first moved here for, would not be enough to keep me in Tennessee. That the silence of my house would overpower all of that, and I would have to leave.

ON ONE OF MY RARE DAYS OFF, I hunted down Mrs. Hansard at the J.C. Penney, having asked her about her shifts there. It took me awhile to find her, and when I did, she was under attack. A well-dressed woman was waving her hands around, complaining about the sales signs being false and that the dresses she was carrying were still full-price at the register, and why didn't someone like Mrs. Hansard know to change the signs?

I saw behavior like this all the time at the hospital, but could excuse it given the life-and-death situations most of my patients and their families had suddenly found themselves thrown into. This woman, I could not forgive. I stood there, grimly fascinated, as she continued to berate Mrs. Hansard, who was stooped over as usual and simply nodding along with everything that was said.

It was Mrs. Hansard's acquiescence—no, something akin even to appreciation—that upset me the most, though. She seemed to be taking in the woman's words as one might take in food or drink, something necessary for survival. At one point, I heard her say, "You would be completely right to do that," and that is when I stepped in.

"I'm sorry, is there some problem here?" I asked as professionally as I could.

The woman was taken off guard. After a moment, she stepped back. "Not really," she said coolly. "I think it's been resolved."

"That's wonderful." I turned to my friend. "Mrs. Hansard, would you mind showing me the scarves? I have some questions about them."

Mrs. Hansard followed me, and when we were standing among the racks of brightly-colored scarves, she said, "Why did you do that?"

"I couldn't stand to hear her talk to you like that. Who does she think she is? You can't allow that, Mrs. Hansard. I'm sure even your supervisor would not want that."

"I don't mind it," she said simply.

I blew air through my nose. "Are you kidding me?"

"Why should they treat me any differently?"

I shook my head. "I don't understand you."

She said, "That's all right."

I bought a scarf from her, though it was only September then, and I didn't need one.

AUTUMN HAD IGNITED THE MOUNTAINS from the top down when Mrs. Hansard met Davy. I remember that the Kroger had a big display of fat pumpkins and scarecrows along its walkway, and that Mrs. Hansard's beat-up old sedan pulled up next to my car just as I was about to climb out. We walked into the store together, commenting on the enormity of some of the pumpkins, and I asked her if she would carve any this year.

"I used to love doing that," she confessed. "But I wouldn't spend money on a thing like that now."

"I guess I probably won't do one, either," I said.

Inside, we went our separate ways, and I found myself an egg and ham sandwich wrapped in foil. A few minutes later, Mrs. Hansard reappeared behind me in the checkout line, and I saw that she was struggling to carry a big bag of clementine oranges, along with a box of chamomile tea.

"Are you getting a cold, Mrs. Hansard?" I asked her, helping her set the oranges down.

"I think so."

I was happy that she was taking care of herself a little, but when I suggested some additional remedies, she waved me off.

The cashier, a young girl named Kelly I'd seen often, called another staff member over and introduced him to us. "This is Davy," she said. "He's in training."

I smiled at the young man, who took his place next to Kelly and watched her as she rang up my sandwich. He was thin and pale in his polo shirt, but good-looking in the way men were good-looking when I was twenty: thick chestnut hair, long-lashed hazel eyes, an expressive mouth. I liked him right away, and worried about the fact that his hands trembled a little, as if from too many cigarettes.

I was swiping my card when I happened to glance over at Mrs. Hansard. The look on her face stopped me; her eyes had widened, her hands frozen around her box of tea. What little color was ever in her cheeks had drained rapidly away and her cheekbones seemed sharper than ever. She looked elfin, almost other-worldly. She was staring at Davy.

"Mrs. Hansard? Are you all right?" I took the box of tea from her and set it down on the conveyor belt.

"Oh—fine. I'm fine," she said, shaking her head. She scrambled in her canvas purse, but for some reason I swept her tea and oranges over to Kelly and said, "Just put hers with mine."

"No problem," the girl said, though she was eyeing Mrs. Hansard. Davy watched Kelly, appearing to have taken no notice of Mrs. Hansard's consternation, and he waved goodbye to us as we exited the store.

"Are you sure you're all right?" I asked her on the walkway.

She met my gaze and I was amazed to see the faintest smile on her lips. She held out her plastic bag. "Here, sweetheart. You look like you could use it even more than me. Some days, you just seem so tired."

I was too surprised to do anything but accept the bag, and later, between shifts, I made a cup of the tea in the staff microwave and drank it as slowly as time would allow, wondering about it all.

A CHANGE CAME OVER Mrs. Hansard after that day. It was a new woman who came to the Kroger to pick out canned fruit and soup. She seemed to move with newfound alacrity, and to be putting on a little weight. She talked more with the staff, especially Davy, and she always went to his register when she checked out. I got in line behind her, listening to her questions, understanding her interest in this young man's life.

She asked him a great deal—what his plans were (he wanted to attend the University of Tennessee and was saving up money for it); where he'd come from (he grew up in Covington, Virginia; this information prompted Mrs. Hansard to ask him about a hidden bridge in the mountains near there, which he did indeed know about); what he liked to do for fun (road trips; he dreamed of driving to Montana one day); even what he liked to smoke (he only smoked American Spirits and he couldn't help himself, he got the habit from his dad). On one occasion, Mrs. Hansard brought a bar of expensive dark chocolate to the register along with her chicken soup, and announced that the chocolate was for Davy, since she'd seen him eating it when he was on his break. He took the bar uncertainly, offering her a slight smile, and I began to worry.

But if Davy found her attentions strange, no one else seemed to, and the others on staff warmed up to Mrs. Hansard as she became more talkative. She even began to crack the occasional joke; I heard her say to a stocker, "What did the fish say when he hit a wall? *Dam.*" I found myself laughing and realized I hadn't heard the sound of my own laughter in months.

In truth, Davy's story interested me as much as any of the others', and so I was happy to listen as Mrs. Hansard asked her questions during those few minutes she had at the checkout line each morning. His father, we learned, had some here to work for Y-12 in Oak Ridge, and did classified work for the government there. Davy had no interest in engineering or the sciences and wanted to study literature instead. I thought this was a bold choice and told him so; he looked at me with appreciation, and I wondered what his life must be like, if his father were constantly on him for his choices. I was happy to be thinking about someone other than myself, and like Mrs. Hansard, I was increasingly interested in what would become of Davy. It was like a novel or a play unspooling slowly beside us both as we carried on with our otherwise uniform lives.

It was scary, the work his father did—that much we picked up on, though Davy could tell us so little. It all frightened him and he always shook his head when he talked about it. His tobacco-stained fingers would move up to his hair and tug at it. He didn't want to live anywhere near a nuke plant, he told us. He wanted one day to teach somewhere out West. He said the Smokies were all right but they weren't high enough for him and he liked the idea of seeing eagles. He confessed one day he didn't know how he was going to afford UT, even working two jobs. He said his father was not going to help him and that the textbooks alone would be a fortune.

Mrs. Hansard asked what classes he'd be starting out with, and he squinted up at the ceiling in the same manner she herself often did when I asked her a question. "Biology, English, algebra, and probably sociology to start," he said. Mrs. Hansard appeared to make a mental note of this, listening intently as he listed off the courses, and then she waved her gentle goodbye and left the store. That day, as on many other occasions, we saw him come out for a cigarette break as we were leaving, and waved to him. He didn't wave back, but I thought he hadn't seen us.

Mrs. Hansard came out of the padded box she seemed to have inhabited when I first met her. Her eyes, once hooded, were quick and expressive. Once, I was there at ten o'clock, actually buying legitimate groceries, and Mrs. Hansard came up behind me in line as I finished setting out my heap of fruits and vegetables, boxes of crackers, coffee, cheeses. At the last minute, I grabbed the plastic bottle of coffee creamer I had set beside the crackers and set it on the candy shelf.

"You don't want that, ma'am?" Davy asked me. "I'll take it, here."

I handed him the creamer, and when I turned back to my groceries, Mrs. Hansard was looking at me. "Why not?" she asked me, her head cocked.

Because I was taken off guard, I answered her honestly: "I forget sometimes there's nobody in my house anymore who uses creamer." Then I bit my lip.

Davy's hands were moving fast, the register emitting its frantic beeps as he rang up my items, but Mrs. Hansard opened her face to me in a look that was profoundly understanding. She said nothing—she merely reached out and rubbed my shoulder, as my colleagues sometimes did—but from Mrs. Hansard, the gesture was worth something more, and it warmed me to my bones.

We stepped out into the autumn air and talked once again of pumpkins, recalling childhood creations like athletes remembering their best games, neither of us letting on that we hadn't made those jack-o-lanterns alone, that the crazy-eyed cats and grinning rabbits had been somebody else's idea. We didn't mention that we hadn't been children at all, but young women partnered with young men, caught up in hilarity as the seeds spilled over our laps and the pulp went into the trash with everything else we thought we could afford to throw away.

IT WASN'T UNTIL LATE NOVEMBER that Mrs. Hansard asked Davy what his last name was. I was behind her in the checkout line, buying a package of energy drinks (exactly the kind of thing I tell my patients to stay away from, but I was struggling to get up most mornings) when she asked.

"Anderson," he told her after a small hesitation. Then, "Did you know the applesauce is buy one, get one free? Do you want to go grab another one?"

She didn't appear to hear him. The look on her face was like a surgeon's after an operation successfully completed: she seemed exhausted, but affirmed.

"Ma'am?" Davy prompted, leaning toward her.

"I'll get it for her," I volunteered.

She looked surprised, as if shaken from a dream. "Thank you, dear," she said to me.

I got the applesauce. When I brought it back, she reached out and swept my few items over into her pile, exactly as I had done weeks earlier.

"Just put hers with mine," she told Davy.

"Why did you want to know my name?" he asked her as he rang up the food.

I was on alert right away, watching him, but he would not look directly at Mrs. Hansard.

"Oh, just curious," she said after a pause. "You get interested in who people are when you live in a place for so long."

Davy did stop then, his hands pausing over my groceries. "You ask me a lot of questions. Any special reason?" He glanced at me, and there was something accusing in his face. For the first time, I realized he was frustrated, possibly even resentful. We'd been too immersed in his ongoing story to realize that he was as sick of talking about his life as we were of living ours.

Mrs. Hansard was flustered. "I'm sorry," she said eventually, reaching up to adjust her glasses and her hair. "I'm sorry if it bothers you."

"It's fine," Davy said with a sigh. "I just wondered." There were circles under his eyes. I wanted to tell him to go home and get some sleep, but of course I couldn't. Still, I hung back as Mrs. Hansard moved toward the exit.

"She's just curious, and lonesome," I said to Davy. "She likes to talk to everyone about their lives. That's all."

"It's just weird," he burst out, slapping down the box of cigarettes he'd just pulled from his pants pocket. "It's fucking strange. She doesn't do that to everyone else, that's bullshit. What is it about me?"

His profanity threw me a little; the words sounded all wrong in his mouth. "I don't know. But she doesn't mean any harm, I promise."

"If you say so." He turned his back on me, saw through the windows that Mrs. Hansard was still just outside, and gave a little groan. He moved toward the other exit at the far end of the store, and once he was gone, I went out to Mrs. Hansard and walked with her to her car.

"That's Davy's car," she said to me as we walked, pointing to a red sedan that wasn't in any better shape than hers. "I saw him get into it the other day. That's his."

I could have said something, warned her that Davy was starting to resent all of the attention, but I didn't. I was stung by what he had said and couldn't imagine relaying any of it to her.

I needed to do something for her. I visited her at the J.C. Penney again the next day I had off, under the guise of buying winter sweaters. I was relieved to find her alone, unbothered, and I engaged her in conversation as long as I could, hoping to shield her from other customers by keeping her preoccupied. When another saleswoman passed by, I changed to subject to clothes, and Mrs. Hansard made the shift with me as though it were perfectly natural, agreeing that three-quarter-sleeves were more flattering but not practical for December. I ended up buying several overpriced sweaters that day, mostly so that she could take credit for the sales. I went home and fell asleep on the sweaters. I was awakened several times by the rustling of the tissue paper she'd wrapped them in, but I was grateful for the noise.

THE LAST TIME I SAW MRS. HANSARD at the Kroger, she was not in the checkout line, but in the parking lot, her rusted sedan parked alongside the car I now knew to be Davy's. Her trunk was open, and she was bent over it, rummaging. I thought maybe she had a flat tire and needed help, and it was terribly cold out, so I went to her. I saw quickly that she did not need my help, that she was deeply engrossed in something I could have no part in: she was taking objects out of her trunk and setting them one by one on the hood of Davy's car, arranging them with great care. She was shivering in a thin coat but did not seem to notice her own discomfort. I said nothing; I could only stand there. On the hood were framed photographs, an engagement ring tawny with age, a family Bible, and then things that were newer, recently purchased: a glossy and expensive U.S. road map; a series of collegiate textbooks, the bindings never cracked, all wearing yellow stickers proclaiming their origin at the University of Tennessee bookstore; a stack of chocolate bars tied with ribbon to a big carton of American Spirits, which would have made me laugh at any other time; and last, a thick manila envelope that bulged with what appeared to be paper. The name *David Anderson* was written in careful script across it.

I did not look up until Mrs. Hansard did, and the reason we looked up was that Davy was yelling. He was on his cigarette break, and from the doors, he was shouting at Mrs. Hansard: "What the hell are you doing? What are you doing to my car?"

I spun back toward Mrs. Hansard, terrified of what might be in her face after this outburst, but nothing had changed. She simply stood there looking at Davy and then went back to what she was doing, pulling more objects out of her trunk. Davy disappeared into the store and within ten minutes, a squad car had pulled up on the other side of Mrs. Hansard's sedan.

If Davy's shouting had not hurt Mrs. Hansard, the sudden presence of police frightened her, and she began to cry. They were two handsome young cops, probably new to the job, and her crying seemed to upset them as much as their questions had shaken her. I stepped in, explaining that I was a doctor, and held Mrs. Hansard's arm as she spoke brokenly to them through her weeping.

"Now, ma'am, it's all right, ma'am," the first cop kept saying, while the other was asking, "Can you just tell us what you're doing with all this? Can you tell us why you're harassing this young man?"

"I think she knows him," I blurted out, and at my own admission, Mrs. Hansard finally told the story, the words tumbling out of her so quickly and in such disorder that both cops stared hard into her face, struggling to keep up. What I parsed out was that she had walked out on a husband and son forty years ago and hadn't gone back, and that Davy, without doubt, was her grandson.

"The spitting image of his father," she insisted loudly at one point, though no one had expressed any doubt. "My son all over again. He is my son, all over again. I would know those eyes anywhere."

"And this?" one of the cops asked, picking up the manila folder. "This is money, ma'am. This is a lot of money. What are you doing with this?"

I saw that he was right—the envelope was straining at its seams, crammed with large bills. It dawned on me that this was no less than Mrs. Hansard's life savings.

"It's for him. I withdrew it out of the bank. It's for him to use for school. Or anything he likes." Her voice was choked with tears, but as the questioning went on, she seemed to regain her strength. Her eyes met mine more than once, wearing the same expression they had the day she saw me put the creamer back. I held her gaze as I held her hand.

Finally, one of the cops went into the store to get Davy himself. But Davy would go no further than the sidewalk, and from there, beside the officer, he shouted once more: "I don't need your money! I can take care of myself! I don't even know who you are," and then turned his back and was gone.

Eventually, the police left us. I had promised them I would help Mrs.

Hansard put everything back into her trunk and then see her home. I was incredibly late for my shift but I hadn't even noticed at the time. The truth is that I did not help Mrs. Hansard move those gifts back into her trunk; I let her leave them where they were, including the manila envelope. I tried to reason with her about that, telling her that she would need that money to take care of herself. She responded, "I know that. That's why I wanted to give it to Davy," and I could find nothing else to say. The last item she placed on Davy's car was a box of tea tied to a little bag of clementines, as if to commemorate the day they met.

I never saw her at the Kroger again, or anywhere else for that matter. I don't know what became of her or how she survived, having given everything she had left to a grandchild who may or may not have one day accepted her gift. But perhaps she already had survived all she wanted to, because her face, when we said goodbye, had softened, gone halcyon with a peace I had never seen before except in a summer sky or the blue depths of a mountain lake.

REGRET WASHES UP IN THE HUMAN HEART like wreckage on a beach. I envy Mrs. Hansard that moment of relief upon first seeing her grandson at the end of the checkout line, as she set down her tea and oranges. I envy her the neatness of finally clearing away those sands, of transposing all that grief onto a plane as literal as the hood of a car. And since I saw her do this, I too have scanned the faces of strangers, in the wards and in crowds, in checkout lines and on trains, hoping to be startled into deliverance by a face that is my own.

20,000 Leagues

OLIVE HAS COME TO LIVE for her predawn dreams. They started almost three years ago and have been coming to her on and off, but with a curious continuity, like an epic poem with great gaps missing but a still-certain narrative. Because these dreams have always involved Olive traveling with a dark, nameless man, there was a time when she feared her husband's infidelities were punishments for her unconscious meanderings. Eventually, though, when Nathan's affairs didn't stop, she started to look forward to her dreams with abandon.

She lies as still as she can now, feeling rather than seeing first light edging in past the curtains. Her husband has left for work by now and the bed is hers. Keeping her eyes tightly closed, she carefully retraces the steps she and this dark man have taken in the past two or three hours. She sees deep woods, the trees very black and spindly, everything waving wildly in a savage rain. She and the man move through this rain, becoming soaked themselves, but his hand stays tight around hers. Faint but promising orange lights peer out from between the glossed black branches, assuring her that there is something ahead of them. The woods open out, revealing a massive field that flashes gold under lightning. Olive is running with the man, but she has time to look up, to really take in this sky. It is impossibly vast, and the lightning moves in a way she has never seen before: endless lines, blazing out from a single centerpoint and moving in parallel streaks to the left and right of this invisible source. She sees that the lines cut through the tiny, round beams of distant stars, and wonders whether the stars' gravity have pulled the lightning into these long, flawless lines, because all together, the streaks of lightning and the orbs of stars create a colossal electric web, too perfect to be accidental.

The man says something to her—his words are not always clear in these dreams—and then they push on. It seems a long time before they press through a smaller, quieter wood, and then stumble into a kind of garden. Ahead of them is a bouquet of houses, their roofs deep blues and reds against a suddenly stormless sky, and Olive can see the rise of dark green hills behind them. The silence is stunning. The moon has backlit everything so that the trees, spiraling up from the ground like cypresses, wear an otherworldly glow, and the ground seems to wave beneath them. The whole place has a powerful sense of rescue, of salvage, and the dark man beside her murmurs something about this place surviving the war. What war? Olive tries to ask, but she can't; she is frozen, mesmerized, by the land's beauty, and trying to understand what it reminds her of.

Finally, Olive sits up in bed and passes a hand over her eyes. Cliff dwellings, she decides. That is what the scene had reminded her of. Its essence, she thinks, was ancient. Something bold and gorgeous, carved into a wilderness. An audacious feat, achieved in the face of violence and impending disaster.

But it is not just the image itself that pulls at Olive. It is the feeling it left her with—a sense of conclusion, as though this might have been the final chapter of the story she has been a part of for three years. She has never woken up feeling this way, and the possibility that the dreams are over makes her ache with sadness. She has craved the company of this man as though he were real.

Only once did she make the mistake of telling a friend about the dreams. Emily, a devout Catholic, believed the dreams had religious significance. "Maybe the man is Christ, walking with you everywhere you go," she'd suggested. Olive had been adamant: "No. It isn't like that. He's a real man, as flawed as I am. I feel like I could lose him at any time." And then, hearing herself, the emotion there, she changed the subject.

She rises and snatches up a raggedy pullover off a chair and yanks it on. The house is small but drafty, and it's a mountain January, beads of ice like unraveled necklaces strewn across the tree limbs that scrape Olive's windows. On a normal day, she would have gotten into a hot shower by now, put on makeup, and left for work at the Clinton library. Today, though, she is not going to work. She can't. Even as she is thinking this, the phone rings, and she picks it up with a grimace.

"Olive?" It's Gracie, Olive's boss. "You're late. You aren't sick, are you? We're going to be busy today with the kids' program."

"I'm not coming in," Olive says dully. "I'm not feeling well."

There is a pause. "Olive? Is everything okay?"

"I'm just sick. I just need a day to get some sleep and I'll be fine."

"Well, all right. Call me tonight, will you? Keep me in the loop. We'll handle things here."

"Okay." Olive sets the phone down. Gracie is a friend, but Gracie doesn't know yet the real reason Olive won't be coming to work today. Nathan has just started his third affair in four years, and though Olive has learned to work through the pain that comes with these affairs, this time it's different. This time, he's chosen one of Olive's own acquaintances—Tracey, a slightly younger woman who also works at the library. He told Olive the truth about it last night, and admitted that he'd be taking Tracey out on her lunch break today. In a way, she was grateful that this time he was open about it, instead of sneaking around until he got caught, but Olive had been speechless. At first, she couldn't understand why he'd choose Tracey, of all people, with her lank hair and her timidity—until she remembered that she'd once told Nathan that Tracey's father was abusive. Nathan had a weakness for this—women who were lost or helpless—and Olive should have known that his interest would be sparked.

It was not always like this. As Olive moves restlessly through the house, picking up clutter here and there, she can't help but look at all the reminders of their beginning: a lacquered and framed map of east

Tennessee, with circles around all the patches of land they had dreamed of one day owning; Olive's woodwork, shelves carved to look like ocean waves lapping over one another, and clocks pieced together from antique parts, gifts she made for Nathan; their wedding photo, taken in an apple orchard in the Smoky Mountains. These are the only really beautiful items in the house, which is drab with its secondhand furniture and dirty windows. Olive used to make gifts from wood for friends and family, even dreamed of one day learning to build a home, but hasn't touched her tools in years.

The dream of land never panned out. They ended up here, in Clinton, a small town that is more of a gateway to I-75 than anything else. Nathan struggled to keep a job; Olive couldn't do much with a major in art history and a smattering of woodworking classes. At the beginning, it was almost romantic they way they'd struggled, but then Nathan had begun to use his pitiful wages to pay for alcohol, and Olive had transformed her woodworking studio back into a spare bedroom so that they could rent the room out to the occasional boarder or college student. Then, later, the affairs started.

She finds their old atlas and sits down cross-legged on the battered sofa with it. She turns to the Tennessee page and bends over the faded blues and greens. She reads the names of towns and highways, but is thinking of small patches of land, houses she saw back when she used to go on long drives alone in the mountains. Often she would photograph the houses, imagining one of them could be hers. She is not a domestic woman, but dreams of having a base to fly back to from long travels. Travel—the idea of passing in and out of the outside world the way a bird touches down on a tree limb and then darts back into flight—fills her with deep longing. The long battle to forgive Nathan's affairs, and to dredge up ways to fill the gaps of her own happiness, has left her stagnant. Once, when sick with pneumonia, she coughed up a murky green fluid and thought to herself, *Thick as pond scum. Makes sense.* Nothing was growing in her. It was no surprise that she and Nathan could not have children.

Something like panic rises in her as she thinks, *I can't handle any more. I have to get out.*

She tosses the map book aside and goes into the spare bedroom. No one has boarded here for awhile, and Nathan rarely enters this room, so this is where Olive hides her getaway bag. It is an old hiking pack, built to carry about 65 liters, and she has filled it over time with everything she needs if she should get up the guts to make an escape. Other women, she knows, would have worked on getting a bank account ready. This was never possible for Olive. Olive is ready to live in the woods if she has to. In the pack is a water filter, emergency blanket, waterproof clothing, flints, a first aid kit, food bars, flashlights, a backpacking tent, a sub-zero sleeping bag, a cup to boil water in, a compass, and more, all safely stored in dry sacks. She knows how to use it all—as a girl she constantly camped and hiked alone in the mountains near her home in Sevierville— and today, she fingers the compass with a kind of wonder. *I could just go,* she thinks. *I could start another life, anywhere. I've got to look out for my own happiness—not his, not ours. Mine.*

But, as always, the thought deflates as Olive herself deflates, leaning over and letting her head fall into her hands. She wonders, how long could she live in the woods like some mountain animal? And—worse— how does anyone make a life worth living anywhere, alone? She sets the compass down and burrows deep in the pack's secret pocket for her revolver. It is a lightweight beauty, nickel-plated, a .38 special that has only been shot a few times for target practice. This is not the first time she has held this gun in her hands and wondered how long she could live alone in the woods before turning it back on herself.

She is just sitting there, holding it, when she hears the mail truck pull up.

GARRETT IS STILL NOT USED to his new second-floor apartment in Lenoir City, a white-walled place he moved into after his divorce three months ago. It still doesn't feel right. Everything is too clean, like an office, and the belongings he's brought in don't fill the spaces. Even the bathroom still feels like somebody else's, and as Garrett stands in front of the little mirror, adjusting his tie, he feels like he's in a motel.

"Really manly, Gar," he mutters to himself as he finishes the knot. The tie is a pastel green, something his ex-wife picked out ages ago, insisting that it looked professional against a crisp white shirt. He hates the sight of himself in his work clothes. He looks just like all the other toadies who work at the dealership downtown—too-clean shirts, ironed pants, silky-but-cheap ties, polished shoes. Really, though, it is his own face and body he has come to hate. These mornings in front of the mirror are becoming harder and harder. Garrett doesn't want to admit it to himself, but he is aging. He's only thirty-five, but his dark hair is peppered with gray, his once-tanned skin is paling, and he doesn't have the physical strength he used to. How could he? The most he has to lift at work is a pen or clipboard, and yet the job wears him out so much that he never has the energy to go on the mountain hikes he did as a young man.

He combs his hair on autopilot, meeting his own brown-black eyes in the glass as his hands move. It is still strange to him to be at the mirror alone. Towards the end there, he and his wife were rarely in the same room, but for years, they'd get ready in the morning at the big double mirror, his wife's hairbrush flashing as she moved. Now, even as he misses the company, he wonders why no one stopped him from marrying Alyson. He supposes they were only too thrilled to see him married and settled.

He'd always been the straight arrow, the one who did everything he was supposed to. Worked since he was sixteen, took care of his parents whenever they were ill, got a college degree, albeit in English which his family didn't approve of. His dream had been to teach overseas, to volunteer in China or South America. But then his brother, a Marine, died in Iraq, and the last thing his parents could handle was another son disappearing. Garrett had his new wife to think of as well at this point.

And so Garrett ended up working for his uncle at the dealership. His uncle's long been retired now, but the job was reliable pay, and if Garrett ever mentioned hunting around for a teaching position overseas, his wife would ask him how he intended to support them making a teacher's salary. She was thirty-two years old when she suddenly wanted children; this, at last, had been what broke them apart. She told Garrett one night that she'd met a man who could be a better provider. Those were the words she'd used. And Garrett felt anger closing his throat like a fist around the tendons. He told his wife that she'd kept him from doing what he'd really wanted to do; she told him she refused to be his excuse anymore. He didn't ask what that meant.

He sets the comb down and after a hesitation opens a wooden box he'd placed on the sink the night before as a reminder. Today is the anniversary of his brother's death, and on this day, Garrett always wears Brendan's watch. He pulls it out of its case and pulls it tightly over his wrist, noting every detail even as he tries not to really look. It is something he forces himself to do, a duty of honor to Brendan, who has been dead for almost ten years now. He'd enlisted three days after the Twin Towers fell, and was dead within the year.

Garrett gives his shirt a final tug and goes into his tiny kitchen to make some kind of breakfast. Though the kitchen is small, it is the only room he likes: it has an oddly tall widow that frames distant hills past the town line, and beside this window, Garrett has placed a reading chair and a slender bookshelf holding all of his favorites. *Angle of Repose. East of Eden. Cold Mountain. 20,000 Leagues Under the Sea.* This last book was a childhood favorite, an epic he never forgot, and the book is the same one he had as a child—bound in green leather, careworn with many bent pages. Garrett sets water to boil for oatmeal and then pulls the book off the shelf.

He had dreamed, as a child, of traveling this many miles, through the mountains but beyond them, to countries he'd never seen. He'd loved books because it was the one way you could do this without permission and without money, the thing he eventually learned made the real rules. Now, looking again at the title, Garrett cringes. 20,000 is a number that's been ruined for him, thanks to his manager, Jeff, and the contest the dealership is hosting today. As of yesterday morning, four hundred little postcards have been mailed to random households in surrounding towns, advertising the dealership's newest gimmick: a scratch-off lottery contest, promising the winner 20,000 dollars in cash. The postcards came with little fake car keys that could be used to scratch off the bubbles; the winner had to come to the dealership to claim his prize.

There is, of course, no winner; the whole contest is a scam, a means of getting people into the dealership to hear about Jeff's "one-time" bargains and specials on the used and new cars languishing in the gray lot out back. The fine print, cleverly hidden on the postcards, explains that the odds of winning the cash are 1 in 59,999; the odds of "winning" the consolation prize, which is a gold dollar and a special coupon, are 59,999 in 60,000. The images under the bubbles match on every postcard. Every recipient is a "winner," but no one will get the 20,000 dollars, for Jeff has the card with the true winning serial number on its back, and that card will never leave the dealership.

Today, Garrett's job is to sit down with anyone who comes in with a postcard, explain that they haven't won the 20,000 dollars, but that they *have* won, because they're getting a gold dollar and a very special deal on a car if they would like to use it. Garrett already knows how miserable this is going to be, and he hates himself for being a part of it.

The water has nearly boiled away and Garrett looks up from the book's cover. "Perfect," he mutters. There is no time now for breakfast. He reshelves the book, grabs a granola bar from his meager snack cabinet, and hurries out.

In the car, he is thinking of the last real adventure he can remember having: getting lost in the Shining Rock Wilderness, out in Pisgah National Forest. He'd been alone out there for nearly four days. He had his water filter, but there was no water that high up, and he was starving, fumbling around trying to find the trail he'd lost. Somewhere in that wild jigsaw puzzle of balds and stands of black pine and winter-hardened rhododendron, he'd hit on a promising trail, and though it didn't take him back to his car, it did take him to Shining Rock. The tower of snow-white stone was shrouded in fog and surrounded by ancient trees. Garrett knew his way home from there. All the way back, he clutched a white stone in his hand, and felt certain that someone was out there, planning everything, showing people the way. He'd never believed in such a thing in his life, and the newness of it shook him. He felt like he'd traveled a thousand leagues, not just in distance but in time, in spirit. In the parking lot, he felt so good that he gave his glimmering stone to a child who was about to start a walk with her parents. Then, running into a hiker who'd lost his dog, Garrett volunteered to hike yet another few miles, helping the man look until the Labrador was back in the man's truck.

When he finally got back to the Blue Ridge Parkway, he saw that he'd missed fourteen phone calls from his parents. Brendan was dead, and Garrett had been in the mountains, completely oblivious. He hadn't done any real hikes after that, nothing more than a couple of miles at a time.

As Garrett pulls into the gray lot of the dealership, he wonders, when was the last time he traveled a single league anywhere?

OLIVE HATES GETTING THE MAIL. On most days, what she finds in the box is oppressive to her: bills she is mainly responsible for paying, letters from her mother essentially saying *I told you so*, notices that her car is due for a tune-up she can't afford, or her mouth is due for a dentist's appointment she has no insurance to cover. Now, she takes the small stack back into the house, bringing the morning's icy air with her, and hip-thrusts the front door closed.

For awhile, the mail sits on the kitchen counter next to some cereal dishes while Olive straightens things up and takes a shower. Finally, Olive reenters the kitchen for some coffee and rifles through the pile as the water heats.

In the middle of it is a glossy postcard from a car dealership in Lenoir

City. Loud yellow letters tell her that she could be the winner of 20,000 dollars in cash, and Olive rolls her eyes.

"Scam," she mutters.

But instead of tending to her coffee, Olive tears the fake car key off the postcard on impulse and starts scratching off the coppery bubbles on the card. When the first four out of five match, she stops.

"Get a life, Olive," she says. But she finishes off the fifth bubble, and realizes they all match.

She rereads the postcard, double-checks the designs she has revealed with the key. She does this several times before it dawns on her that this might be legitimate. She turns off the heat under her coffee water.

The postcard instructs her to call the dealership to confirm that she is a winner. With a slightly shaking hand, Olive picks up the phone and dials. An automated voice welcomes her to the dealership and encourages her to press 1, then input the number she sees on her postcard. Olive does so, and then another automated voice says brightly, "Congratulations, our records show that you are a winner. Please come in to the dealership to claim your prize."

Still doubtful, Olive hangs up, finds the phonebook, and calls the dealership's main number.

"Evanston's Ford, Jeep, and Chrysler of Lenoir City," a woman's voice chirps. "What can I do for you?"

"I, uh, received one of your postcards? About your contest? I wanted to try to clarify whether I actually won or not. I just wasn't sure-"

"Did you call the number on the card, ma'am?" The voice is buttery smooth, too warm. "Yes? Well, let's set you up with an appointment with one of our gentlemen here. They'll confirm what you've won. What's a good time for you today? We have openings at ten, eleven, noon, and every half hour after that til seven."

She is talking too fast, and Olive is confused. "So then it's possible I didn't win?"

The woman laughs. "It sure sounds like you're a winner, ma'am. The thing is, you can't really confirm unless it's in person, you see? Just stop by to find out what you've won. Now which time works best? We've got three folks on duty today—Ted, Eric, and Garrett. I'll set you up to meet with one of them."

"Eleven o'clock," Olive hears herself say, glancing at the wall clock. Suddenly, she wants to get on the road, find out what this all means, before the day is gone. "Eleven works for me."

"That's Garrett you'll be meeting with, then. We look forward to seeing you, ma'am. Give me your full name again, and I'll give you directions out here if you need them."

Olive gives it to her, and only realizes after she hangs up that she's given her maiden name, Olive Holston. But why not, she asks herself, feeling a twinge of excitement. What if it's real? As she picks through her closet, looking for an outfit, the possibilities start to occur to her. If she has won 20,000 dollars, she can do almost anything. Go back to school for a graduate degree. Get a better car and just go. Travel until the money runs out. Or . . . she stops, holding a sweater. She could stake out her own home on her own piece of land.

The emptiness threatens her again—she has caught herself imagining that the dark man might actually come with her to this place—and she strips almost violently and pulls on her nicest underwear, her favorite white bra. Over this goes a silky camisole that she has not worn in years. Then, a deep blue sweater and a pair of dark jeans with brown boots. She spends some time on her hair—a thing she rarely does anymore—coaxing some of the long, wild tresses into a clip. Her hand, applying mascara, trembles.

"What is the big deal?" she says aloud. "It's probably just a scam. And if it is, so what. It's a nice drive out of Clinton and it's something to do today. For the heck of it."

When she gets into her car, though, clutching her scrawled-out directions, her stomach is in a knot. She ignores her neighbors, many of whom sit out on their porches this time of day even in the worst weather.

On the road, she is hyperaware of everything: the ice below the wheels, the wind caressing the sides of the vehicle, the distant mountaintops with their sunlit glaze of summit-snow. The moon is barely visible, a sliver of pearl hung from the neck of a lonely cloud, and the air is clear. Olive pictures a swath of land fringed with frosted woods. A brown house with puffs of smoke emerging from its chimney, determined as a pioneer locomotive charging through newly-blasted tunnels in the hills.

She is thinking furiously. With this money, she could change everything. She could go back to where she went wrong, and fix it all. But where *had* she gone wrong? *Nathan, that's where*, she tells herself, but bites her lip, knowing it isn't quite true. Something else is wrong and it isn't all his fault.

She takes the exit for Lenoir City. On her way into town, she passes a man who has parked his truck on the side of the road and is holding up a sign that she doesn't have time to read. She catches a glimpse of the little wares he has spread out across the rusty hood—they look like toys, a smattering of trash like a microscopic yard sale—and she shakes her head. It's a sad world, but after this, things might not be so sad for her. After all, she is driving with a postcard and a key in her purse, both of which promise twenty thousand dollars.

She presses down hard on the accelerator and checks her directions for the next turn.

AT THE DEALERSHIP, the other salesmen like to call Garrett "The Professor," poking fun at his habit of reading on his lunch breaks. They of course don't understand how much the nickname stings in light of what Garrett actually wants to be doing, and he doesn't bother to tell them. Ted yells, "Hey Professor, you've got office hours today," as Garrett enters, and Garrett forces a smile. He looks up and realizes he is passing under a gargantuan banner that reads *20,000 CASH PRIZE GIVEAWAY!*

"How many appointments am I stuck with this morning?" he wants to know.

Ted says, "Five already for you, six for me, five for Eric. The phone calls are already coming in like crazy, just like El Jefe said they would. This should be fun." He rolls his eyes.

"Real fun. Telling people they've been had." Garrett goes to his desk and drops into the swivel chair there, half-heartedly turning on the computer. He pushes aside a stack of papers and fiddles with his calculator. He eyes the others—Ted is talking to Eric, Jeff is nowhere to be seen—and leans down to open the bottom drawer of the desk.

"Hey, Gar," Eric shouts. "What are you doing Friday night?"

"Working," Garrett says, sitting back up.

"After that," Eric says, moving over to Garrett's desk. "You want to come out with us? We're meeting some of my wife's friends at this new place in Knoxville. Might be good for you to get out a little."

Garrett tenses. "No, thanks. I'm always wiped out by the end of the day here Fridays."

"So am I, but come on. You're a free man, now," Eric reminds him, and the phrase pricks at Garrett. Eric goes on, "You're lucky. Not stuck like the rest of us. You might meet somebody new," and he winks at Garrett. The gesture seems obscenely childish.

"I'll think about it," Garrett says, to get rid of Eric, who finally does move off.

A free man. In Eric's world, this means that Garrett is "free" to screw other women. Garrett doesn't know how to tell him that this is the last thing on his mind, or a match for his personal definition of freedom. In what way, he wants to ask Eric, is he free?

No, he will do what he always does this Friday night: watch the History channel on his little TV, and sit there in awe of ancient people who had no phones or computers but lived life more vividly than anything Garrett can conceive of. Even the evil ones, like Julius Caesar, impress him. Their fearlessness is as mystifying as the ocean; their zeal for life, something ordinary men were too small to contain. It seems to

Garrett that some of these men could have scooped a hole out of the ground and birthed whole sparkling galaxies from a single seed. This, he is sure, is what made them not angels or demons, but humans at the height of human potential. He has loved stories about the ancients since high school, and still can't let them go, though he tends to think of them more as children's stories now than history.

A customer wanders in—clearly, not for the contest—and Eric attacks the man immediately, steering him outside toward their SUV's.

Eric gone, Garrett looks around, and finds that Ted is talking to Jeff just outside Jeff's office. Jeff loves to talk about himself, and Ted is certainly trapped. Garrett takes advantage of the time to bend back down and open the desk drawer. He shoves aside the old brochures he uses to disguise what he really hides in here, and pulls out a small yellowing envelope.

Inside is a photograph of his brother, Brendan. The photo is the last one taken of him. In the picture, Brendan is in a military hospital, standing in a dark corridor with only a faint orange light behind him. He is posed is if for a fight, both his fists up, and his mouth wears a tight smile. His hands and wrists are tightly bandaged, as though he'd tried to slit them himself, but really, he'd been hit by shrapnel from an exploding mortar. He'd had his hands over his head when it happened and they said at first it had saved his life, but it didn't. A blood infection killed Brendan right there in the hospital a week later, and the friend who took the photograph sent it to Garrett.

Even now, Garrett can't get over the image of his brother in this dark hallway. Brendan's dark-blond hair is sweaty but bright, like a sun-seared field under a fresh rain. His eyes are fevered. His chest is bare, and those bandaged hands gesture fiercely at things Garrett can only guess at. Most likely, Brendan was about to collapse, the infection just beginning to take root in him, but in the moment this picture was taken, he seemed ready to take on anything.

Garrett rarely looks at this photograph, fearing what it does to him.

It makes him almost resent his brother, for showing Garrett, even from the grave, his lack. Something in Brendan's look, the intensity there, always strikes Garrett as accusatory: *Everything you do—your work, your love, even your hate—is buried. Every move you make is mired.*

"Professor!" Jeff strides his way over, his chest puffed out like always, and Garrett stuffs the photo back in its envelope and shoves it under the brochures.

"You've got your first appointment in five minutes," Jeff says, looming above Garrett. He smells strongly of cologne. "Guy's name is Jack Hudson. Two or three more guys after that—I'll give you the list. Then some woman named Olive. With a name like that, I bet she's seventy years old. Have fun."

"Great. Thanks."

Jeff drifts away, and Garrett looks at his brother's watch. It was designed to be worn in the backcountry, and it bothers Garrett how ridiculous the watch looks on his thinning wrist, against the crisp cuff of his sleeve.

He looks up, and a man in coveralls is standing in front of his desk.

Garrett rises, holding out his hand. "Hi there. You must be Mr. Hudson?"

"That's me." The man settles into the chair Garrett offers, and looks expectantly at Garrett. "I've got one of them tickets here. All my symbols match. They told me you'd confirm the win."

The man looks about forty, with oil-streaked skin, dirty hair, calloused hands, and good-natured blue eyes that right now are glittering with a half-hidden hope. Garrett swallows.

"Well, that's what we're here for. May I see that card? Here." Garrett takes it and gestures toward the reception desk. "Let me run these numbers through, and we'll see what we've got here. It'll be just a minute." This is what he's been told to say. He goes through the motions, taking the card up to the desk and handing it to Mary, their receptionist, who gives him a tiny eye roll and files the card away. She hands him a gold dollar out of a box and a thick brochure with vivid advertisements for a sale they're about to have. He takes it and resists the urge to shred it.

Back at his desk, he sits down across from Jack Hudson and forces his salesman's smile. "Well, your numbers show that you're a winner, but not the grand prize winner," he explains brightly. He hands over the gold dollar, which the man takes but looks at with open disdain. Then he holds out the brochure. "We'd like to treat you to a special discount for a very limited time on our Jeeps, starting this week—"

"No thanks." Jack Hudson stands up heavily, pocketing the gold dollar with a small laugh. "I had a feeling. Worth a shot, anyway. I won't be affording a new car anytime soon—sorry."

"We have a great used selection," Garrett begins, but the man waves him off.

"I can barely take care of what I got," he says. His mouth is tight, like he's holding in another laugh or maybe a curse. "Like I said, worth a shot." And he's gone, moving slowly away from Garrett, his right hand visibly toying with the gold dollar deep in his coveralls pocket.

Garrett stays where he is. *I cannot do this again.* But he does. The next two men are painfully similar to the first—barely concealing their hope, their excitement, and then barely concealing their disappointment and embarrassment when the scam is revealed. Nobody shows interest in buying a car here, and for this, Garrett is grateful. At least he doesn't have to literally rob anyone today.

At five to eleven, Garrett leans back in his chair and eyes the door, expecting the seventy-year-old woman. No one comes through the doors, though, and for a moment, Garrett turns his chair toward the showroom window and watches his favorite tree move in the January wind. It is a river birch growing in a bizarre spot, and even from here, Garrett can see the flutter of its papery coral bark in the breeze. It looks like butterflies are kissing the tree. He shakes his head at his own thought.

When he looks up, a woman is standing in front of his desk, and the light behind her sets the auburn in her hair on fire. Her eyes, amber-green, find his, and register something like shock.

"Do I know you?" he asks politely when he can find his voice.

OLIVE COLLECTS HERSELF as this man, this stranger, speaks to her. His dark hair, and the way he was sitting in his chair when she walked in, threw her off balance, and she wasn't sure why. At first she thought she recognized him from somewhere. Now, convinced that she's never seen his face before, she holds out her hand briskly.

"I'm Olive," she says. "I've got one of your postcards. It says I've won—I've won the cash prize. But they told me I had to come in to confirm it in person."

Garrett holds out his hand, and grips hers tighter than he intended to. "Garrett. You're right, I just have to check your numbers up front. Can I have your ticket?" But even as he asks, he feels his heart sinking. This woman with her eyes like a mountain stream looks so feverish with hope that he doesn't know how he can go through with this. She is about his age; God only knows why she is here, what she hopes to get from this money that won't be hers. God only knows how trapped and miserable she, too, might be. He stops.

"Is there a problem?" Olive asks, her hands twisting nervously in her lap.

"No problem. Just give me a second." He walks away, holding her ticket, and Olive watches him go. She is a house of cards, she knows. Ready to collapse here at this desk if this isn't what she wants it to be. She is angry with herself—when did she become so irrational? She'd told herself from the beginning that this was just something to do during the day. Now it's too late to go back to that way of thinking.

She is lost again in her fantasy of a square of land in the wilderness when Garrett returns. He sits down slowly and extends his hand; on his palm, glinting in the fluorescent light, is a gold dollar.

"Your ticket is a winner, but not a grand prize winner," he explains. His voice is toneless, but his eyes—very dark now—are fastened on hers. "We've got this gold dollar for you, and this—" He stops, looking down at a glossy brochure in his other hand. "This—"

Garrett finds he can't finish his own sentence. Olive doesn't take the gold dollar, only stares at it for a long moment.

"No, thanks," she says faintly. "I figured. I knew it was a scam." She tries to laugh and brushes back her hair. "You'd think most people would know right away. I bet most did. I bet I'm the first idiot to come in here today."

"No," Garrett starts, then, "I mean, no, you're not an idiot, and you weren't the first to come in. Lots of people have come in. I'm sorry it isn't what you thought it would be."

Something in her face hardens at this. "You're sorry? Really? This is your job."

"I wish it wasn't."

She does laugh now, an ugly bark. Garrett realizes with alarm that her face is turning red, her eyes filling. "Sure you don't. How long have you been here, anyway?"

"Longer than I should have been." He scrambles through his second drawer and finds a box of Kleenex, holds it out to her. She stares at him and shakes her head.

"The whole thing is cruel," she says simply, and rises. She is openly crying now, and her voice is louder than before: "The whole game is fucking cruel."

Garrett also stands; the other men are looking their way, Ted's mouth hanging open. "I'm sorry," he says again, speaking rapidly. "I truly am. I didn't invent this—contest. It wasn't my idea. I don't have a choice in this."

"Of course you do." Collecting herself, Olive squares her shoulders and shakes her hair back. "Thanks for nothing. Garrett."

He watches her stalk out of the showroom. Her hair bounces in wild curls down her back and she looks like someone who was born and bred in the mountains. He looks down at the gold dollar, then back up. He can see her climbing into her beat-up sedan.

Garrett sets down the brochures and breaks into a run. As he bolts out the showroom door, Ted shouts at him, "What's going on, Gar?", and he sees Jeff jump out of his office, his mouth opening to call after Garrett.

In the lot, Garrett rushes alongside Olive's car as she pulls out past the used cars. He catches her eye, waves both hands, but she doesn't stop until she reaches the pullout where she has to look for oncoming traffic. Garrett uses the pause to dart around the front of her car and pull open the passenger side door. He can hear Jeff yelling.

He has never done anything like this in his entire life. His heart is pounding so fast he can barely speak, but when Olive gapes over at him, he manages to say, "Just let me in. Please."

A car speeds past them, and Olive, flipping on her turn signal, says, "Are you out of your mind?"

"Just let me in. For God's sake."

"I don't even know you. What do you want, a ride?"

Jeff is outside, his hands cupped at his mouth: "Garrett, what in hell do you think you're doing?"

Garrett ignores him. "Please," he says again. He holds out both hands. "I'm not crazy, I'm not a psycho, I just want to talk with you. For a minute."

Olive glances in the rearview mirror and then shakes her head. Tears are still beaded on her cheeks. "Oh, my God." She gestures for him to get into the car, and Garrett, stunned, slides into the space beside her and slams his door closed. She pulls onto the road just as Jeff comes bolting up the drive.

THERE IS A LONG SILENCE as they drive west. Twice Olive opens her mouth to ask him something—she isn't sure what—and both times she stops.

It is Garrett who breaks the silence. "I've never done anything like this," he says.

Olive says nothing.

"I swear it. It's just—God, I hate that place. I hate what I do there. I can't ever see a way out. None of this is what I pictured. When I was young, I mean." He is babbling: "This isn't at all the way I meant for things to turn out. My life."

Her hands tighten on the wheel. "I think I can relate to that. What was it you pictured?"

"I'm not even sure. I just know it was different."

"Why can't you get out?"

"Well—it's a long story. My brother died, in the war. I wanted to leave but it would've killed my parents. Then it was my marriage. I was stuck, you know? Supporting us. I didn't have much choice. I'm divorced now, but . . . "

"But what?"

Now Garrett is silent, feeling his stomach turn over. The truth, he knows, is that he is just afraid. He is as afraid of living his life as vividly as his brother did, as he is afraid of dying, as his brother did. He fears that the ancient heroes really were larger than life, not children's stories, exaggerated in their glory. He is afraid he's just not up to the task of truly living. That whatever it was he felt as a young man, climbing trails in Pisgah National Forest, was just an illusion. He was neither a capable man nor was he a good one. And the magic of what he felt out there was only a boy's imaginings.

"I'm a coward," Olive says suddenly, speaking precisely the words Garrett is holding in his mouth.

"You? You seemed pretty brave in there," Garrett says weakly.

"Brave? Crying all over you like a child? Please." She glances his way; her mascara has run a bit, but strangely, it makes her even lovelier, wilder, in his eyes. "I wanted that prize money because I thought I could use it to pull myself out of my stupid life. My shitty marriage and my pathetic job and my hopeless inertia. And every day I tell myself that everything I hate is somebody else's fault. Like my husband's."

Garrett opens his mouth to say, *Ditto*, but is still.

"I can't figure out how to look at things any differently than I do," Olive says. "I keep looking for a key but there isn't one. I thought that money was it. I'd buy myself a piece of land and then make romantic journeys all across the country. I'd look at sunsets over the water and climb mountains." Then she laughs bitterly. "I'm boring the hell out of you. I guess that's what you get for jumping into my car. Where should

I take you? How about I just drop you back off and we'll pretend this never happened. This whole day."

"No," Garrett says, so forcefully that Olive looks at him, startled.

He says, "I used to fantasize about all that, too. Travel and owning land and going everywhere. Did you ever read *20,000 Leagues Under the Sea?*" He shakes his head. "I wanted that to be my life."

She gives him a wry smile. "I don't think I ever want to hear that number again."

"I don't blame you." Then, "How far is it to where you live?"

"It's kind of a long haul. I live all the way out in Clinton."

Garrett studies her profile and then looks down at himself, finally realizing how truly insane this is, and how lucky he is that she did not call the police or shove him out of the car on the highway. He must seem like a freak to her. He says, "I'm sorry. I've acted crazy. I don't really know what came over me. You can take me back now if you want. I'll never bother you again."

"Now that's the first disappointing thing you've said," Olive tells him, "other than when you explained how I was a winner, but not."

"Disappointing?"

"You had some guts back there. Where'd they go?"

Both are slightly in shock. Olive doesn't know where her words are coming from, or why she isn't afraid of this stranger in her car; Garrett is amazed that he is still here, and wondering at himself as well, at his burst of courage back at the dealership. And now, Olive's words seep into him, and he looks away from her, at the trees whizzing by.

"What exactly are you saying?" he asks at last.

But she doesn't hear him; she's pointing up the road, at a pickup truck parked in the grass just off the pavement. "He's moved," she says. "He was in a different place when I drove in."

"Who is he?" Garrett sits up in alarm as Olive guides the car off the road, pulling up behind the truck.

She doesn't answer, and so he gets out when she does. Big cardboard signs against the windshield and in the rusted bed read, *FAMILY NEEDS HELP. I HAVE A JOB, JUST NEED SOME HELP RIGHT NOW. HANDMADE CRAFTS, 2.00.* Dotting the hood of the truck are crocheted potholders, keychains, tiny stuffed animals, handmade pins and brooches, and coffee mugs with flowers painted on their sides. A man hops out of the truck and Garrett sees that he is missing a hand. Something turns over in him.

"Hi, folks," the man says, waving. "Have a look, see if anything strikes your fancy. I appreciate you pullin' over. Most don't."

Garrett, struck silent, finds himself hovering close to Olive, as though they are husband and wife. Olive mulls over the objects on the hood and then starts plucking them up, one at a time, filling her hands. She holds out the stack to the man, who smiles and nods at her. "Guess you like crochet," he remarks. His eyes move over the items. "That'll be eighteen dollars, ma'am."

Olive places the crafts in Garrett's hands as naturally as though they have been together for years. She rummages in her purse and while the man is turned away, looking for a plastic bag for her, Garrett sees her take out a twenty and then fold an additional twenty inside it. She hands it to the man, who helps Garrett drop the little gifts into a bag.

"Thanks so much, ma'am," the man says. "We do appreciate it. My wife makes these. We're making a go of it, but it's been a rough year for us."

"I understand. Tell her they're lovely." Olive smiles at the man, and waves as she and Garrett make their way back to the car. Her eyes are radiant with some secret.

"Hang on," Garrett says to her. He turns around and walks back to the man, unclasping his brother's watch. He hands it to the man, who looks carefully at it.

"You sure?" he asks Garrett, frowning. "This looks expensive."

"It's a good watch. Better you get something from it than me. Just take it."

"I thank you." The man pockets the watch, and gives Garrett a broad smile. The wrinkles in his face ripple outward as though his face is a stream Garrett has dropped a tiny stone into. "You and your wife, you've got a good way of living. Don't let that go."

Garrett doesn't know what to say, so he just waves as he turns away. Once back in the car, he turns to Olive. "Did you know him?" he asks.

"I should have," she says. "I should have paid attention to him before. What did you give him?"

"Nothing. Something I thought he could use."

They pull back onto the road, and Garrett is still holding the bag. He looks at Olive, waiting for her to meet his eyes.

"I used to do woodwork," she says finally. "Mostly gifts for people I knew. Can you make anything?"

"Not really," he admits. "But maybe I could." He laughs. "I once carved a scale model of Mesa Verde into clay. I spent three months on it. That was in high school, though."

She slows down and looks at him strangely. "The cliff dwelling?"

"I know. It was a weird obsession, I guess."

Olive clears her throat. "Do you want to go back?"

"Not unless you want me to."

They drive on, and the distant mountains glow a fiery blue.

Acknowledgements

I would like to thank my family -- Frank for the stories we've created together, Chris for all that he has built with his hands and his heart, and my parents for their continual support. I am grateful to Neil Connelly, my mentor, who taught me that reality has an even greater capacity for beauty than dreams. Finally, I want to thank my friend Kate Klein for every wise word she has sent my way over the years.

ABOUT THE AUTHOR

Elizabeth Genovise is a graduate of Hillsdale College and of the MFA program at McNeese State University in Lake Charles, Louisiana. Her first collection of stories, *A Different Harbor*, was published in 2014 by Mayapple Press. She currently lives near Knoxville, Tennessee, where she is happy to be teaching English while spending her weekends on the trails in the Smoky Mountains.

Photo: Chris Hodges

Fomite

A fomite is a medium capable of transmitting infectious organisms from one individual to another.

"The activity of art is based on the capacity of people to be infected by the feelings of others." Tolstoy, *What Is Art?*

Writing a review on Amazon, Good Reads, Shelfari, Library Thing or other social media sites for readers will help the progress of independent publishing. To submit a review, go to the book page on any of the sites and follow the links for reviews. Books from independent presses rely on reader to reader communications.

Visit http://www.fomitepress.com/FOMITE/Our_Books.html for more information or to order any of our books.

As It Is On Earth
Peter M Wheelwright

Dons of Time
Greg Guma

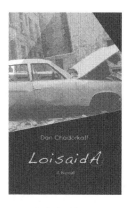

Loisaida
Dan Chodorkoff

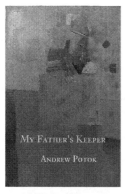

My Father's Keeper
Andrew Potok

My God, What Have We Done
Susan V Weiss

Rafi's World
Fred Russell

Fomite

The Co-Conspirator's Tale
Ron Jacobs

Short Order Frame Up
Ron Jacobs

All the Sinners Saints
Ron Jacobs

Travers' Inferno
L. E. Smith

The Consequence of Gesture
L. E. Smith

Raven or Crow
Joshua Amses

Sinfonia Bulgarica
Zdravka Evtimova

The Good Muslim
of Jackson Heights
Jaysinh Birjépatil

The Moment Before an Injury
Joshua Amses

Fomite

The Return of
Jason Green
Suzi Wizowaty

Victor Rand
David Brizeri

Zinsky the Obscure
Ilan Mochari

Body of Work
Andrei Guruianu

Carts and Other Stories
Zdravka Evtimova

Flight
Jay Boyer

Love's Labours
Jack Pulaski

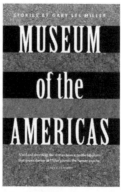

Museum of the Americas
Gary Lee Miller

Saturday Night at Magellan's
Charles Rafferty

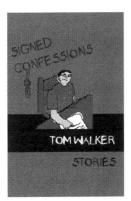

Signed Confessions
Tom Walker

Still Time
Michael Cocchiarale

Suite for Three Voices
Derek Furr

Unfinished Stories of Girls
Catherine Zobal Dent

Views Cost Extra
L. E. Smith

Visiting Hours
Jennifer Anne Moses

When You Remeber
Deir Yassin
R. L. Green

Alfabestiaro
Antonello Borra

Cycling in Plato's Cave
David Cavanagh

Fomite

Fomite

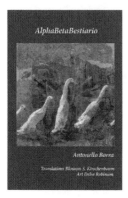

AlphaBetaBestiario
Antonello Borra

Entanglements
Tony Magistrale

Everyone Lives Here
Sharon Webster

Four-Way Stop
Sherry Olson

Improvisational
Arguments
Anna Faktorovitch

Loosestrife
Greg Delanty

Meanwell
Janice Miller Potter

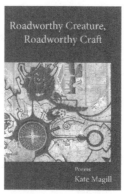

Roadworthy Creature
Roadworth Craft
Kate Magill

The Derivation of
Cowboys & Indians
Joseph D. Reich

Fomite

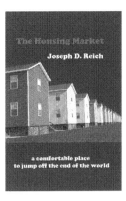

The Housing Market
Joseph D. Reich

The Empty ▯otebook
Interrogates Itself
Susan Thomas

The Hundred ▯ard
Dash Man
Barry Goldensohn

The Listener Aspires
to the Condition of Music
Barry Goldensohn

The Way ▯one
of This Happened
Mike Breiner

Screwed
Stephen Goldberg

Planet Kasper
Peter Schumann

My Murder
and Other Local ▯ews
David Schein

Picking ▯p the Bodies
James F. Connolly

Fomite

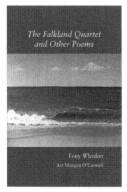

The Falkland □ uartet
Tony Whedon

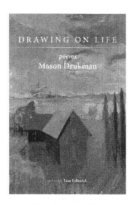

Drawing on Life
Mason Drukman

Among Angelic Orders
Susan Thoma

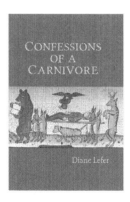

Confessions of a Carnivore
Diane Lefer

Principles of □ avigation
Lynn Sloan

Derail Thie Train Wreck
Daniel Forbes

Free Fall□Ca□dalibre
Tina Esca□a

A Guide
to the Western Slopes
Roger Lebovit□

Planet Kasper
□olume Two
Peter Schumann

Fomite

Nothing Beside Remains
Jaysinh Bir␣patil

Foreign Tales of
Exemplum and Woe
J. C. Ellefson

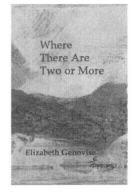

Where There Are Two
or More
Eli␣abeth Genovise

The Inconveniece
of the Wings
Silas Dent ␣obal

Made in the USA
Middletown, DE
15 June 2015